The Dark Paladin

By CW Lamb

I would like to thank my Readers for their patience in waiting for this book. 2019 was a long year for me with several significant life changes.

Cover Design: www.art4artists.com.au

Copyright © 2019 by CW Lamb   WWW.CW-LAMB.COM

All rights reserved. No part of this publication may be reproduced, distributed, or transmitted in any form or by any means, including photocopying, recording, or other electronic or mechanical methods, without the prior written permission of the Author, except in the case of brief quotations embodied in critical reviews and certain other noncommercial uses permitted by copyright law.

First Edition

14 13 12 11 10 / 10 9 8 7 6 5 4 3 2 1

Contents

Chapter 1	4
Chapter 2	14
Chapter 3	23
Chapter 4	32
Chapter 5	42
Chapter 6	52
Chapter 7	61
Chapter 8	71
Chapter 9	82
Chapter 10	91
Chapter 11	99
Chapter 12	107
Chapter 13	117
Chapter 14	126
Chapter 15	134
Chapter 16	142
Chapter 17	151
Chapter 18	157
Chapter 19	166
Chapter 20	174
Chapter 21	184
Chapter 22	195
Chapter 23	204
Chapter 24	213
Chapter 25	221
Chapter 26	230
Chapter 27	238
Chapter 28	248
Chapter 29	258

Chapter 1

Alex Rogers awoke to the repeated strokes of a tongue against his cheek and forehead, sure the activity intended to get his attention. He was positive it was Kinsey, his dog turned wolf, looking to wake him. Likely she wanted breakfast, and this was her way of making it known.

"I'm awake," he mumbled as he raised an arm in an attempt to brush her away.

The motion sent waves of discomfort through his back and arm. Before opening his eyes, he realized he felt stiff and damp, his warm bed suddenly cold and hard against his back. Reaching out to his left, he searched for the warm body of Cassie, his new bride, only to find what felt like a fern. A sudden panic set in as he turned his head and opened just one eye, his new bride not where he had left her the night before. Rolling back, he was treated to a view of partially obstructed sky, the surrounding evergreen trees intermingling their branches against the blue sky above him.

Struggling to make sense of the message his eye was relaying to his brain, he opened the other and turned his head the other way to find a small black dog sitting patiently nearby, staring intently at him and tail flying wildly behind her.

"Kinsey?" he blurted, spurring the dog to begin her licking once more.

"Enough ok," he added as he brushed her away, pushing her to one side while sitting up.

The motion caused him to wince once more as the cold, hard, ground he had been lying on had done its work on stiffening his muscles. Scanning the area around him, Alex was worried, disoriented and confused. With no Cassie in sight, he had a quick flush of fear that it had all been a coma induced dream.

Dismissing that thought as unacceptable, he pushed the rising panic aside and tried to focus on his circumstances. The dense undergrowth of the forest rose up all around him, with just him and Kinsey in the small clearing more than large enough for the two.

"Where the hell are we?" he asked the dog as he paused to consider his situation.

The last thing Alex remembered was going to bed with his beautiful wife Cassandra, in their bedroom inside Castle Windfall. As Lord Protector and regent there, representing King Ben of Great Vale, he was directing the recovery of the city. Left in shambles after Prince Renfeld's misguided war, Alex was working to rebuild the local economy and restore its peaceful place in the world.

Their wedding had been a major event in the couple's newly adopted home, the celebration lasting for days. It was several more days before all the visiting dignitaries finally departed for their own parts of the lands. Even Elion had spent several days in the couple's company, almost as if he were hesitant to leave the pair. In the end Alex was happy to see them all go home, allowing him time to focus on his new wife.

Looking at himself for the first time, he discovered he was no longer in the sleep attire of the Lord Protector, but instead bore the jeans and flannel button up shirt of Alex Rogers, Seattleite and forest wanderer. The attire forced him to reconsider once more that he had dreamt the last one plus year of his life as he lay unconscious here in the forest? As he struggled to reconcile his current predicament, a weak groan to his left drew his attention.

Jumping to his feet, he was elated and relieved to discover Cassie was no more than a few feet from where he lay. A wave of relief passed through him as he knelt down beside her prone form. His touch caused her to stir and he was greeted by her confused expression as she regained consciousness and scanned her surroundings.

"Here, let me help you," Alex said as she tried to sit up on her own.

Turning to him as he spoke, he started to ask her more questions when a second sound drew both their stares. Alex watched as first Leander appeared, still partially hidden in the plant life, followed by Abrianna. Both had supposedly been in Great Vale and were surely not expected here, wherever here was.

"Are you guys ok?" Alex asked, as he watched the two displayed the same looks of confusion and lack of understanding that he had seen on Cassie's face.

A sound beside him drew his attention back to his wife, as he watched her reply to his question. The problem was, he didn't understand a word of what she was saying.

----*----

Cassie shivered in the cold as she struggled to wake. The bed felt hard beneath her and she could hear someone nearby spouting gibberish as she tried to sleep. A slight groan escaped her lips as she tried to move, reaching out to try and find Alex, sleeping beside her. It was then that she opened her eyes to find her husband hovering over her, the greenery all around them a clear indication they were no longer in their Windfall bed-chamber.

Watching Alex as he helped her up, she struggled to shake the disorientation she felt. The strange noises he made as he spoke added to her confusion.

"Alex, what happened? Where are we?" she asked in reply after she watched Leander and Abrianna appear nearby, the tall groundcover concealing their presence earlier.

She could see a look of confusion on his face as she spoke.

"I don't think he can understand you," Leander commented as he crossed over to check on Abrianna and then the pair closed in on Alex and Cassie.

"Where are we?" Abrianna repeated as she looked about them.

"I have never seen these woods before," Leander replied as they watched Alex stare at them all in confusion.

Once more they watched as Alex spoke gibberish at them, the noises he made having no meaning to any of them.

"Brie, the learning spell, did it wear off?" Cassie suddenly offered, referring to the spell Abrianna had placed on Alex when they first met.

"Possibly, let me try another," she replied.

Approaching Alex, she gently took both of his hands in hers and closed her eyes. Evidently Alex understood what was happening as he nodded in comprehension and closed his eyes as well. Cassie watched as the two stood motionless, Abrianna chanting quietly as she worked the magical spell.

"It's not working, I can't feel it," Abrianna blurted as she opened her eyes, releasing Alex's hands as she did so.

"What do you mean, you can't feel it?" Leander asked.

"I mean, there is no magic here, we aren't in A'nland."

----*----

Alex recognized Abrianna's attempt to work magic. Unable to understand any of his three companions, it was clear he had lost the ability to communicate with them. Now, he could tell she was repeating the learning spell that had enabled him to quickly come up to speed last time.

Previously, as she had performed this action, he had blasted both of them with an unintended, but instinctive, protective spell. In order to not repeat the event, Alex tried to relax, closing his eyes and reaching out to her with his senses as he had been taught. As he did so, he noticed that there was something different about the experience. Where he normally felt the rush of power as he opened himself to the world around him, now it was only the slightest trickle, no more than a gentle tingling at best.

Hearing Abrianna speak, he opened his eyes to see the frustration on her face, and he was still unable to understand the words. Scanning the woods about them, the familiarity forced Alex to come to the conclusion that they were, in fact, back in his world. That realization made him reassess each of his companions standing before him.

All were dressed in typical Pacific Northwest fashion, he and Leander in T-shirts with flannel long sleeve shirts over them. Both women had light jackets over fashion T-shirts and all four were in jeans and hiking boots. He now confirmed that these woods were the very same that he had wandered many times just outside of Seattle.

Standing there, watching his three companions discuss what he presumed was the same conclusion of where they were, he started running the explanation of who through his head. For some unknown reason the four had been transported back to Alex's home realm. Likely an action by the elves, he had to assume it was a Dark Elf reaction to his success in squashing both Prince Renfeld and Tantalus's attempted rise to power.

His Earth, abandoned by both races of Elves long ago, or so he had been told, had seen the rise of technology replace magic and that was why Abrianna's spell had failed. Alex didn't even bother to try one of his own as he could feel the lack of the free energy that fueled his efforts in Cassie's realm. It was a sudden bark from Kinsey that drew all their attention back to the present.

All four watched as the little black dog dove for the underbrush, chasing after some unseen creature. Just as quickly, she returned, reaching Cassie first, who knelt and stroked the dog affectionately while speaking unintelligibly.

"Look, I know you won't understand a word of this, but follow me," Alex said as he motioned to the other three.

Before departing, he then gave Cassie a quick kiss of reassurance, as much for himself as for her. While unhappy at their circumstances, he was delighted she was still by his side. Indicating they should follow, all three nodded in understanding as they headed in the direction Alex indicated. Taking the lead with Kinsey at his side, he retraced the steps that would take them back to the primitive dirt road that brought him to this place so long ago.

Walking along the barely discernable path, he could hear his three companions talking quietly amongst themselves. Likely giving voice to all the questions running through his own head, Alex had to wonder what they would find ahead. Doing the math, as he had learned from King Ben, the time he had spent away from here likely equated to sometime between five and six years. That time difference had allowed a former Confederate Officer from his world to reign as King in Cassie home realm over 150 years later.

Alex had no hope whatsoever that anything he had left behind was still around. His Jeep would have either been stolen, vandalized or simply towed off years ago. His home would have fallen into foreclosure and his job filled by another after his disappearance. All in all, he had no idea what he was going to do once they cleared the trees ahead.

Eventually stepping out onto the dirt road, Alex waited for the other three to join him before turning left and heading back to the spot where he had left his Jeep. The others had stopped talking as they studied the forest roadway cut between the trees. While rough by Alex's standards, it was wider and flatter than most of the routes they had traveled in A'nland.

Following the road, Alex began to pick up his pace as he became anxious about their situation. It was a very long walk back to Seattle. His only hope was they could hitch a ride once they reached where this trail intersected I-90.

Rounding a bend in the road, Alex stopped dead in his tracks. There before him on the side of the road, sat his black Jeep, nosed into the woods and still where he had left it, apparently untouched.

----*----

"What do you mean no magic?" Cassie asked when Abrianna ceased her efforts with Alex.

"Just what I said. I can't feel anything," she replied in frustration.

"How can that be?" Leander asked.

"We aren't in our world any more. I think we are in the realm where Alex comes from," she said while indicating the trees around them

"Don't you recall his descriptions of the forest," she added.

"How did we get here?" Cassie asked while glancing at her husband, frustrated at her inability to talk to him.

To her, the language barrier felt like an invisible wall, keeping the pair apart.

"Dark Elves?" Leander stated more than asked.

"Maybe," was all Abrianna would say.

It was then that Kinsey let out a bark and darted for the underbrush. Cassie hadn't really noticed the little black dog, but instantly recognized her face as she reappeared once more.

"Can you understand me little one?" she asked as she knelt and stroked the dog.

It was then that Alex began speaking, motioning in a fashion that made Cassie understand he wanted them to follow. Accepting the kiss, her heart ached with desire to hear his words once more instead of the rambling nonsense.

Turning to follow her husband and the little black dog, Cassie scanned the area as she walked.

"I wonder what dangers lie in these woods? We are unarmed and without magic," she commented to her companions.

"Alex once told me there wasn't much to fear in his world outside of the cities. It was the villains not the creatures that presented the greatest dangers," Leander replied.

"Why do you think we were all sent here?" Abrianna asked, changing the subject.

"It is quite odd that we were in Windfall and you in Great Vale, yet we all awoke here together?" Cassie offered up for consideration.

"I would have thought the Dark Elves would want Alex alone removed from power, and not all of us. What is to be gained by moving us all to a place of no magic?" Leander stated.

"It's not just about magic, my love, or they need not include you. There is something greater afoot here," Abrianna said softly, trying not to insult her intended.

"In Gundor Stronghold, the dragon warned Alex that the elves were not his friend. Do you think King Elion had something to do with this?" Cassie asked out of the blue.

"It is one of the possibilities," Abrianna replied with a nod.

The three then traveled in silence until Cassie watched Alex step out onto an open area ahead of them. Following suit, they found themselves on a wide, relatively flat dirt road. Cassie was surprised at how consistently wide the path was cut through the trees in both directions. There was hardly any rutting in the roadway where the cartwheels should have pressed their way into the earth. She suspected it was not well traveled.

She watched Alex turn left and so they followed him and Kinsey as they worked their way down the road. Soon enough Alex stopped before them, staring at the way ahead.

"By all the gods, what is that?" they heard Leander say as they halted behind a stationary Alex.

----*----

Moving up to the driver's door of the Wrangler, Alex found it locked. Inside, he saw several items on the driver's seat, one of which was his keys. With the hardtop on rather than the canvas soft-top, he wasn't going to simply slide a hand inside. Pausing for a moment to consider his options, he thought through the situation.

There was no way his Jeep had set here for eight plus years like this, so it had been set up for him to find. As such, the locked vehicle had been provided specifically for him alone and recently or some opportunist would have smashed the window and taken it long ago. Stepping back as the others watched him, he slowly began circling the vehicle, checking the wheel wells and bumpers.

He found what he was looking for behind the spare tire mounted to the back of the vehicle. A magnetic hide a key box was secreted inside the tire carrier, up underneath the top of the hollow mount. Removing the key from the box, he opened the door and retrieved the loose items on the driver's seat.

The keyring held not only the ignition key for the Jeep, but also several others he recognized, including his house key. In addition, he found his wallet, holding a valid driver's license and a considerable amount of cash. There were several credit cards as well, all current and in his name.

Finally, there was an envelope with a note inside, handwritten and addressed to him.

Alex, your service to A'nland can never be repaid. Remember all that you have learned there and we hope that it will serve you well in the challenges to come.

There was no signature, but the cryptic nature of the message confirmed to Alex that the elves had to be behind the whole thing. The most disturbing part was the gentle tone indicated it was the Woodland Elves, not the Dark Elves behind this.

Remembering those around him, Alex passed the page to Cassie, who in turn passed it to Abrianna. From their looks he could see the scribbles meant nothing to either of them. Moving to the passenger side of the Jeep, he unlocked the door and then motioned for Leander.

Sliding the passenger seat forward to allow access to the rear seat, he pointed to the opening. Indicating Leander should climb inside, Kinsey brushed passed both men and quickly leaped in first, demonstrating how it's done.

Leander quickly followed suit with Abrianna a hesitant third. Placing the seat in its upright position, he then assisted Cassie into the front passenger seat. Before closing the door, he grabbed the seatbelt and started to buckle his wife into her seat. He could see the hesitancy in her eyes as she watched his motions, but made no move to stop him. Waving for Leander and Abrianna to repeat the action, he had to point out the buckle receivers next to Kinsey as each pulled the belts from the retractors.

Satisfied all were securely belted in, while noting the looks of confusion on all three faces, he closed Cassie's door firmly. Rounding the front of the vehicle, he quickly climbed inside and inserted the key into the ignition. Belting himself in as well, he gave everyone a weak smile.

"Well, here goes nothing," he declared as he turned the key.

The engine fired right up, the action startling all three passengers while Kinsey sat happily between Leander and Abrianna, familiar with the sound and its meaning. Alex did a quick check of his passengers, putting on his best smiling face before he put the Jeep in reverse and backed out. Turning tightly as he backed the vehicle out of its notch in the woods and onto the road, he easily cleared the trees.

Putting it in first gear, he started off down the road, doing his best not to jar his passengers as he picked up speed. Moving into second gear, he set a steady pace as he traveled the dirt path, slowing for the occasional washout or rut. He could hear his passengers passing comments back and forth as they made their way steadily through the trees.

At long last, they emerged onto asphalt, indicating they were nearing the I-90 freeway. Alex glanced at Cassie as she stared wide eyed at the broad concrete curve in the road that led them onto the freeway, heading west. Shifting as he gained speed, he soon had them westbound at 70 miles per hour. From the looks on their faces, he was sure all three with him were terrified as they made their way toward the city.

Chapter 2

King Ben Griffin of Great Vale was not in the best of moods as he stared out the window of the keep. The discovery that his precious daughter was missing, apparently snatched from her bed-chamber during the night, was compounded with the disappearance of the Ranger's Guild Master. Under normal circumstances, he might consider that the young couple, engaged to be married, might have secreted off on some romantic adventure.

He was well aware that this was not the case, however, as a message bird from Windfall declared the Lord Protect and his new bride were nowhere to be found in Windfall as well. Considered a powerful, but a somewhat untrained magician, it would have required someone of extraordinary skill to overcome Alex. Taking into account that he would also be defending his beloved Cassie, Ben's niece and the center of Alex's world, it would have to be several someones.

Deliberating on all of this as he stared absently at the fields beyond the city walls, he knew what he needed to do, but was unsure how to proceed. Only the elves would be so bold as to snatch so many notables without concern for impact or repercussions. Be it either King Elion or King Avenstore, Ben knew he was at a disadvantage.

Though a wizard himself, he was no magical match for either of his Royal counterparts. He would not be able to force whichever had performed the deed to return that which had been stolen. His best option was to convince one of the two to side with him in the conflict that had required Alex to be banished from A'nland.

It was no mere guess that had led to that conclusion on Ben's part. He had seen both the Elven Kings in the gallery above the throne room floor during the wedding of Alex and his niece. A rare sight indeed, Ben could not recall ever seeing the two together so closely, standing side by side as one might a brother or trusted friend. He knew then that there was trouble ahead, but chose to keep that thought to himself.

His mind made up, Ben turned away from the window and began preparing for a trip north. One did not simply summon an Elvin King, so he was going to have to go to them.

----*----

Cassie now understood where her husband's innate bravery came from. He calmly navigated the noisy metal carriage at breakneck speeds while others darted in and around him, seeming oblivious to their presence. She was amazed at the various sizes and shapes of the other traveler's carriages, and their sheer numbers.

The restraints across her body, holding her in place, did little to buoy her confidence. They seemed far too loose to be of any real value and the lack of a buckle or tie made her unsure that she could quickly escape their grip should she need to.

At first, as they traveled the dirt path, somewhat familiar to her and her companions, she marveled at the rate of travel the carriage was displaying. Now on the broad, flat stone roadbed, it seemed all of Great Vale was rushing past at once. She watched Alex as he hardly noted the massive metal box as it flew past them. She imagined several families could live inside as they moved from place to place.

"This is insanity," she heard Leander say as he watched the people in a similar vehicle next to them look over and wave at him.

"I never really believed the stories..." Cassie replied.

"Look there," Leander said as he pointed out the front, looking through the glass window.

Cassie could see something high in the air, almost birdlike.

"Should we be worried?" Abrianna asked as all three stared at the strange object in the sky. Alex must have noted their gestures as he pointed to the same object and commented. His casual tone led Cassie to believe it was of no concern.

The longer they traveled, the more people they saw around them and eventually they started to see buildings mixed in the trees lining the roadway. Cassie noticed that some of these had big rigid banners with illegible script and images of people or animals. At one place they saw the carriages all lined up as if waiting their turn for something. There was a freckled faced girl with bright red hair and braids on their banner giving her no indication of its function.

Finally, Alex selected a smaller road that took them off the main path. Every so often he would stop with the others around them and watch as others traveled in the perpendicular direction before stopping and allowing them to return to their path. Little by little the stone path got smaller, changing from gray to black. Eventually they entered a village, where all the buildings were near the same size and lined up quite nicely one after another.

Alex slowed at one point, studying one of the red stone buildings, before turning and stopping right in front. He declared something that Cassie couldn't understand, while turning to look at the three. He had done something to stop the carriage, the silence noticeable.

----*----

"Well, home sweet home," Alex declared as he pulled the Jeep up into the driveway and turned off the engine.

Making his way back home to the Renton Highlands in good time, he wasn't sure what to expect as he turned into his housing subdivision. He was surprised to see that his house looked very well cared for considering it had been abandoned for several years now. Positive he was in the right place and assuming it still was his house, he had to trust that the elves had provided the key for a reason and it was unoccupied.

Motioning for everyone to stay put, he slipped out of the vehicle, but not before Kinsey leaped into his unoccupied seat and then jumped out behind him. Walking slowly to the front door, in an effort to confirm if the house was vacant, he peered into the front window, looking for any movement inside. Seeing none, he crossed over to the door, eventually inserting the key into the lock and opening the door. Stepping inside, he could see the house was exactly as he had left it, maybe a tad cleaner, but otherwise untouched.

Stepping back outside, he motioned to the others to follow, but soon realized they didn't know how to operate the seatbelts or doors. Rushing over to the passenger side, he opened the door and assisted Cassie, releasing her seatbelt and watching as she slipped out, almost falling. He suspected her legs had fallen asleep, unused to the long ride in the seats.

Moving her seat forward, he then helped Leander and Abrianna unbuckle, both also appearing stiff from riding in the cramped quarters with Kinsey. Closing the Jeep door behind them, he then led all three through the front door and into the house. Once inside, he could see the mixed looks of confusion and curiosity on their faces as they scanned the surroundings.

A simple design, the red brick single story was your typical 1960s track home that Alex had renovated after moving in. Entering at the center of the front of the house, you found yourself in the open living room, dining room, kitchen in front of you and to your right, with a wall on your left.

About in the middle of the house, splitting front to back, a hallway shot off to the left mid wall, providing access to the three bedrooms and two baths that made up the rest of his home. To his far right, past the living and dining rooms, an oversized two car garage completed the structure.

The kitchen was partially open to the living room at the back of the house, with a breakfast bar separating the dining room from the kitchen, and a half wall on the living room side. With the three watching him as he moved about the house. He first went into the kitchen where he found it fully stocked as he checked the cupboards. Everything inside appeared fresh, with the milk in the refrigerator good for another week.

Motioning for the others to follow him, he reopened the refrigerator, indicating its contents. He then opened several of the kitchen cabinets, displaying the dinnerware and drinking glasses. Finally, he opened the pantry where he heard Cassie gasp as she scanned the selection of items stored within. Even though she was unable to read the labels, the food items displayed on the packing made it obvious what was inside.

Next, he began a tour of the house, starting at the bathroom accessed from the hall. He flushed the toilet and ran the water, probably overdoing things in his efforts to demonstrate. Nods from all three indicated the understood the use of the room. When they reached the bedrooms, he emphasized that Leander and Abrianna could share or not, moving each to their own room and then dragging Leander into hers before shrugging indifference.

Finally, for Cassie, it was easy as she understood straight away which room was Alex's. Still filled with his clothes in drawers and closets, he led her to the ensuite bath, repeating the demonstrations performed earlier. He then brought Leander and Abrianna in, opening his closets and drawers, indicating they should take whatever they required. Confused at first, he had to hold up shirts and pants in front of Leander before he caught on. Though smaller in stature than Alex, the shirts, sweats and gym shorts would do in a pinch until they could get more appropriately sized clothing for the group.

Returning to the living room, Alex waved them into the kitchen, indicating they should take what they wanted while he headed to the last space in his house. Using a door at the far back corner of the dining room, he entered his office, where he had worked from home, once upon a time. Rather than usurping one of his bedrooms as an office, he had taken a part of his oversized garage and closed it off.

Exceptionally deep as the garage space was, the loss of the parking floor space wasn't missed at all. His Jeep, sports gear and tools all still fit nicely into what remained. In the office he found his laptop still on his desk, his files and papers all undisturbed. Sitting at the desk, he powered up the computer as he noticed Cassie peering inside the open doorway.

"Come sit here," he said as he pulled a chair over next to him.

He waited as she crossed over and took the offered seat. Turning back to the PC, he began banging away at the keyboard. Surprised that his login still worked, he checked the date in the corner of the display.

"Five years, ten months," he said aloud confirming the length of time he had been away. Using Ben's age as the yardstick, he and Ben had long ago calculated that every year in A'nland was about five years here at home, or rather their home realm. Neither considered their birthplace home any longer, both committed to A'nland. Cassie just smiled, uncomprehending about what he was doing or saying.

Alex continued to scan his laptop, searching the device for data on their current state and possible clues as to why they were there. The first thing he noted was the thousands of unread emails in his inbox, suggesting a source of information. Dismissing that for the moment, he next logged into his bank account. What he saw there threw him for a loop.

"$14,876,325.89!" he read off the balance.

"Looks like we won't be starving!" he said to his wife with a smile.

Next, he went to the transaction section. There he found that the house loan had been paid off and the taxes, utilities and property maintenance charges had been set up for automatic payment withdrawals. In addition, he had been receiving almost $3 million dollars a year in deposits over the time he was missing. Notes attached to the deposits referenced taxable deductions already diverted to the IRS for quarterly earnings. Had someone been planning on sending him back home all along at some point?

"Damn, these elves are on it," he said sarcastically. Unsure of how to relate the information to Cassie, he just kept going.

Flipping back to the earliest emails, he was surprised to find where someone had been impersonating him. The first thing he found was his resignation letter. It had been sent the day he disappeared, and his boss had replied a few days later.

"Dear Alex,

While I am sad to be losing you, I certainly understand the circumstances. The gentlemen from the Government stopped by to answer any questions and deliver the company assets you had in your possession. Whatever the top-secret project is they have dragged you into, rest assured you are welcome back here anytime.

Best Regards"

"So that's how they covered up my disappearance," he thought.

In a way it was pure genius, as anyone who might know him would see the house maintained during his absence and not question it. The rest of the emails that were not spam were the occasional friendly voices from the past or a business contact trying to get a hold of him.

Closing his email application, he turned to look at his beautiful wife patiently sitting at his side, watching his every move. Red hair framed her angelic face as she gave him a hesitant smile. Likely her acceptance of magic made it much easier for her to digest all this, but the language barrier was a huge issue. Turning back to his laptop, he began looking for English language tutorials.

He quickly realized that all the free ones were based on a reference language, like French to English or Russian to English. All the top selling programs were reference based translators as well. Changing his search parameters, he set the query to learning a language with pictures. It took him several try's before he found the software package he was looking for. Using something called "The Cloud" it provided both images and an audio pronunciation for each word.

Once he paid the fee with one of the credit cards provided him in the wallet he found in his Jeep, he walked through a few lessons with Cassie. Selecting the beginner level, he was rewarded with a menu listing various categories. Selecting the general category, the display contained a flood of small images, all suggesting everyday items. There was a mix of animals, foods and things one might see as they walked down the street.

Looking to Cassie before he traded places with her, a quick kiss passed between them, then he began demonstrating the program. Assisting her by placing his hand over hers as she moved the mouse, they selected an image resembling the Jeep outside.

"Car," he heard the computer say in an overly enunciated tone.

The word would appear over the image as the voice sounded.

"House," came the next declaration as Cassie selected another image, one depicting a home similar to his.

Cassie suddenly brightened as she apparently understood the action. Calling out to the others, Alex heard both Leander and Abrianna enter the small office as the three exchanged words.

"Car," Cassie said as she selected the image once more, nodding to the display as it repeated the word.

With a kiss on Cassie's cheek, Alex got up and surrendered his seat to Abrianna. All three A'nlanders were speaking as Leander moved to the other side of Cassie, pulling another chair over to the desk. Once seated himself, Leander pointed to another image for Cassie to trigger.

"Horse," came from the computer's speaker.

Abrianna next spoke in a string of sounds that only provided car and horse as intelligible words. Alex smiled as he backed away, noting that they were the first understandable things any of them had uttered. That was how Alex left the three, as he exited the room and began preparing lunch for everyone.

----*----

Cassie had no idea what Alex was doing, but he seemed quite focused on the magic window before him. As he poked at the numerous buttons all clustered in rows, he starred at the changing images. A couple of times he spoke in the nonsensical language they had heard earlier, but from the tone in his voice, she suspected he was more surprised than angry at what he saw.

She sat patiently as he continued to work through whatever information the magic window delivered him. After a bit, she could tell he was finished with his initial work and had started something new. As he worked, she could see him going through display after display, searching for something.

Then she saw the little images of animals she recognized and other things she had no words for. Alex made one of them grow big and she heard the window speak for the first time. Confused at first, she recognized the thing in the window as the carriage they had traveled in to come here. Next came one that looked very similar to the outside of this building.

"Brie, Leander, come here," she cried out as she understood what Alex had been doing.

Moving the small object in her hand as Alex had shown her, she pushed on the part that made the clicking sound.

"*Car*," she announced with a smile before the magic window could repeat the word.

"Isn't that the carriage Alex brought us in?" Abrianna asked as everyone shifted places.

"Yes, I think this is some sort of learning magic. I can select an image and it will speak the name," she explained.

"Do that one," Leander asked while indicating the Chestnut horse similar to Rose.

"*Horse*," was the reply.

"So that is a *car* and that is a *horse*?" Abrianna asked, forming the unfamiliar words as she motioned at the images.

"So it would seem. We are currently in a *house*," she repeated as she picked the one that looked like the place they had entered with Alex.

"What is that?" Abrianna asked as she picked another unfamiliar image from the display.

With that, the three sat, working their way through the entire group of images. Cassie was surprised when, after selecting the last image, the entire window filled with new selections. While working their way through the new group, Alex appeared with drinks and food for everyone.

"*San Which*," Leander declared as he held up the plate Alex had set in front of him.

Cassie had remembered the image of sliced bread, filled with what looked like meat and cheese. The nod of approval from Alex had confirmed the statement. Food in hand, all three continued their studies.

22

Chapter 3

Kelby sat in the private study of the Lord Protector, waiting on word from the King of Great Vale, their adopted Uncle. It had been her that sent the message bird notifying King Ben of the disappearance of his niece and her half-sister, as well as the Lord Protector himself. Leena, her twin sister, sat at the small table nearby, eating.

"I don't know how you can eat at a time like this?" she snapped in frustration.

"Starving yourself will not help the situation," she replied in turn after swallowing.

Both women, mermaids actually, had been invited to live with their half-sister Cassie once their relationship had been uncovered. All daughters from the same father, Cassie's mom had taken the twins in as her own children, their mermaid mother killed by Tantalus and his dragon in Freeport for defying him.

Amelia, Cassie's mom, had offered to have the girls come to Great Vale to live, but neither wanted to be so far from the water. Here in a castle by the Western Sea, the three, both nymph and mermaid, found happiness.

The adoption of the twins had placed them both in the Royal Family and by title made them Ladies of the Court. Kelby struggled with the newly found prominence, her previous low-key lifestyle in the tavern much more to her liking. Leena however, was wallowing in the luxury her new position provided. Having almost anything she wished delivered to her on a silver platter was not even close to growing old for her.

Before Kelby could offer a retort, a fluttering at the window signaled a possible reply. Opening the pane, she was rewarded by a small black bird that vanished in a puff of smoke once it landed in her open palm.

"What does it say?" Leena asked after another bite as Kelby studied the message.

"Going to see the King of the Woodland Elves for assistance. Sending Amelia to help you. Hold the fort until she gets there"

"What does that mean? This is a castle, not a fort," Leena asked as Kelby read the message aloud.

"I think he wants us to run things until our new mom gets here?" Kelby said nervously.

"How hard can that be?" Leena asked casually with a shrug before taking the last bite.

----*----

With his three companions safely studying English in his office, Alex finally took a breath and went about reorienting himself to the hometown he had left behind. Gone from here a little more than one year in his mind, the five plus years local time had been more pronounced. New faces in the houses nearby, all friendly, but unfamiliar, had represented a turnover in the neighborhood home ownership.

A quick run to the local market turned into an exploration trip, as new construction supplanted some of his local haunts. Sports bars, restaurants and grocery stores were all either gone or bore new names and owners. Some things were still familiar, though, as he dropped down from the highlands and into downtown Renton proper.

There he could see the library building that still straddled the river. Cutting over a few blocks, he saw the Sam's Club Wholesale discount was still there as well as the Renton City Hall. Checking everyone's elf supplied clothing for labels and sizes before he left, he made a list of essentials to collect while he was out. Stopping at several of the local shops, he was able to quickly purchase several days' worth of outfits for each of the three.

Underwear had been a bit awkward as the A'nlandians had a more relaxed concept of such. Both women had been provided modern earthly solutions and it had been Alex's uncomfortable duty to get Abrianna's sizes. In the end he had taken Cassie into their bedroom and had her remove her undergarments. He then demonstrated what he needed from her cousin. Redressing, Cassie soon returned with Abrianna's garments for Alex to record their sizes.

After wandering the community and completing his chores, he could feel himself falling back into the old familiar patterns of Alex Rogers, Seattleite. The culture shock came when he decided to stop at one of the many drive-through coffee stands he had seen all afternoon. Espresso Stands had been fairly common before his departure, White Mocha's being his go to coffee drink. Pulling up to the window of a particularly colorful stand, he was completely unprepared for the reception he received.

"Hi, what can I get you?" asked a pretty young woman wearing only pasties and a thong bottom. The stickers on her large bust line did nothing to hide her charms as they danced before his eyes.

"Ah, a white mocha, please," he replied while trying not to stare. In doing so he spied another girl serving a customer on the other side of the stand. From behind, all he could see covering her was a string that appeared at the top of her ass and split in two directions around her hips.

"Tall, Grande or Venti," His barista asked cheerily.

"Oh, Grande, please. Hey, forgive me, but I've been out of town for a while. When did this all happen?" he asked while motioning at her lack of clothing.

"You must have been gone for a long time. This is pretty much the norm around here," she replied with a giggle that caused her body to move in extremely appealing ways.

As she made his drink, she continued to chat with him, always staying in view.

"Where did you go?' She asked as she topped his mocha with whipped cream.

"Oh, you know, all over, strange places and stranger people," he replied, not sure what more he could say on the topic without sounding crazy.

"Staying in town long?" She asked invitingly as she leaned out the window, handing him his drink and giving him a show in the process.

"Not sure. I have a lot of unfinished business back where I was and my wife has never been away from her home before this," he replied as he handed her a $10 bill for a $4 drink.

"Keep the change," he said with a smile.

"Come back again," she replied with a smile, blowing a kiss as she waved at him with the $10 bill.

Alex turned the Jeep around and headed back home, resolved in one fact. He was not going to take Cassie out of the house until she understood English well enough to avoid any misunderstandings with the locals.

----*----

Pulling into the drive, Alex finished the coffee and grabbed his packages from the passenger seat. Opening the garage with the remote on his keychain, he dropped the empty paper cup in the trashcan before hitting the door closer and entering the house. The door from the garage opened into his office and there he found his three companions as he had left them, all huddled around his laptop.

"Alex," he heard Cassie exclaim, as she jumped up from her seat and rushed to greet him.

Expecting a kiss, he was disappointed to see her rush past him and into the dining room.

"Chair," she declared while pointing at one of the dining room chairs.

"Table, door, window," she rattled off while moving from one object to the next.

By now the others had joined them in the common area formed by the living room, dining room and kitchen. Not to be left out, Leander and Abrianna each grabbed a nearby item.

"Cup, plate," the two added.

"Excellent," Alex replied with a smile as he placed his packages on the kitchen counter.

As the three left him there and returned to their studies, Alex went about unpacking his food purchases and putting things away. Separating out each of the clothing purchases, he placed the appropriate items on the bed in each recipient's room. His mind wandered as he performed the tasks, thinking about the situation they were in and the circumstances that had gotten them there.

He was surely being removed from power in A'nland due to his growing abilities, but why now? His role as explained to him by Elion was to help restore the balance there. Now more than ever the influence of the Dark Elves was in check, their forces in full retreat. He was being pulled from the game before he even got a chance to solidify the gains made across the lands.

And, while thankful that Cassie and the others were here at his side, it confused him even more. Were it just the pair of them, he and his wife, he could see the reason of it. Without his love there with him, the pair would move heaven and earth to be together once more, but Leander and Abrianna? Why banish those two with him and Cassie, for surely Ben Griffin was probably frantic with worry over his beloved daughter.

The loss of magic was another concern. He recalled that the Elven King had explained to him on his earth, magic was not as it once was. The Elves had abandoned this realm, thinking it beyond saving, its corruption and chaos irreversible. Still, there was something in the explanation that troubled Alex. The cause and effect were missing in the message, why was the magic gone? What had happened to make it go away?

His tasks finished, he returned to the kitchen. Moving outside through the sliding glass door to start his Barbeque, as he had burgers on the menu for an early dinner, he uncovered the gas fired grill. Standing before it, he questioned the words of the Elven King as he went through the motions of preparing it for use. If magic were completely gone, how is it they were able to continue to move back and forth between the realms. What were the elves drawing on to continue to operate in this realm? There would have to be something left for them to draw on, wouldn't there?

Opening the lid of the grill, he stood lost in thought as he reached for the burner knob. Pausing, he opened his senses, searching for the telltale signs of the wisps of free energy as Abrianna had taught him to detect so long ago. As hard as he tried, he couldn't find anything he recognized to pull from, he sensed only darkness around him.

Closing his eyes, he searched deeper, wider, broader. There was something there, something on the fringes of his understanding that he couldn't quite grasp. It was as if the magic he was looking for had been changed into something unrecognizable, masked or hidden from detection.

Concentrating like never before, he reached for the burner knob and turned on the gas. Pulling from deep inside, he was able to focus his effort from the energy he had inside himself and those small sparks he sensed. Opening his eyes, he stared intently on the burner, envisioning the gas as it escaped the many ports along its length.

He was startled to see it burst into flame before his eyes. Did he actually do that or did he hit the igniter without thinking? Looking at his outstretched hand, he couldn't remember.

----*----

"Good!" Leander commented as the four sat at the dinner table in Alex's Renton home.

Before each of the four was a plate of food, all prepared by Alex and hot off the grill. Each platter held a cheeseburger with homemade fries and a side salad. The simple fare was as familiar to him as it was exotic to his housemates. All seemed to be enjoying the experience, as the finger food was a novelty for the three. Usually, even in the field, one used a knife or a spoon to eat.

His experimentation while working to make dinner had debunked the notion that all magic had been driven from his world, thought the slightest results took tremendous efforts and concentration, and left him with a terrible headache. In part, it confirmed the Elves stance that the magic might as well be gone, as all Alex had been able to do so far was light the gas grill and a few candles. The amount of concentration required to perform those simple tasked left him light headed, but the effort would have leveled a forest in A'nland.

The exercises did provide some hope that there was a way to get back home, this realm no longer holding that name for him. He was excited at the prospect, but he also felt he needed to keep his discovery to himself, as the inability to explain the complexities of his efforts was a huge obstacle.

"San which?" Cassie asked as she held her burger up for another bite.

"Cheeseburger. But yes, I suppose it's a kind of a sandwich," Alex replied with a smile while nodding in agreement.

He listened as the three exchanged familiar and unfamiliar words while they ate. The general demeanor suggested they liked what he had placed before them. He smiled to himself as he remembered the surprise he had stashed in the freezer for later. He didn't think their world had anything like it.

Kinsey, having finished her own food, sat curled up in one corner of the couch, watching intently for any indication she might get a handout. As best Alex could tell, his little dog was taking their return home in stride, not at all upset at losing her wolf identity. He suspected she had always considered herself a wolf all along so nothing lost.

----*----

Cassie took another bite of the thing Alex called a Chee Burger. Unlike the San Which they had eaten earlier, this one was served hot and had vegetables and sauces mixed in. It was a novelty to eat a proper meal without utensils, the mixed vegetable dish called a Sa Lid being the exception.

"What are these things called again?' Leander asked as he held up one of the long slender fried vegetable sticks.

She had seen Alex dip his in the red sauce before eating it.

"Fries?" Abrianna replied tentatively.

"Yes, that's it. I like them," Leander added as he followed Alex's lead, dipping his it a pool of red on one side of his plate.

"Me too," she added as she mimicked the action.

"Have either of you considered why we are here? I mean why we got sent away with Alex?" Abrianna asked as she paused from her meal.

"I had assumed the Dark Elves had something to do with it. Besides removing Alex as a threat to their plans, you and I are the only heirs to the Great Vale Throne. In one action they have cleared the way to both Great Vale and Windfall."

"Perhaps, but why now. There is no threat on the horizon and no one to assume power should something happen to father. It is almost as if we all came here because it is safe for us to do so," Abrianna said speculatively.

"I am not sure I follow?" Leander asked after swallowing.

"If King Elion needed to send Alex home, for whatever reason, now is the perfect time to do so. The Dark Forces are driven back across the lands, even in the west, and by sending all of us, it lessens the sense of urgency Alex might feel in getting back to you," Abrianna finished, indicating Cassie as the object of Alex's motivations.

She could feel her cheeks flush at the inference, her feelings for the man beside her just a strong.

"You have to admit; things were set up pretty nicely for Alex to return here. I have no idea how it works though, but were anyone to disappear for years back home, I would expect little to remain of their holdings," Abrianna explained.

"You suggest someone else besides Avenstore sent us here? Who and for what purpose?" Leander asked as he finished the last of the food on his plate.

"That is what we need to figure out if we ever hope to get home," she replied as she passed looks between Cassie and Leander.

----*----

Dinner over and the kitchen cleaned, Alex led the trio into the living room to test out another learning tool. Placing everyone where they could see and sit comfortably, he turned the TV on and began flipping through the various channels.

With far more options available to him than he remembered, he eventually found what he was looking for. Located on one of the prime pay channels on his cable TV system, he selected an early season of shows, before television became so politically correct.

Turning to the three seated nearby, he launched the 1970s Sesame Street intended for children's early learning. He watched as the characters talked through letters and numbers. His three companions were confused at first, but began showing understanding as the alphabet streamed across the display. Soon all three were repeating the lessons provided to them.

    Leaving them enthralled, he returned to the kitchen where he broke out the ice cream he had purchased earlier and began filling bowls. Toppings added to increase the decadence of the experience, he passed out the treats to the three humans, dropping a Frosty Paws in front of Kinsey for her own enjoyment. That's how the group spent the evening until exhaustion finally overtook all five and they retreated to their beds for the night.

Chapter 4

Ben Griffin was not particularly excited to see the King of the Woodland Elves. While Elion had been a good friend and ally to him over the years, that relationship had not come without cost. Wars and death had been the currency with which the pair had paid one another for the favors bestowed.

Using one of the two winged horses provided to Alex and Cassie as gifts, he had taken flight to E'anbel. The magical Elven city, one that could only be accessed by elven invitation, usually an escort, or by magical transport. Shadows, a jet-black mare, was one such magical transport.

Amelia had taken the other mount, Rose, west to Windfall to help the mermaid twins in their attempt to rule the city in Alex's absence. He knew Amelia was well up to the task of governing, he was more concerned about the adopted daughters she had recently acquired. The pair had only lately abandoned the larcenist lifestyle of their mermaid sisterhood.

"I would ask to what I owe this unexpected visit, but I won't insult you by playing that game," Elion said as he greeted Ben in the open area where Shadows had landed.

No sooner had hooves hit stone than two of Elion's retainers had appeared to take Shadows to the stables. Following the Elven King as he waved him inside the nearby structure, one Ben knew to be Elion's home, he remained silent until the two had settled in a quiet anteroom.

"My daughter?" Ben asked both cryptically and emotionally.

"I could ask you to just trust me, but when it comes to matters of the heart, more is required."

Ben nodded, acknowledging both the statement and its meaning. Before Elion could say more, a servant came into the room, setting a pitcher and two cups on a nearby table and then retreated silently.

"Would you care for something?" Elion asked, motioning at the tray.

"Please," Ben replied, accepting that good manners required patience.

"So, to the question at hand," Elion started as he poured for the two and then offered Ben a cup.

"Were you aware that Avenstore was at your niece's wedding?"

"I was, you two seemed deep in conversation," Ben replied, recognizing the Dark Elf King's name.

"And you know that the dragons are back, free to roam the skies once more," Elion added after a sip from his cup.

"A few," Ben replied, acknowledging the facts reported to him after Alex and Cassie's last adventure.

"But do you truly understand the significance? They were once bound to the Dark Elves, controlled in absentia via the departed Renfeld and Tantalus. They are now truly free, a neutral power in the war for maintaining the Balance," he explained.

"How does this involve Abrianna?" Ben asked, not really interested in discussing the politics of elves at the moment.

"Since arriving in A'nland, Alex has grown in strength and ability, possibly greater than anyone anticipated," Elion replied, apparently ignoring the question.

"And as he has, he has restored the Balance to a point where we are now in the advantage. His continued presence here would only work to insure our eventual dominance over the Dark forces in this realm. Those he holds close to him, Cassandra, Leander and Abrianna, generate the base of his power."

"So, all were banished from A'nland? To where?" Ben asked, astonished at the revelation as he put it all together.

"Yes. To your earth, a place where there is supposed to be no magic, thus neutralizing his advantage."

"If there is no magic, why send all four?" Ben stated more than asked, his frustration evident in his tone.

"Without his friends, how else could he return here?"

----*----

The following day Alex went back out once more after settling everyone in for the day's lessons. Finishing breakfast, he had Cassie and Abrianna in his office on the laptop once more while Leander and Kinsey sat in the living room watching more Sesame Street. The dog was particularly fascinated by the talking Muppets.

The previous night's viewing had them all counting from one to ten and familiar with several letters of the alphabet before they called it a night. Not wanting to impose on Leander and Abrianna's choice of sleeping arrangements, he simply locked up the house and led Cassie to their room, making his goodnights in the process.

Closing their bedroom door behind Kinsey, who found her spot in one corner, he kissed Cassie gently before leading her into the bathroom. There, he offered his wife, her choice of shower or bath. The inability to communicate with her chafed at him, as he had never given much thought of how much they shared with one another until now.

"Sink, toilet, bathtub," she rattled off with pride, as if she knew his thoughts and was challenging his concern.

"Yes, and this is a shower," he replied as he started the water and then turned the valve redirecting the flow upward to the showerhead.

He could see her surprise and confusion as he motioned for her to undress. She quickly caught on and was soon stepping into the tub, the water directed to the wall, her clothes a mixed pile on the floor. Alex reached up and demonstrated how she could direct the water before closing the shower curtain.

Leaving her to her shower, he reentered their bedroom and began pulling out his earlier purchases, laying out options for her to sleep in. Next, he returned to the bathroom, hanging a towel over the bar for her to dry with when she had finished. Slipping from their room, Alex was headed to the kitchen to get them both drinks. Unfortunately, he was just in time to catch Leander and Abrianna in a passionate embrace at her open bedroom door.

"Pardon me," he quickly offered, trying to retreat back into his room, but the damage was done as both broke away from each other.

Swiftly moving past the two as they made room for him to pass, he vacated the hallway to give them privacy. Spending more time than needed in the kitchen, but eventually needed to leave. Returning to his room, he could see both the guest room doors were closed, indicating Abrianna and Leander had chosen to remain separated for the time being.

He was not surprised at the decision, Leander even more steeped in class traditions than Abrianna, but he was disappointed for the pair. Even though they couldn't talk, he took some comfort that his wife was there by his side this night. He wished the same contentment for his friends, but that was something they needed to work out for themselves.

Closing the door to his own room, he noted the water was off and he heard the sounds of someone drying. Peeking into the bath, he could see Cassie as she finished drying herself.

"Like shower," Cassie offered as she pointed to the showerhead with a smile.

"I thought you might," he replied, not expecting her to understand every word.

Swapping places with her, he undressed and started his own shower, indicating the things he had laid out for her on the bed. The sound of running water next door suggested either Leander or Abrianna had commandeered the other bathroom, as the two shared a common wall. A quick shower had the forest grime off him, and the hot water had worked wonders on aching muscles. Once he had dried himself, he wrapped the towel about his waist and passed his wife, having decided on one of his t-shirt, a toothbrush. Both made quick work of the task.

With that, he led her back into the bedroom where he found something to sleep in and then climbed into bed with Kinsey curled up at their feet.

"Love Alex," she declared as she slid up next to him under the covers.

"Love Cassie," he replied as she wrapped herself around him and they settled in for a night's rest.

Today he was headed out to find an electronics store. All three of his companions were making great progress with the language software and Sesame Street, but he needed his computer for research of his own. With a bulging bank account, according to his online balance, he felt more than comfortable with the extravagance of purchasing three new computers.

Locating one of the larger chain retailers, he cautiously approached one of the sales staff, intent on getting in and out as quickly as possible. He had acknowledged to himself that the technology at home had changed significantly since his last purchase. He recognized the laptop and television were not the same models he had left behind, however similar they might have appeared, so he decided to play dumb.

"How can I help you?" the young woman asked as she stepped out to greet him from behind the counter.

"I need three laptops for some friends starting a language class," he explained.

"You are buying laptops for your friends? Nice guy!" she commented with a smile.

"Well, they are more like family really. They are going to be using language software and need internet access," he explained.

"Well, are you sure you want laptops, or do you really need tablets?" she asked.

"Uh, I don't know," he answered truthfully.

For the next twenty minutes Alex received a primer on tablets vs laptops. The major differences and similarities as well as cost concerns of each type. Some had detachable keyboards and external disk drives.

In the end he selected a model of laptop that could be flipped to work like a tablet including a touch screen or used like a regular laptop with its attached keyboard. The internal SSD, or solid-state disk drive was more than large enough for his needs and the memory and processor could run anything he might consider useful.

He looked at both the Apple and Windows machines, considering the Apple as a more user-friendly option, even with its higher price tag. In the end, cost not really being a concern, he still selected the Windows machines as that was what they all were all used to and changing things up on everyone now added to the learning curve for all involved, himself included.

While he was waiting for the saleswoman to complete the transaction and pull inventory from stock, Alex wandered over to some of the display computer systems. Browsing the various models, his mind began to wander as he absently poked at one. Thinking of his life far from here, he began to make comparison of A'nland and his earthly realm. He focused on Elion's comments on the loss of magic here as the realm had spun out of control.

Looking at all the technology around him, he thought that in some ways the magic wasn't gone, it was simply transformed. Any of the devices here would be as mystical to Ben and Amelia as a conjuring would be to the saleslady. Approaching another of the machines, this one apparently powered off, he imagined turning it on with a wave of his hand.

Alex suddenly stopped, as the display before him flickered to life, a small charge of unexpected energy escaping his fingertips. Quickly glancing around, he noted no one was paying him the slightest attention. He rapidly checked the machine, typing in a few commands and receiving the expected responses. Then, just as quickly the machine went as dark as before.

Unlike his previous attempts here on earth, where he had been trying to force the magic, this came without thought. He had been relaxed and not even trying to gather magic, it was more of a whimsical afterthought than a real attempt. He was also mentally comparing technology and magic, thinking of the two as one rather than separate things. Reaching out with his senses, he thought he could detect just the slightest wisps of free magic floating about.

"Did you want to see this desktop computer as well? I can plug it in for you if you like, we just set it out, but it's not getting power yet," the sales clerk said as she reached past Alex and recovered the power cord, still unattached to the machine.

"No thanks, I was just killing time," Alex replied quickly as he turned and headed to the checkout counter.

The sales woman's confirmation that the computer wasn't even plugged in was the icing on the cake. He had done magic here without trying and in a way completely different than in A'nland. Maybe magic wasn't gone here after all, maybe it was just hidden or took a different form than he was familiar with? Then again, maybe it was him supplying the energy the magic required after all.

Packing his purchases into the Jeep, he quickly found his way home and shuttled everything inside the house where he found everyone as he had left them. Not pausing to try and explain, he simply set all three laptops up on the kitchen table and connected them to his wireless home network.

Next, he led each of the three to their particular machine, receiving an enthusiastic smile from Leander as he realized he had his own computer. Once everyone was settled, Alex returned to his office where he began his own research on earth magic. Working with an assumption that myth was actually recorded history, he looked for references of magical locations.

Why did it take so much effort to light a candle here at home and almost nothing to power the computer at the store? Maybe it wasn't him, maybe it was where he attempted his efforts.

----*----

Emma sat behind the counter of the Tribal Elf, a shop she ran with the other members of her Wicca Coven. The 23-year-old had been a member of the Coven since her mother had first introduced her to the group at age 14. One of several Wicca shops in the greater Seattle area, they also operated as a thrift store and novelty shop, adding to the diversity of their activity and income.

Often confused as witches, she frequently had to explain to friends that she was no such thing. Really a form of modern Paganism, her coven had its roots in a much older belief than was common to other Wiccan groups. More like nature worshipers, they were less focused on gods and goddesses and more the yin and yang of how contrary forces balance one another. Equal but opposite, they provided harmony.

Alone at the moment, she casually flipped through one of the many illustrated books they offered on the magical world they believe existed beyond the obvious. In its pages, she scanned many of the familiar mythical creatures from legends around the world. She paused on a page that held an elf maiden, bow in hand and apparently hunting in the woods.

Ever since she was a little girl, Emma had been fascinated by the natural world around her, both the visible and the imaginary. She would wander the small wooded lot near her home for hours. She drew on her surroundings, letting it energize her when she was sad or lonely. When her mom asked her what she was doing, she always gave her the same response.

"Looking for Fairies."

Obsessed with thoughts of fairies, pixies, nymphs and elves, she would read everything she could find on the subject. On days when she couldn't go outside, she would sit in her room reading or drawing her own pictures of mythical creatures of every kind. It was after one such episode that her mother took her into her confidence.

"Where did you see this?" she asked Emma, holding up one of her pictures, recently completed.

That particular drawing was of an elf girl, sitting sideways in a stream with her knees drawn up to her chest and arms wrapped around them. The water had not quite reached her waist, and a rocky bank behind her giving way to the darkened woods beyond. The face on the page stared back at the observer, head cocked to one side as if evaluating the onlooker.

Her bare legs and exposed back had an elaborate set of tattoos, and her face had a complementary set of markings, starting at her eyes and dropping down over her cheeks. Her long brown hair only partially concealed the markings. Mostly unclothed, she had the distinct pointed Elven ears, tartar eyes and simple jewelry. Earrings, a feathered waist belt and a delicate chain around her head like a crown or Tiera were her accessories. At the center of the chain, a small gemstone centered on her forehead.

"Nowhere, I just made it up in my head," she replied, anxious at her mother's intensity.

"Do you see her in your dreams?' she asked much more softly and with much less emphasis.

"Yes, sometimes," Emma replied slowly.

"Has she spoken to you yet?" her mom asked with a smile.

"You see her too?" she asked her mother urgently.

Emma had been afraid to tell her mother of the elf girl in her dreams. She assumed it was all part of her obsession.

"Yes, I do, but your brother does not. We must keep this to ourselves, do not even tell your father," she replied softly but with an edge that Emma took to add importance to the statement.

"OK," she replied hesitantly.

Her mother had never asked her to keep secrets before, especially from her father.

"Is she real?" Emma asked of her mother, the question one she had been asking herself since the first night she appeared in dreams.

"I don't know for sure, but I think so. Rather, I think she was a really long time ago. My mother explained to me that she is our elven ancestor. She is our connection to magic."

"Magic?" Emma had asked.

"You can feel it, I know you can. When you walk in the woods, you can sense the life all around you. You feel the tingle of excitement with the energy that is all around you," her mother stated.

Emma nodded in agreement, her voice escaping her as her mother had put into words the feeling and emotions she had been struggling to understand.

"Tomorrow you are coming with me, to the shop. There are some people I want you to meet."

And that was how her education had begun. The other women of the coven were like her, they too had dreams of elven ancestors, reaching out to them. A small group, under the 13-member guideline for a Wiccan Coven, they were actually not true to the core belief as outlined by Gerald Gardner and Doreen Valiente in the 1940s and 50s. Wicca was what most closely aligned to their principles, so they just ran with it.

All of these women had images of elves in their heads, but the images were not all alike. It was almost as if they were all members of different elven groups. And because of that, it was magic that drove the common beliefs of this group of women. Well, magic and a core belief that they were descendants of ancient elven tribes of some sort. They worked tirelessly to try and connect with the magical energy they believe connected all life force, rooted in nature.

Emma was extremely proud of the fact that they had adopted her drawing as the logo for the shop. She had done others after joining but it was her first image that everyone agreed embodies the spirit of their Coven.

As she stared at the page before her, she suddenly felt a tingling, as if she had been electrically charged. Before she could focus on it, trying to locate the source, it faded. Part of the reason they had chosen this location for their shop was a strong sense of magic. Abigail, their leader, had explained that some places were better than others for working magic.

"Did you just feel that?" Madison asked as she appeared from the back room where she had been working.

Almost ten years older than Emma, Madison had been with the coven since her 16th birthday when her father had brought her to the group. While the magic flowed from both men and women, this group focused on the female aspects of the influence.

"I did, it was stronger than anything I have felt before," she replied.

"We need to get the others, call a gathering," Madison instructed.

Chapter 5

Sitting in his office, Alex could hear the three talking in the dining room as he continued to do his research, the door open between the two rooms. The event at the electronics store had him confused but hopeful. As he bounced from website to website, he looked for any references to magic users in the here and now. There were tons of references to medieval wizards or Salem witches, but the more modern references were fringe religious sites.

"Alex. Please come," he heard from the other room as he stopped to stretch after crouching over his laptop for so long.

Getting up from his seat, he stepped into the other room where he found the three huddled over Abrianna's laptop. On the screen was a series of symbols and images that took him aback. It appeared that Abrianna was doing an internet search outside of the lesson software and had come across a local Wiccan website, The Tribal Elf.

"Elf magic," Abrianna said while indicating one particular symbol on the site.

Looking over her shoulder, Alex read what the site had to say about the image. Sure enough, the image, a seven-pointed star, was labeled the Elven Star. It was referenced as an ancient symbol from time immemorial of the sacred number seven. In a more modern reference, it was adopted to reflect not only the four points of the compass, North, South, East and West, it also added Above, Below, and Within.

Next to it, was the better known five-pointed star referencing air, water, fire, earth and spirit. There were other images of what Alex knew as Celtic knots and things that looked distinctly Egyptian. All had the two women very excited.

"Why are you looking at magic?" Alex suddenly asked, sure this was not a coincidence.

"Got feeling before Alex come home," Cassie replied and Abrianna nodded as well.

Scanning the site, Alex found references to earth magic and Wiccan rites. Hitting a few of the hyperlinks he came across something that caused the two women to comment once more.

"Dragons!" Cassie and Abrianna blurted in unison.

The exclamation spurred a flurry of conversation between the three A'nlanders while Alex continued his investigation of the website. The webpage had several images of various dragon novelties, some interwoven in symbols while others were standalone figurines. The page referenced Dragon Guardians. Scanning the text, it described dragons as protectors and made references of humans who work with them in harmony.

Finally, the three stopped talking and Abrianna got Alex's attention.

"Alex. Elves' magic, Dragons' magic," she said simply, but with a motion of her hands.

He watched as she continued to repeat the phrase while motioning from one side to another. Suddenly the significance hit him.

"Dragons can move between realms like elves can," he stated while repeating Abrianna's action.

----*----

Amelia arrived in Windfall to a raucous crowd in the courtyard of the Windfall Castle. On the steps of the keep were the redheaded twins, trying to get the gathered group to listen while a line of palace guards stood between the two parties.

"What in the name of all that is holy is going on here?" she announced in a royal tone as she climbed the steps after emerging from the parting crowd and passing through the line of guards.

"We were holding court as we had seen Alex do and they turned on us," one of the two identical redheads shouted.

That seemed to incite the assembled men even more. From the looks of the gathering, Amelia assumed them to be merchants or other tradesmen.

"SILENCE!" Amelia shouted over the din.

"You, what is your name?" she announced while pointing at a rather well dress man in the front row.

"My Lady Amelia, I am Adad and I run a trading house of eastern goods. These two charlatans dare suggest that I employ mermaids to transport payments to and from my buyers across the Western Sea," the man said angrily.

"I will remind you these girls are my daughters and Ladies in the Royal court!' she replied sternly.

"My apologies, my Lady," the man replied, duly chastised.

"And you?" Amelia continued, point to another in the front of the crowd.

"I am Doirend my Lady. The Ladies wanted me to allow mermaids to direct my fishing fleet, and then pay them for it!"

"Did they now? Listen to me everyone, there will be no changes in the trading laws or fishing practices today. Everyone return to your businesses and come back tomorrow where I will hear your petitions."

Amelia watched as the crowd dispersed before turning on the twins and waving them inside the keep.

"Mother…" started one of the two

"Not a word!" she snapped as she waved them in through the double doors before heading to one of the small anterooms and closing the door behind them.

"Sit!" she said to the twins as she pointed to a couch.

Taking her own seat across from the girls, she took a deep breath before speaking.

"Look, I am sure you meant well…"

"Mother they wouldn't listen to us. That man, Adad, he was complaining of the pirates and his loss of payments returning from Freeport. We suggested that he use mermaids to transport gemstones rather than gold and silver. They have higher per piece value in smaller quantities and would be moved in a fashion inaccessible to pirate raids."

"And the other man," the second girl started.

"He wanted magical help in locating better fishing grounds. We suggested he pay the mermaids to find the best places to fish instead," the other finished.

Amelia gave out a deep sigh before replying to the sisters. As she studied their faces, she realized she needed to spend more time with the girls. She still had no telltale clue as to which was Leena and which was Kelby. She knew Cassie could tell the difference but she hadn't shared that little secret with her mother.

"While your ideas do have merit, do you not see that these people are not yet ready to accept mermaids the way you know them to be. The merchant only knows them as thieves, and you propose he trusts them with great wealth. And you, it is well known that mermaids slit the nets of the fisherman to frustrate their efforts."

She could see the girls considering her words as she paused for effect.

"It will take more time for you to gain their trust, you can't just dictate your desires to them. Let's see if we can't come up with a way to demonstrate your ideas to them," Amelia finished gently.

"It looks so much easier when you and Alex do it," the one she thought was Kelby replied before standing to hug their adopted mother. The one she thought was Leena joined in the embrace after nodding her agreement.

----*----

Cassie and Abrianna were doing their best to get Alex to understand them. Before he had returned with the new lap tops, both had recently felt, well, something that triggered a familiar tingling. Abrianna had been the first to sense the energy of magic, calling attention to the event.

"Did you just feel that?" she had asked Cassie earlier as the pair shared the magic window while Leander remained in the other room. They were going over yet another panel of images, working to memorize the meaning of each.

"Feel what?" she asked as she shifted her attention away from the images before her.

"Did you just feel a tingling? You know, like a discharge of magic?"

"I did feel something, but I thought it was from sitting here so long," Cassie replied after considering the question.

What she didn't want to expand on was, she had been feeling many new sensations lately. She wasn't sure what was going on inside her, but things were different somehow. She had been attributing it to the transformation of coming to Alex's home realm from her own. A magical creature herself, she worried that prolonged exposure here was doing her harm, but feared giving voice to her concerns.

"Well, it's gone now," Abrianna sighed.

The two continued to work together until Alex returned home. Not wanting to get in his way, she continued to work with Abrianna as he busied himself in the other room, pulling strange objects from boxes and stringing the strange black rope everywhere. Once he was finished, he gathered everyone and placed each with their own magic window.

"These are laptops," she heard him explain as he placed something called a headset on each.

Cassie was surprised to hear the sounds, removing hers once so see if the others could as well. The silence she discovered, explained that each of them could only hear their own devices. She went back to working on her language skills until Abrianna got her attention once more.

"Cassie come look at this," she said while waving her cousin over.

Removing the headset and moving over to the other side of the table where Abrianna had been working, she could see that her cousin was not doing the same thing she had been. Looking at the thing Alex called a Lap Top, she saw something surprising.

"Brie, what are you doing?"

"I watched Alex earlier, and he put words in that thing called *google*. I tried elves and magic and this is what I found," she explained as she displayed images familiar to them both.

"Those are sacred magic symbols. Your father has books on that," Cassie commented.

"Do you think Alex knows about this?' Abrianna asked.

"Alex. Please come," Cassie shouted.

The pair waited until he turned the corner of the table before continuing.

"Elf magic," Abrianna said while pointing to her Lap Top.

They all watched, Leander being drawn into the conversation by now, as Alex flipped through the screens. Cassie could see her husband reading the words that were only now beginning to become legible to her.

"Look, Brie, Dragons!" she blurted as Alex changed screens.

She watched as Abrianna attempted to make Alex understand that Dragons, like Elves, could move between realms at will. That could be their way back home.

----*----

Captain Regas stood at the railing of his ship, Sea Rapier, as he scanned the horizon. Fresh from a port call in Windfall, he was unsettled by the news from the castle. The disappearance of the Lord Protector was a bad omen for Windfall and made his duties all the more important. Of all the ships made available to him since his appointment by the Lord Protector, this one was by far the fastest and most maneuverable. That was very important to him as he was now responsible for protecting the very waterways he once pirated himself.

His methods were proven, almost exactly same as he used as a pirate. He would use the smaller, faster ship to overtake his target, disabling the vessel only enough to allow the larger, more heavily armed warships to catch up and subdue their prey.

Unfortunately, lately business has been a little too good, that was why he returned to port. In the very short time since the disappearance of the Lord Protector and Lady Cassandra, the Western Sea pirates had returned in mass. Part of him longed for the old days where he was the one chasing down the fat merchant ships. His thoughts were interrupted by the lookout.

"Mermaid on the port side!"

The announcement reminded him of one of the reasons he was glad he wasn't pirating these days. Earlier that day he had received a message bird instructing him to expect such a visit. Moving quickly to the left side of the ship, he peered over the railing to see the delightfully bare torso of an exquisite young woman, easily keeping pace with the moving vessel.

Her piercingly beautiful green eyes were framed in jet black hair. Only visible from the waist up as she rolled over on her back to more easily talk to the ship's company, Regas could only imagine the powerful tail that was easily propelling her to keep pace with the ship's progress.

"What's the word?" he asked the vision of loveliness.

A smile crossed her face as she scanned the ship's railing before speaking. The number of sailors manning the port railing was increasing with every second. After ensuring her appearance had garnered a respectable audience, she turned her attention back to Captain Regas.

"There are three small ships lying in wait, hidden in the islands off the west end of the Northern Mountains. They appear to be planning to attack the trade ship from Nyland. Do you know the place?"

"Very well," Regas replied as he recalled the place she described.

It was in a bay not far from there that he had encountered the Lord Protector, negotiating a meeting with the Dwarf King and gaining a leadership position in the Royal Navy. Part of that assignment was now chasing off his former comrades in arms, inspiring them to look for safer waters to practice their trade. Now helping in that effort were the mermaids related to the wife of the Lord Protector.

A paradox to sailors, the mermaid community had always been considered a love/hate relationship. The sailors loved the attention they received in their presence, and then hated themselves the next day when they found themselves flat broke. The message from the bird explained that Lady Kelby, newly adopted member of the royal household, had brokered an agreement enlisting mermaid help in policing the local waters.

Regas understood the newly formed relationship was intended to align the two groups in a common cause. Before this new arrangement, she had initially helped some with the thievery against His Majesty's sailors, but with this last port call he had caught one particular mermaid ignoring the instructions. Regas called her on it, reminding her of the truce.

"Hey, a girl's gotta make a living!" had been the reply.

A word to the head mermaid had found the offender reassigned to other tables.

"Anything else?" Regas asked the girl below as he watched her flirt with his men.

"Tell Leena, we miss her!" she replied and then blew a kiss to those on the railing and now in the rigging high above as well.

With that, Captain watched her turn over and disappear into the depths with a parting wave.

"Back to work!" he bellowed at the crew without bothering to look in their direction.

----*----

Alex was not sure this was the greatest idea, but his companions were not to be denied. After their stilted conversation, both Cassie and Abrianna insisted they visit the Wiccan shop on the website. The site had indicated that the shop was open until 9pm today and was located in the University District area of downtown.

While not terribly far from his Renton home, it was still in a heavily traveled area close to the University. The fact that this was a workday for most people also meant the roads would be filled with commuters heading home. Fortunately, their route had them going an opposite direction from those leaving their offices downtown.

"Alex, boats?" Cassie said to him from the passenger seat up front next to his.

Leaving Kinsey at home, they were crossing the I-90 floating bridge and there were a small number of small pleasure boats out on Lake Washington. Given the wet, yet warm weather, he suspected they were playing hooky from work. A common practice in the summer, people took advantage of the warmth even in the rain.

"Yes, boats," Alex replied before they entered the I-90 tunnel, blocking them from view.

Emerging into the light on the other side of the tunnel, he heard the audible gasp from all three passengers as the downtown high rises came into view. Transitioning from I-90 to I-5 Northbound, the traffic slowed, giving them all plenty of time to gawk.

"That big house?" Abrianna asked from the back seat.

Alex could see her pointing to Columbia Center, a full 76 stories tall.

"No, not a house, People work there," he replied while mimicking typing on a keyboard and watching her face in the rear-view mirror.

He could see the confusion on her face until Leander repeated the typing motion while saying something. The only word Alex understood was laptop. With that, her face brightened.

"Work, not house," she repeated with a nod.

Alex was pleased to see that the three were picking up the basics of English, hopefully enough that they could soon do more than identify objects and basic needs. The three still talked to one another in what Alex called A'nlandian, but their intermixing of English words was increasing.

By now they had edged their way past downtown and were approaching Lake Union on the left of I-5. Alex could see the University on the right as they crossed the Ship Canal Bridge and he prepared to exit. Not overly familiar with the U District himself, he wandered around several streets before he found parking near their destination.

"Oh great," he commented as the four exited the Jeep into a light rain.

A normal occurrence in Seattle, the overcast skies had opened up into a constant mist, soaking anyone unprepared for the event.

"This way," he said to his companions as he led them on the short walk to the shop.

Nothing more than a typical Seattle drizzle, it was enough to get the four of them more than damp before they reached The Tribal Elf's front door. Waving everyone in before him, he was just in time to step into the open area of the shop where a group of women were all standing, staring at Cassie.

"Why is she glowing?" the closest asked while pointing at his wife.

Chapter 6

Rather than a direct return to Great Vale from his trip to the Elvin city, King Ben had diverted to Windfall to check on Amelia and the twins. While King Elion had been no more helpful regarding Alex than his insinuation that the four together had the ability to return home, it was relayed with optimism. However, the rest of Ben's visit was not so positive.

Elion had warned him that with Alex gone, he feared the dark forces would once again try to press for their advantage. There had been rumblings in the north, as the Vassal King was not happy with how things had fared with Tantalus and his dragons. Normally an unorganized group of individuals, Elion had seen a change in the North that had him concerned.

Shadows set down lightly in the courtyard inside the keep walls, startling several guards and a few unsuspecting businessmen crossing the open space.

"Forgive me," Ben commented as Shadows did her best not to run down the pair of unfortunate traders in her path.

One of the two appeared to be preparing a sharp retort, but halted once he recognized the rider.

"Sire, we didn't hear your approach," the other replied as they scanned the closed gates behind Ben, confused where he had come from. Shadows wings had disappeared at her landing, so for anyone not watching, it would be as if she appeared from thin air. With a parting wave, Ben reined her over to one side where a stable hand had rushed to meet him.

"See that she is well cared for," he instructed the young lad.

"Yes Sire," came the simple reply as the boy led Shadows over to the stables.

"Ben!" came an exclamation from behind him as Amelia appeared at the top of the steps of the keep. He was sure someone must have rushed to fetch her at his appearance in the yard.

"Amelia," Ben replied as he quickly climbed the stairs to embrace his adopted sister.

"How is it?" he asked quietly, motioning toward the inside as the pair turned and entered the keep.

"Much better now that I am here," Amelia replied, understanding the question concerning the twins.

"I have assigned each of them special duties that are better suited to their current understanding of how a kingdom is run," she added with a quick smile.

"Good," Ben replied with a smile of his own.

"I have also instructed them not to take on any additional duties without checking with me first!" she added with a broad smile.

Looking around, Ben could see a great deal of activity in the public area of the keep. Peering into the great hall, its ceiling long since repaired from the gaping hole Alex had created in his battle with the red mages, he could see the twins busy with various groups. He passed a questioning look to Amelia.

"They actually had some great ideas; they just didn't understand how to communicate them. Kelby is working with the bankers and merchants devising a pilot program for mermaid transported payments between the various ports," she said as she motioned to the crowded table on one side of the room.

Ben could see several dour looks on the men she was speaking with. As he considered the proposal, he could actually see the brilliance of it, but understood the skepticism of the men. He could hear Kelby patiently answering their questions one by one.

"I told her to think of working the bar, more subtly and without the thievery," Amelia said with a grin.

"Leena is working with the fishing boat Captains," she said simply while pointing to another group.

Here, Ben could see the twin walking among the seated men, her actions far more like a barmaid. She would pass from man to man, pausing to rest her arm on their shoulders as she too answered questions. The fact that she had a lot more exposed skin than her sister was not lost on the group of men. He had to suppress a laugh as he scanned the faces of the seated participants. All were entranced with her actions.

"Why are you here?" Amelia finally asked, pulling his attention from the twins.

"Elion warns that trouble is coming. He believes the Northern Lords are organizing for action, though I am not sure what size force they can field. He also talks of troubles in the west, with Tantalus gone and his dragons free to do as they wish."

"Ben, you now have strong relations with both the Northern Dwarves and those in Two Thorns. In addition, all of Great Vale and Windfall follow your lead, that is probably the largest consolidation of support in ages. Who would dare to directly challenge such, Alex or no?"

"That is what has me worried."

----*----

Alex surveyed the women lined up before his group. All were mesmerized as they stared at his wife, glowing a beautiful aqua.

"You see light?" Abrianna asked in broken English as she motioned to her cousin by her side.

"Yes," one of the younger women finally replied with a nod of agreement.

The women were all passing confused looks as they glanced to one another for confirmation.

"Who are you people?" a second asked.

Before Alex could reply, a sound from behind caused him to turn. Entering the shop after the four, an older woman absently entered the space, not looking up until she noted the standoff between the groups.

"Why is she glowing?" she asked as she passed over to the others, while staring at Cassie.

"Do you have a towel or something she can dry with?" Alex asked without further explanation.

With everyone else standing quietly, the young woman who had spoken earlier rapidly sidestepped out of the room, never taking her eyes off Cassie. She quickly returned with a towel in hand.

"Here," she said with an extended arm.

Alex took the towel and handed it to Cassie, motioning for her to dry herself. She did as she was told and he could soon see her telltale aqua colored hue begin do die until it was almost imperceivable. He realized at that point that they had not showered together since their arrival here so he had never seen the telltale flair of magic he had come to expect from her when wet. The realization gave him hope.

"Who are you?" the woman repeated.

"My name is Alex Rogers, and this is my wife Cassie. That's Abrianna and Leander," Alex supplied, pointing to each in turn.

"That's not what I meant," she started.

"Yes, I know, but we need a little information first before we go there. Who are you all?" he asked in return.

It was then that the older woman who had just entered, stepped up to Alex and started examining him closely. He could see Cassie watching her every move as she began to touch his face with her hands. He heard Cassie say something to Abrianna in A'anlandian and receive a nod in reply.

She closed her eyes as she stood with his face in her hands, everyone else quiet as they watched.

"It was you, wasn't it?' she said more than asked as she stepped back.

"Lock the doors, we are closed for the day," she said to the others as she motioned to the young woman who had retrieved the towel.

"This way, please," she motioned as she indicated that Alex's group should follow.

Leading them into a back room, he heard an audible gasp from both Cassie and Abrianna as they scanned the space. All around them were symbols and images similar to those they had seen on the website.

"We are Wiccan," was all the older woman said as the group filed in.

"Please sit," she then said as she pointed to the chairs surrounding a great open space in the center of the room.

Alex guided Cassie to one of the seats, taking the one next to her. Abrianna and Leander sat next to him. With everyone seated, they sat quietly for a moment before the woman spoke once more.

"It was your magic we felt, wasn't it?" she asked Alex.

"Magic gone," Abrianna said firmly.

"What she means is we were under the impression magic was gone here," Alex added.

"Here?" one of the others repeated as a question.

"I am a local but they are not," he answered indicating his companions.

"Ireland?" someone asked while indicating the green-eyed redhead at Alex's side.

"A'nland," came Cassie's reply.

It was then that Abrianna stood up and went over to the older woman who had inspected Alex. Repeating the actions of the older woman, she echoed the performance on her. Abrianna stood motionless for several seconds before opening her eyes and turning to her companions.

"Elves," was all she said.

----*----

Abrianna had been surprised as anyone to see Cassie glowing as the four walked to the shop they had seen on the lap top. Still unsure if it was a merchant shop or a temple, she just hoped it was a lead on how to get home. It took her a moment to remember that, unlike her and Alex, who just manipulated magic, Cassie was actually a magical creature herself, at least in part. If any of the four of them were to have some form of residual magic in this realm, Cassie was more likely due to her heritage.

It was the realization that the women of the place could see her glow, as well as the sacred symbols on the walls that convinced her it was a temple. What she now wanted to understand was, were the women like Cassie, magical themselves, or was it the place that held some of the old magic supposedly long since banished.

The room they sat in held all the things she would expect to see in a place of worship. Beyond the symbology on the walls, there were small figures and statuary of creatures and races familiar to her. There were also candles and crystals used in ceremonies and spell casting. It was the dragon imagery, though, that had her greatest interest.

Long ago, before the great war that had seen dragons in hiding or enslaved to do others bidding, they had been free to roam the many realms. In the seas, on land or in the skies, they had the magic required to pass through the boundaries that kept the realms separate from one another. It was for that reason that the folklore here in Alex's home realm held tales of their existence.

That thought was interrupted by the conversation between Alex and one of the women.

"Magic gone," she stated flatly.

She hadn't caught all of the words the two had exchanged and now heard Alex adding to her comment. Abrianna was extremely frustrated at the inability to communicate beyond simple concepts. She longed to speak with Alex about how he was able to source his magical energies back in A'nland before coming here. While she had been the senior practitioner in terms of longevity, he had both Elven training and a natural ability to draw in the power he needed from other sources, like no one she had ever seen.

Since their arrival, she had been attempting to work any kind of magic, but the emptiness around them left her with nothing to manipulate. She could draw from within, but didn't have the magical strength to do more than a simple reading of the health and welfare of her companions. That was how she knew something was up with Cassie, she just hadn't the time to identify what it was.

Glancing at Cassie as she replied to something, she could see the Nymph's glow was gone, her clothes dry so the nymph magic dissipated. She had relished the slight sense of magic her cousin had radiated earlier. That thought suddenly had her up and standing before the older woman that appeared to lead the others of the gathering.

Closing her eyes, she reached out with her senses, straining to find any sense of magic. As her mind wandered over the woman's presence, she could detect a fleeting panic in the woman until she relaxed at Abrianna's touch. For them to see Cassie's magical aura, there had to be some native magic in the woman, just like Cassie's nymph source.

It took her several tries, but she touched something deep in the woman's being that brought it all together for Abrianna. This woman was touched by Elf magic. Somewhere in her past, she had an elven ancestor.

"Elves," she announced as she pointed to the women in the room.

----*----

Alex rose as Abrianna waved him over to her. Mimicking the movements that she had just performed once more, he heard her instruct him.

"Feel Elf inside," she said as she motioned for Alex to repeat her actions.

Doing as he was told, he closed his eyes and let his senses roam over the woman before him. Not exactly sure what he was doing, he did as Abrianna had shown him before, when the two were working to save Cassie from the dragon venom in the tunnels beneath the Northern Mountains. This time, however, he wasn't looking for the angry red of the dragon poison, he was looking for, well, he didn't know what he was looking for.

Scanning the woman carefully, he gently probed deeper and deeper until he spotted something different. Turning to Abrianna, he repeated the action with her, looking for a similar effect. Sure enough, Abrianna had a similar trait, although hers was more pronounced. Deep inside her being, he could see a light green glow, he supposed the essence of her magic. The woman he scanned earlier had one similar, only hers was more of a brown color.

"Well, I'll be damned," he said as he nodded understanding to Abrianna.

"Are you all related to Elves?" he asked as he scanned the assembled coven.

"Who are you people?" another repeated for the third time.

"I am Lord Protector Alex Rogers of the city of Windfall," Alex started with a bit of pomp.

"This is my wife, Lady Cassandra. Next to her is Crown Princess Abrianna of Great Vale and her betrothed Leander, Grand Master of the Rangers Guild," he finished.

As he spoke, each of his companions acknowledged their name as spoken.

"I knew it, I knew the fairy world still existed! That's where you are from, right, the fairy world?" a young woman burst out.

"In a manner of speaking," Alex replied hesitantly.

"Why are you here?' the older woman asked, attempting to quell the exuberance of the young woman beside her.

"Dragons," both Abrianna and Cassie said in unison.

"Dragons?" the woman repeated.

"We find ourselves stranded here in this realm and are trying to get back home. Both Cassie and Abrianna think that we can use a dragon to return home as they can pass between the realms using their innate magic," he explained.

"Realms," another woman asked.

So now it was that Alex's turn as he walked the group through the last 1 plus year of his life, skipping over much of the details regarding the war and anything about why they found themselves stranded here. As he spoke, the older woman had drinks served and cut several questions short to prevent him from getting sidetracked.

"So there really are dragons?" she said absently as she shook her head slowly in amazement.

"Alex free dragons from slavery," Cassie said in broken English.

"Slavery?" came a concerned question.

"Not really slavery. There were a few dragons where we are from who were forced to fight against their will or risk losing their eggs. We were able to return the eggs and free them from the villain holding them hostage," he explained, wondering where in the world Cassie had learned that word.

"Your website talks about Dragon Guardians and attracting them. That's why we came here," he explained, anxious to get off the topic of hostage dragons and slavery.

Now it was the older woman who looked uncomfortable.

"I'm not sure how helpful we can be, most of that material you saw online comes from old documents we have. There are some papers here as well, written in Runes, we believe them to be quite old. Unfortunately, none of us can read them and everyone we have taken them to for translation say they are fake. They have been part of this coven since its creation."

"Can we see them?" Alex asked.

The woman motioned to one of her members, and the other bolted from her seat. Alex could see the anticipation in the women as if they were waiting for some great revealing event to occur. Returning quickly, the woman handed a small stack of yellowed parchment sheets. Alex did a quick scan of the sheets only to confirm they were completely illegible to him, though the characters were clear and easy to see.

Passing the stack to Abrianna, he hoped she might be able to understand the contents. With all eyes on her, Abrianna scanned each sheet, occasionally nodding her head in understanding. After taking several moments to study each of the pages provided her, she set the pile down on her lap and looked up at those gathered around her.

"Elf words," Abrianna declared after scanning the sheets.

Chapter 7

The Vassal King, Ailmer, was not in the best of moods as he sat eating dinner with his wife Vennala. After that disaster with Tantalus and his cursed dragons, the couple had laid low lest the southern King march his troops, already afield, north and take his lands as well as Windfall's. Fortunately, there had been no such effort made to dethrone the couple and so they breathed a sigh of relief.

"Any word from the west my love?" Vennala asked after she had waited for the servants to leave.

Since their near-death experience in this very room, Ailmer had ordered all servants vacate the room during meals. Only one at a time was permitted at the doorway to respond when summoned. That damn redheaded enchantress had nearly blown them all to pieces with the Wizard's black magic packages. A good part of his living area was still under repairs from those explosions.

"Not a word, nor a declaration of support from Avenstore himself."

"He had promised to make amends for the failures of Tantalus. Does he not know of the restlessness of the Northern Lords? Assurances have been made, commitments to be honored," she replied with an edge in her voice.

"I have received a message from the south declaring the demon White Wizard and his nymph wife have disappeared," Ailmer offered to help mollify his wife, it would not do for her to get spun up unduly.

"Good riddance," she snapped in reply.

With that, the two sat in silence for several minutes, eating. Ailmer watched his wife, for he noticed a sudden softening in her manner.

"The White Wizard is gone from Windfall you say?" she repeated.

"Yes, gone in the night. Rumors are the Dark Elves are to blame, retaliation for the losses incurred and dragons freed," he said as he watched her consider the information.

"There you have it, Avenstore's support," she said as she brightened into a smile.

"How so?" Ailmer asked, not seeing where his wife was going with the comment.

"Avenstore will never appear before us declaring you heir to Renfeld's legacy. He has, however, cleared the path for you to step up and take it for yourself," she said, building in her excitement.

"I am not so sure…" Ailmer stated in reply.

"Nonsense. Call a gathering of the Lords so we can spread the news and begin planning the conquest of Windfall! Imagine, we would hold both deep water ports on the coast!"

Ailmer began a reply, but was cut short as his wife sprang from the table and began to hurry from the room.

"I must go select what I will wear for the gathering. I do wish that girl hadn't left with the wizard, she had a real talent," he heard her say to herself as she left through the doors leading to the usable part of the upper floors.

Ailmer wasn't as convinced as his wife that the path was clear. He would need a lot more from Avenstore before he dared challenge King Ben for Windfall.

----*----

Abrianna had separated the papers provided her, into three separate stacks. After rereading each and every one, she was positive they were on the right track for finding a way home. Only one of the piles applied to dragons though. The others related to the history of Elves in this realm and the last more specifically to the ancestors of the members of this coven.

Unfortunately, each pile held a fraction of the total information relating to the aforementioned subjects. Abrianna would start on one page and the next would jump ahead, leaving a considerable void in the narrative. Just as she found reference to the methods for summoning a dragon, the next page discussed the temperaments and characteristics of several breeds.

Looking up from her work she could see every eye in the room watching her work.

"Not all," she said in frustration, her broken English adding to her agitation.

"What Brie?" Cassie asked nearby in A'nlandian.

"These are all in the ancient elven tongue, but they are only partials. Each stack refers to different subjects, but none of them are a whole tale."

"What about the dragons?" Leander asked.

"This pile here refers to dragons. This page starts on how to summon one, but the following pages are missing."

"What about the others?" Cassie asked while motioning to the greater share of parchments before here.

"This group tells the tale of the Elves history in this realm. It talks mostly about Woodland Elves and their interactions with ancient humans. That pile describes the mixed breed children of elves and humans. Apparently, as they saw the magic leaving this world, there was a move to have more children of mixed race blood."

"Does it say why?" Cassie asked.

As the three talked, they could see the others, Alex included, waiting for them to finish.

"It starts to but the next page isn't here. All it says is, *The ties that bind us together*."

----*----

Avenstore sat behind a large glass and steel desk, located in a spacious office high in the Columbia Tower building in downtown Seattle. His corner office had a spectacular view of the city below, including downtown and the Space Needle. The glass workspace before him was devoid of clutter, only an office phone and a monitor with a keyboard was visible.

The remainder of his office was decorated in a similar fashion, all very modern and lacking the traditional wooden furniture and dark paneling found in most stiff senior executives' offices. Unlike the Woodland Elves who had abandoned this reality, he had chosen not to hide his presence, but rather embrace its culture. It took very little effort and even less magic to adjust his appearance to fit in with the humans surrounding them.

His fine suit and expensive shoes made him look every bit the successful businessman he was. He was in fact the CEO of a very successful corporation, diverse in its holdings and almost entirely run by Dark Elves. With the bulk of his employees consisting of humans, it was only the senior management that were his loyal subjects.

"Sir, here is the report you requested," he heard as his assistant entered after a brief knock at the door.

"Thank you, Roberta," he replied with an easy smile and acknowledgement of her statement.

"Will you require anything else? I was thinking of going home for the night," she replied.

"No, thank you. Have a nice evening," he replied, the smile never leaving his face.

He watched as she turned and left, closing the door behind her as she did so. It was only then that he opened the folder before him, leafing through the pages as he scanned each. He had no sooner completed the last page when there was another tapping at the door.

"Come in," he replied as he closed the folder.

"Is that the report Sire?" a well-dressed man asked after he closed the door behind himself and approached the desk.

"Sit," Avenstore replied as he pointed to one of the chairs opposite his desk.

Sliding the folder across his desk to the elf, his second in command here, he waited until the other had an opportunity to scan its contents in full before speaking.

"What is Elion up to?" Avenstore finally asked after the other looked up from the papers.

"The reconnaissance team reported that Lady Cassandra, Princess Abrianna and the Ranger Guild Master were all relocated with the Wizard?"

"Yes, that was not part of my discussion with Elion, but in a way, it makes sense. If the Wizard had been returned without his bride, his motivation to find a way back would be immeasurable. His efforts to do so could upset our activities here," Avenstore said with a knowing look.

"But the Princess and Guild Master, what of them?"

"Yes, that is the question now, isn't it? I feel this is some sort of power play by Elion, however on the surface, it makes little sense," Avenstore replied as he considered the situation.

"Perhaps a ruse to get the King of Great Vale more involved?" the elf asked his king.

"Perhaps, however, that notable will soon be swept up in events at home. I think it's time I took things up a notch there."

"What about the recent burst of magic? That was felt far and wide. I fear it may have been the Wizard," his subordinate speculated.

"It will take more than that to expose our operations here. OK, enough of this for now, maintain surveillance, but keep your distance. The four are not to know they are under observation. Oh, and keep all information on this activity off the network, no electronic copies, we are not the only one's capable of intercepting such information," he added while waving the folder in the air.

----*----

The ride home had the three passengers actively talking among themselves as Alex sat listening to the gibberish with the occasional English word mixed in. They had stayed at The Tribal Elf until well after dark and Alex did his best to help interpret Abrianna's findings. While everyone watched the three A'nlanders talk among themselves, each of the coven members had quietly approached Alex, asking him to confirm the Elf ancestry within.

All the members of the coven did contain some remnant of Elf magic, but Alex could tell they were not of the same source. Some had the brown he had sensed in the head of their coven, while others had blues, greens and various shades of all three. He secretly feared he would find the black of the Dark Elves in one of the members but was relieved there was none in this group.

He was surprised to find that the leader of the coven, Abigail, was not the strongest of the members either. Emma, a young woman that appeared no more than 21 or so, had a very strong light blue in her. Unsure of how the information would be received, he kept that part to himself, only assuring her he could see the elf in her.

"Alex, how far Enga Land?" Cassie asked, breaking his train of thought.

"It's pretty far. We would need to fly, which will present its own problems," he said absently, unsure of how much Cassie could understand.

It wasn't just the flying that was troubling Alex, unsure of how his companions would fare in a plane for hours on end. In the here and now of his world, people did not just jump from country to country without papers. Specifically, he needed to find a way to get the three passports to travel abroad.

Once Abrianna had described the papers and indicated they were incomplete, the excited group had explained that they had been brought to the US from England. The home of the modern Wiccan movement, it had started in the early 20th century and expanded to the US and the rest of Europe from there. It was suggested that the missing pages could be found in the archives there.

----*----

To move between realms was as easy for Avenstore as it would be for the average human to make a run to the corner store. That was not to be his challenge on this trip. The realm he was visiting was one where the dominant life form, roughly human in appearance and skeletal structure, was hunted almost to extinction.

The cause of that was the reason for this trip. The Realm's state of affairs had drawn the Elvin King here in the first place.

"Love what you've done with the place," Avenstore opened as he stopped before the organized mass of metal sitting on the roughhewn stone throne before him.

Looking all about, he could see the remnants of the death and destruction wrought by the object of his interest. What wasn't dead or destroyed, was burning, crumbling or in a general state of decay. Skeletal remains were piled everywhere, the vanquished adversaries of the throne's occupant.

"I have a job for you, think of it as an all you can eat opportunity" Avenstore explained as he turned his attention back to the armored Knight sitting splayed in the only organized stone structure left standing.

Leaning slightly to one side, it appraised the Elf with blood red eyes, peering through the only openings in his horned helmet. Its armor was ornate but functional, the occasional mark embedded in a fold or ridge indicating use in combat. The helmet carried more decorations, the horns protruding from the top gave the king an impression of an Ibex, in the way they curled unwavering to the rear. The look was more animalistic than demonic.

A massive sword was held in one hand, so long it stood crosswise, acting almost as a barrier between the two. The blade was intricate but certainly not ceremonial as its length was stained with the blood of those that lay rotting all around.

"A new realm for you to feast on, one that will prove no great challenge, but I do request a tad more restraint," Avenstore added with a sigh as he motioned about them.

He watched as the creature stared back with the red orbs it called eyes. After a pause, he detected the slightest nod of acceptance.

"Excellent," the Dark Elf King replied with a smile.

----*----

After leaving the temple of the women, Abrianna had hope that they were on the path to returning home. The residual magic she found inside the temple members disputed the claims that all magic was gone from this realm, however, her inability to summon magical energy outside of herself was still a problem.

"So those women were all descendants of elves?" Cassie asked Abrianna.

"Yes, both Alex and I could see the telltale residual magic. Like you, they have their ancestors' magic buried deep inside," she replied.

"And those documents?" Leander asked.

"They were very old copies of Elven Histories. Someone long ago had access to an Elven Archive where they documented their life here. I suspect the complete original works still exist, hidden away somewhere as they are practically indestructible."

"How do you know they were copies?" Cassie asked, curious on why her cousin was so sure of herself.

"Father has a few tomes of elven history, gifted him from Elion. They are very rare and extremely valuable. In the original you can feel the magic infused in the pages to insure their survival over the ages. These pages lacked that energy."

"Alex, how far Enga Land?" Cassie asked her husband as they traveled in his vehicle.

Abrianna understood his reply to mean it was far from here and would require some form of winged transport. She recalled seeing that object in the sky on their first day here and assumed that was the common means of air travel in Alex's world. Here, one thought in terms of machines, not creatures, for transportation.

She could see the concerned look on his face and assumed there were other challenges he had not given voice to. The language barrier was a real problem, and even with all their studies, one she didn't see resolved anytime soon. If they could just get one of their party fluent in both languages, it would go far in resolving the impediment to their returning home.

----*----

Elion was quite pleased with himself as he went about his duties. While unhappy at the distress he was inflicting on his friend and ally in Great Vale, he knew that Ben would persevere. There were bigger issues afoot here than just the temporary loss of one's daughter and heir.

Unable to Scry across the realms, he had to rely on regular reports from his resources there. He refused to call them spies, the word leaving a negative connotation. He preferred to think of them in a term of the realm, news reporters. There to observe, but take no action, their steady stream of information had Elion up to date on all the latest events.

As expected, his people had identified a second group shadowing Alex and his companions. Doubtless minions of Avenstore, the interlopers had made no effort to interfere with the exiles either, they had simply monitored their every move. Elion was sure his people would remain discreet, their orders very specific regarding being discovered or overt support of the subjects involved.

He did, however, provide a certain amount of latitude for the indirect backing of the efforts to set things right. Alex's discoveries around Magic and the Wiccan Coven were positive indicators that he was on the right track to the bigger picture. The Wiccan Coven in particular was an element well known to Elion, one created long ago to secure an Elven anchor in this realm of man.

The Elven heritage they carried was a seed planted by his ancestors in ancient times, one intended to lay dormant until the return of magic. It seemed that time was now possibly close at hand, so long as Alex was able to follow the clues and unravel the mysteries to repair the damage done so long ago.

----*----

Kelby was happy to see her adopted Uncle as they sat around the table for the evening meal. Both she and Leena had felt a true affection for the man, both fatherly and protecting. It was a feeling he shared with them as well, treated as daughters. As they had never known their real father, this was foreign to the pair, but very welcome.

"Amelia tells me you two have made quite an impression on the locals?" he said with a knowing smile.

"Mother explained to us that is not just the message, it's how you deliver it," Kelby replied, not wanting to expand on the near riot they had caused.

"So it is, but tell me, what do the mermaids hear from the North and the West?" Ben asked more seriously.

Kelby looked to Leena, a shrug passing between the two.

"Nothing significant. The pirates have increased their raiding, but that's not news?" Leena replied.

"Is there a problem?" Kelby asked.

"I'm not sure, can you ask them to keep an ear out?" Ben asked in return.

"Yes, Uncle," both answered as one.

-----*----

Once home, everyone seemed to scatter. Kinsey was there to greet them at the door, her joy at their arrival replacing her earlier irritation at being left behind. Alex watched as Abrianna and Cassie headed straight to their laptops, Cassie diving into language studies while Abrianna appeared to be looking for more Rune sites.

Leander stood watching the pair for a moment before heading to the kitchen. He asked the pair of women a question in A'nlandian, receiving a dismissive wave from the pair before continuing on.

"Alex?" he asked as he held up a loaf of bread that had been resting on the counter.

"Sure, let me help," Alex replied as he headed into the kitchen as well.

With that the two men made something to eat, while watching the women pound away on the laptops. Alex could see the frustration as both struggled with the language. After several minutes of consideration, Alex grabbed his laptop and began doing a little research himself leaving Leander to fend for himself.

Chapter 8

There are many realms that make up the universe known to all living creatures. Not all realms were controlled by Elves and many did not contain humans. In some of these realms, the laws of nature, magic or physics didn't translate well, making the movement from one to another fatal to most beings. One place of fire and brimstone was the source of human myths of hell while a vaporous cloud realm of pleasure and plenty became heaven.

Avenstore knew well the many realms they had influence over and the occupants residing therein. It was from one of those realms that he chose his champion, his Dark Paladin. Roughly human in form, its bipedal symmetrical body contained two arms and two legs, but the head contained eyes but no mouth.

Feeding off the energy of those it killed, a mouth was unnecessary as the creature would draw in the life force like a sponge soaked up water. Communicating telepathically, it made its intentions known to friend or foe alike. Coming from a place where survival meant the death of others, its skills with weapons were beyond compare. In the realm of Ben Griffin, it would be near unstoppable so long as it's one weakness remained undiscovered.

The creature was intelligent, though simple in its wants and needs, so Avenstore needed someone of greater ambitions to act as its handler. It would be introduced as the champion of the Vassal King, and the beast would be supervised by him. Once its mission was complete, the disruption of the reign of King Ben, it would be unnecessary. Avenstore needed someone like the Vassal King to continue to disrupt the realm once the balance had shifted in the favor of the Dark Elves, but the champion would be returned to the realm it came from.

With that decided, Avenstore went about setting part two of his plan in motion. That required a trip back to A'nland and a trip to the West Lands. Some things could not be delegated and had to be handled personally.

----*----

It was early morning as Alex pulled the Jeep up in front of The Tribal Elf. The four had promised the coven they would return first thing in the morning to continue their research together. At this hour of the morning the traffic was light and he was able to find a spot to park right in front of the little shop. The four had hardly exited the vehicle, Kinsey left behind at home once more, before one of the Wiccans opened the shop door, excitedly waving the group inside.

"We've been expecting you!" she said with enthusiasm while motioning the group into the shop and then locking the door behind them.

Alex noted the Closed for the Day sign hung in place once they all had entered.

"Thanks," Alex replied, the last to enter.

Inside he could see the other members of the coven, all busily moving about. They had set up a table to one side of the room and laid out a simple serve yourself breakfast.

"Hungry?" someone asked as the four moved further into the shop.

"Yes," Leander replied enthusiastically, surprising everyone as it was the first English words he had spoken to the coven.

"Please, eat," Abigail said as she motioned for them to step forward.

Alex motioned for the others to step up, the Wiccans included, as he slid over to speak to their leader.

"Abigail, can you tell me more about the Casting Circle? I understand it is a Wiccan practice to come together for certain spells?"

Alex had been researching Wiccan magical practices until everyone had finally retired to bed. He could see the older woman appraising the question. He suspected that under normal circumstances she might be wary of sharing their traditions and ceremonies with an outsider. After a moment she let out a deep breath and then replied.

"Yes, we believe that the circle is a sacred shape. With it, we can create a high energy space that allows us to safely practice magic. After yesterday's disclosures about our ancestors, I can see now there is much more to it than I ever imagined."

Beyond the symbology of the act, Alex was interested in how it might enable the participants to share their meager residual energies into one substantial act of magic. He had learned a considerable amount last night researching all he could find on wiccan magical practices, but wondered how useful the information truly was. Translating the mythology to what he knew of magic, he created a hypothesis on how he might fix one of their many problems.

"I have an idea about how we might address the language barrier, but I am going to need everyone's help," Alex said while indicating the assembled group.

"I'm all ears," Abigail replied, the eagerness in her tone matched the excitement in her eyes.

"Abrianna?" Alex said aloud as he waved the young woman over.

She had been standing with a group of women, doing her best to answer questions. Alex could tell by the way she pointed to various objects in the room that she was being quizzed on various creatures. Excusing herself in broken English, she made her way over to the pair.

"Abrianna, I want to try a learning spell," Alex explained upon her arrival.

"Learning?" she repeated.

Alex then motioned to the collective gathering.

"Magic circle," he added while taking her hand in his and then grasping Abigail's as well.

He could see Abrianna considering the proposal. Slowly she began to nod.

"Maybe work," she responded after a moment longer.

Alex's thought was that the small amounts of magic the coven could perform where due to their combined energies, focused on a single task. The problem was, he had no idea how to perform the learning spell, as it was something done to him, not one he had done to others.

"Paper?" Abrianna asked Abigail, making a motion as if she were writing.

"Oh, sure," the older woman replied as she moved over behind the counter to snatch a pad and pencil from a shelf.

"Here," she said as she handed the writing materials to Abrianna.

"Cassie," Abrianna said while waving her cousin over.

After a brief conversation that only the two understood, Cassie nodded understanding and they moved over to the counter. Alex watched as the pair began to write word after word in English. Several times they had a protracted conversation as they struggled to find the word they needed. Finally, after about half an hour, Abrianna took the pad and handed it to Alex.

He scanned the contents, confused at first until he realized it was a spell. Unlike himself, Abrianna used words and chants to help with her magic. Taking the pencil, he replaced a few words, writing his above her original. After a brief conversation, both Abrianna and Cassie nodded, understanding at his corrections.

Image to word, word to sound. Pass understanding all around. Share the knowledge, share the fun. Let us all speak as one.

Reviewing the verse once more, he had to help pronounce the word knowledge to the A'nlandiers, where Abrianna and Cassie had used thought.

"Now I need a big glass of water," Alex asked Abigail.

No sooner had he finished his sentence than one of the young women appeared with a pitcher in hand, off the table.

"Even better," he replied as he took the offered vessel.

By now everyone in the room had been watching their activities.

"Should we go next door?" Alex asked, indicating the room they had all used the night before.

Without a word, Abigail began shepherding everyone into the coven's ceremony room. The last to enter, Alex was in time to see Abrianna moving people about the circle, placing the coven members in between herself, Cassie and Leander.

"Alex explain," she said as she took her place in the circle of people.

"We are about to try a learning spell using the collective magic each member of the circle holds within."

Leander started to speak up when Abrianna waved him quiet. Alex knew the man was without magic, but for this exercise it wouldn't matter. He needed to be part of the circle to be included in the spell, so he was along for the ride whether he liked it or not.

"These are the words to the spell, I need each of you to memorize them and chant with Abrianna," he finished as he passed the paper to Abigail and watched as each scanned the sheet, mouthing the words, and then passing it on.

The final part of Alex's plan was a bit of a surprise to everyone, Cassie in particular. Stepping over to his wife, Alex gently kissed her before dumping the entire pitcher of water over her.

"Alex!" she said in surprise, gasping as the cold water was a shock to her system.

Kissing her once more, the turquoise glow of her magic was in full bloom, evident to all but Leander. He then walked over to his assigned place in the circle. Taking the hands of those women on either side of him, he nodded at Abrianna to begin.

Starting softly at first, Alex could hear the collective chant as all the members of the coven quickly sync'd up with Abrianna.

Image to word, word to sound. Pass understanding all around. Share the knowledge, share the fun. Let us all speak as one.

The chant droned in his ears as it increased in tempo. Alex could feel the gentle tingling as the magic started to flow throughout the circle. He heard more than one of the women squeal with delight as they too felt the power of the circle's magic pass through them, though none stopped the chant.

Now was the time for the last piece of the puzzle. For this to work, Alex needed to act as the battery, combining his magic with Cassie's to power Abrianna's spell. Closing his eyes and opening himself up to the flow of energy, he drew from his inner reserve, amplifying the amount of energy he received. By now, a ringing in his ears drowned out the women's voices and he felt light headed.

Opening his eyes, he saw a whirring combination of white, turquoise, green and sandy brown as the energy flowed from one person to another. Suddenly there was a white flash as he released his reserve and Alex felt himself falling forward, passed out before he hit the floor.

----*----

Ailmer was not too keen on this plan to take the Northern Mountains. Driving the dwarves from their tunnels beneath the stronghold made sense from a strategic perspective, but the Dark Paladin provided by King Avenstore made him very uncomfortable.

They were sitting in the throne room of Gundor Stronghold, Avenstore seated in the place of honor, Ailmer's throne. Ailmer and his wife were standing nearby as the three looked down from the raised dais at the thing the Elf King had brought for them. It looked roughly human, clad in dark armor with only eye holes in the helmet.

Half again as tall as a man, the thing could look at the three without raising its head. Ailmer could tell that the many guards lining the walls were doing their best not to stare as he did, not all were successful.

"You are sure the dragons have been driven from the area?" Avenstore asked once more.

"I'm sorry, Sire?" Ailmer replied, his attention still focused on the aberration standing nearby.

"You say the dragons are all returned to the west after Tantalus's death," Avenstore repeated.

"Yes, yes, all turned tail and departed with their eggs, supplied by that horrid White Wizard," Ailmer's wife Vennala replied as her husband stared at the armor-clad monster, speechless.

"Good, then neither will be of concern as you move your influence south," Avenstore replied, implying the wizard was also gone.

"How so?" Ailmer asked, the words escaping his lips before he realized it.

"He is yours to command," Avenstore explained as he motioned to the warrior before them.

"He is but one warrior?" Vennala commented dismissively.

Vassal Queen or no, Ailmer didn't like it when his wife challenged the Elf King. If he took offense, he didn't show it.

"He is worth an army. No weapon in the realm can kill him."

"All things have a weakness," Vennala replied.

"True, however, his does not reside within these lands," Avenstore said lightly.

"But war is not fought one man at a time, we need an army," Ailmer replied, redirecting the conversation lest his wife upset the King and taking care not to offend the elf himself.

"This is not going to be a war; it's going to be an adjustment. You simply need to find a way to get the beast before you in single combat with the King of Great Vale," Avenstore replied before standing.

"I will be in touch. In the meantime, use him to clear the dwarves from the Northern Mountains. That should be sufficient to get everyone's attention for the next step."

Apparently finished with the conversation, the elf strode from the room and disappeared from view.

"What now?" Ailmer asked of his wife as they both stood staring at the armor-clad atrocity before them.

"You heard him, start with the dwarves," she said emphatically before hurried off herself.

----*----

Captain Afis was third in line, as the column wound its way through the tunnels beneath Gundor Stronghold. Before him was the scout and another soldier, while directly behind him was the abomination he was assigned to oversee. In the rear was less than a dozen more soldiers, all with instructions to assist the Paladin as needed. Their orders were simple, find the dwarves that inhabited the mountains and let the Paladin drive them out.

"Sir, contact ahead," the scout whispered as the pair had stopped before him.

"Let the beast lead the way, then," Afis commanded as he waved the towering hulk ahead of him and the others.

He watched as the armored monster passed them by and then disappeared into the darkness ahead of them. It was only a matter of moments before the sound of shouting and the clash of steel filled the tunnel from ahead.

"Let's go," Afis ordered as he waved his small force forward.

No more than one hundred feet further down the tunnels, they came into an open cavern, man, or rather dwarf made and dimly lit by torches. As his men fanned out behind him all were treated to a gruesome sight.

In each hand, the Paladin held a struggling dwarf by the throat, feet thrashing in the air as it held them high over its head. At his feet were two more dead, their bodies, shadows of their former selves, and across the void the last of the combatants was regrouping. The Captain watched in morbid fascination as the Paladin held first one dwarf and then the other before his face, visibly draining each of the life within. As it did so, Afis swore he saw the creature grow in size and strength.

Tossing the bodies aside, the Paladin looked back at Afis, and then headed at an even pace, chasing the retreating dwarves.

"Follow him," was all the Captain could put into words as the men took a wide path around the dead dwarves, as if afraid to touch the withered bodies.

----*----

King Teivel of the Northern Dwarves was not at all happy with the report from his men in the tunnels near Gundor Stronghold.

"What kind of meshugana news is this?" he asked as he read the parchment passed to him.

"Who is this nudnik?" he asked again as he set the missive down.

"Sire, we don't know. The gonif just appeared in the tunnel and started attacking us."

"Anyone killed?" he asked with great concern.

"Yes Sire, and the drek took all we could give without a scratch. Once we retreated, I saw troops from Gundor behind the teivel. Sorry Sire," the man added as he realized his faux pas.

"Teivel to teivel it is then," the king said firmly as he thought devil to devil it is!

----*----

Alex could hear people speaking as he lay on the floor, his eyes still closed and his head pounding. The sounds around him added to the pain as each word spoken drove deeper into his skull.

"Can you please keep it down," he murmured, the sound of his own words adding to the discomfort.

"You will never learn," he heard the familiar voice of Abrianna say.

Opening one eye, he found both Cassie and Abrianna hovering over him as he lay in the center of the room. Accepting the offered water, he drank, taking several swallows before waving it off.

"So, it worked?" he asked, both eyes open now.

"Well, Cassie, Leander and I can now speak English," Abrianna started.

It was then Alex noted several women of the coven talking excitedly among one another. Each was passing the parchment pages back and forth, the ones Abrianna had read the day before.

"We still can't read these," one blurted dejectedly to Alex.

"Those were written in Elven. It would take a much different spell to teach you that," Abrianna explained.

The thing was, none of them were speaking English.

"They were affected too?" he asked as he started to sit up.

A sharp pain in his head caused him to wince and rethink moving just yet.

"The problem with spellcasting in a language you are not fluent in is precision. I now see the error in the wording, but at the time it seemed correct," Abrianna advised.

"And then your little burst of energy pushed it over the edge. When you doused Cassie, we actually had all the magic we needed for the three of us. I was working to focus the flowing magic to discrete subjects, where only Cassie, Leander and I would be impacted."

"Wait, I thought you couldn't spell yourself?" Alex asked.

"I can't. I was attempting a trick I learned from my father. I had set you up as a trigger to spell me back as I was spelling you when you dumped the surge of power into the circle. Instead of just spelling me, you overran us all."

"That's my husband. If a little is good, a lot is so much better," Cassie said, the sarcasm in her voice doing little to hide her concern over his condition.

"Well, it was a lot all right. All I could do was pass it along, half the circle between us was already impacted by the spell," she finished while motioning to the rest of the room.

By now he felt good enough to get off the floor and let both Cassie and Abrianna act as stabilizers. Moving slowly, he first sat up and then worked to regain his feet.

"Thank you so much, thank you," Abigail said as she rushed to help Alex's rising form.

Alex recognized the words were not English, the woman speaking Cassie's native tongue.

"Don't mention it. No, I mean really, don't mention it to anyone. Listen to me a minute everyone," Alex said aloud, pushing through the pain of the self-inflicted headache.

He waited until everyone had stopped to hear his next words.

"I appreciate that you can now speak what I call A'nlandian. However, beyond the walls of this room, anyone else who can speak it will most likely not be your friend."

He paused to be sure that got everyone's undivided attention.

"We were sent here as part of a longstanding dispute between the Dark Elves and other Elven factions. I have no idea how they would react to all this."

"What are we, what faction?" came the expected question after the information sank in.

"Not Dark," Abrianna replied.

"None of us?" Emma asked, a look of concern on her face now.

"No, Abrianna and I checked for that yesterday. None of you are of dark elf descendent," he answered, taking some liberties with its accuracy.

A brief nod of agreement from Abrianna confirmed the statement. He couldn't actually tell what types of elves they really were, but he could say not dark.

"We will be careful. From this day forward, we will only speak the language here in the safety of the coven walls," Abigail answered for the group.

While still a little unsteady on his feet, Alex had to brace himself as Cassie slid up next to him, wrapping both her arms around his arm and squeezing.

"You need to take me home now, we have a lot to discuss," she whispered into his ear before planting a kiss on his cheek.

Chapter 9

Avenstore made his way through the darkened tunnels of the Dragon's Teeth as he worked his way deeper into the mountain range. His elven senses made lighting a torch unnecessary as he worked through the maze of tunnels intended to confuse trespassers. Never wavering from his course, he soon reached the master chamber deep inside the range that was his goal.

"What is your business here Elf King?" he heard boom in his brain while his ears remained untested.

"A moment of your time is all," Avenstore replied politely as he stood in the darkness, his voice the first to disturb the silence.

"More than you are due," came the response in his head.

As he watched, Avenstore could see the red dragon appear from behind the great stone pedestal that acted as the center of a stone ring. He had sensed her presence long before entering the cavern, but this was the first time he could see her with his eyes. Both dragon and elf had no need for the artificial illumination that humans required. That was a good thing since most of it had been destroyed earlier when the ceiling gave way. Avenstore could just make out the molten rock where Naga had sealed herself in once more.

"I was not your jail master Naga, that crime is laid at the feet of the House of Tantalus. Humans stole your offspring, not elves."

"But a word from your lips and the wrong would have been addressed," she hissed, her steamy breath forced between bared teeth.

"You know we no longer take direct action. Your kind almost perished the last time we did," Avenstore replied with emphasis to the last.

"So you say, Elf King. Is that your business, to explain away your inaction, looking for forgiveness?"

Avenstore knew the dragon was intentionally disrespectful, attempting to goad him.

"No, my visit is only to suggest that dragon kind might benefit from a similar policy of nonintervention. It is beneath our status to allow the lesser life forms to drag us into their petty squabbles."

Avenstore could almost hear the dragon's thoughts in the silence that followed his statement. He imagined the beast considering all the possible meanings of his words.

"Fear not Dark Schemer, I did not go to all the trouble to reseal my chamber only to burst forth once more. I have my eggs here, safe from those who would attempt to bend me to their will. If you have nothing further, I suggest you make a hasty retreat."

"As you wish," Avenstore said as he turned in place and left the dragon's lair at the same relaxed pace he entered.

----*----

Naga was not at all fooled by the Dark King's words. She understood the elves had something planned that her involvement might put at risk. Her words had been true, though, as she had no intention of placing herself or her offspring in jeopardy. In the back of her mind, however, there were debts to be paid on both sides of a potential conflict.

Should the White Wizard request her aid, she would be hard pressed to refuse. If perhaps, it was also in an effort to foil the Dark Elves, she had a score to settle there, as well.

----*----

Considering everyone had the ability to speak the same language once more, the ride home was unusually quiet. Cassie had been quite insistent that they needed to excuse themselves from the Wiccan's hospitality and retreat to their home. Pulling up in front of their house, Alex was surprised to see Cassie all but leapt from the vehicle and lead the group to the front door. Opening the door and then stepping back to allow the others to enter, he fended off the excited greeting from Kinsey.

"Please excuse us," Cassie announced to their companions before taking Alex by the hand and leading him into their bedroom.

Entering first, she waved him past and then he watched as she closed the door. Spinning in place, she launched herself at him, taking them both off their feet. Landing on the bed with Cassie on top of him, Alex accepted the heated kiss from his wife.

"By all the gods, I have missed you," she whispered before smothering him with another passionate kiss.

It took little effort for Alex to slip her shirt over her head as she worked on his. Fumbling with the unfamiliar undergarment, Cassie surrendered to Alex's silent offer to assist. In no time at all the couple had completely disrobed each other and were locked in a lover's embrace.

----*----

"I never realized how much we rely on talking," Alex commented as he lay with Cassie at his side.

The warmth of her bare skin against his was an intimate welcomed alternative to the distance the two had experienced since their arrival here. Alex hadn't really thought about it until now, but he had been so focused on finding a way home had been quite neglectful of his wife's needs, emotional or otherwise.

"I was going crazy, it was like you were here, but not really here," she explained, her head on his chest with one arm wrapped across his stomach.

"So many times, I just wanted to retreat to our chambers and talk of my fears," she added as she squeezed him.

"Fears?" Alex asked curiously.

"Yes fears. Alex your world is terrifying. For someone who can't speak the language, even more so. I was positive we were going to die in your car as we raced here on that great stone road."

"Jeep," he replied absently as he considered her words.

"What is a Jeep?" Cassie asked, in return, confused at his reply.

"My car, it's actually called a Jeep. Sorry, I was just trying to imagine how it must have been for you three."

"Well, you had a similar experience," Cassie started to say.

"No, I can see where it was not the same. I woke up in a world of my imagination, you were completely unprepared. Here, let me show you," he said as he rolled out from under her so he could reach the drawer of the nightstand beside his bed.

Pulling out the top drawer, he extracted a couple of the paperback books he had stashed there so many years ago. Rolling back to a confused Cassie, he handed her the books, covers depicting wizards, flashing swords or enticing young women. These were all 70's and 80's titles where the men were over muscled and the women showed more skin than not.

Alex watched as she studied one after another, pausing at one point to scan the pages of a Burroughs novel about Mars.

"This looks like the eastern desert, but the women do not dress like this," she commented after closing the book and pointing at the cover.

The woman on the cover was pretty much naked except for an elaborate leather harness and skimpy bikini bottom. She was holding two swords, one strategically placed to conceal her breasts from the observer. The male companion was similarly attired, only his modesty was protected with a loin cloth.

"You have more of these?" Cassie asked with curiosity while waving one at him.

Slipping out of bed, Alex went over to an armoire he had in one corner of the bedroom. To the casual observer, it might have appeared redundant considering the opposite wall had closet doors running its length. Opening both doors, Alex exposed row on top of row of hard and paper-backed books lining its interior.

"You have read all of these?" Cassie asked in wonder as she slipped out of bed and crossed the room to stand next to him.

"Pretty much, some twice," he replied as she scanned the titles.

He watched as she reached for a larger book, one set to one side of the rest.

"Ah, that was a gift," he started as she began to flip through the Boris Vallejo art book.

She paused after scanning a few pages.

"Do people here think women in the other realms are always naked? You must have been very disappointed," she asked, shaking her head in mock disapproval.

"At least they got this one right," she said with a smile as she displayed the page entitled "Mermaids".

On the page Alex could see four very beautiful topless mermaid women, all brazenly posing on a rock. While very attractive, there was an edge in their expressions that gave one pause to consider their intentions. Next, she stopped at one entitled "Water Nymphs" where the three women were only slightly more modest, their attire similar to the Baristas he had encountered in town.

"Why do fairies get clothes, but nymphs do not?" she asked after flipping through a few more pages.

Before he could reply, both heard a soft tapping at the bedroom door. Crossing over to the door, Alex opened it slightly while hiding behind it to allow for some modesty.

"Alex this thing keeps making noises. I found it on the table beside the lap tops," Abrianna said while offering a small flat device to him.

"Thanks," he replied after taking the phone from her and watching her turn and leave.

"What is that?" Cassie asked as she climbed back into bed, the art book still firmly in her grasp.

"It's a phone I think, but not mine," he said as he climbed into bed beside her while examining the phone.

Suddenly the phone lit up, the audible ring tone startling them both. Pushing the circle on the screen marked answer, he held it up to one ear.

"Hello?" he asked hesitantly.

"Mr. Alex? This is Emma at The Tribal Elf. Abigail asked me to call you and let you know a package arrived here with your name on it."

"How did you get this number?" he asked, the curiosity of it, overriding the question of the unexpected package.

"It was written on the package," she replied.

"Ok, I'll be right there," he answered before checking the phone for the disconnect button.

"Who was that?" Cassie asked as she watched her husband talk into the box in his hand.

"That was The Tribal Elf, someone sent us something. I'm going to go check it out."

"I'll go with you," she said as she started to get out of bed.

"No, I should go alone. This phone, and a mystery package mean someone is letting us know, they know we are here. If they are not friendly, I need to be able to act fast and you all don't know the rules of this place. The last thing we need is to get arrested for assault, or worse, murder."

----*----

King Teivel was not about to let one bulvan kill his people and drive them from their own tunnels. They had been fighting a war of harassment, unfortunately, as any direct confrontations with the nudnik proved useless. The teivel could take everything they could dish out and still keep coming. The King was fortunate that so far, no more of his people had been killed, though a few came close to meeting their end.

"Sire, we are ready," one of his men whispered as he settled down beside him.

"Excellent!" the King replied as they sat silently in wait.

The plan was a simple one. They had lured the nebekh into a section of the tunnels they had booby-trapped. The tunnel from Gundor hit a T section where one could travel right or left from the intersection. Once they drew the small force into the section of tunnels on the right, Teivel and his men would pull on ropes attached to supports holding the tunnel roof in place. Another group in the left branch had ropes of their own to assist in the trap.

"I hear them now," someone whispered.

Pitch black with no illumination, the dwarves had no trouble seeing the movement ahead as the unwelcome visitors advanced. The fact that the humans following the long antagonist carried torches made it that much easier to know when to trigger the trap.

"NOW!" Teivel bellowed to the men on the far side of their victims could hear as well.

As one, both groups of dwarves pulled hard on the ropes tied to deadfalls in the center of the tunnel. With a rumble of falling dirt and rock, the dwarves felt the rush of passing air as it was forced from the tunnel. It took several moments for the dust to clear enough to make out the wall of stone before them.

"That should be the end of that schlemiel!" Teivel said with satisfaction.

With that the groups started to gather their weapons.

"Sire, what is that?" one of the dwarves asked as the group began their trek out.

Turning to look at the newly blocked tunnel, he could see a faint glow beginning at its center. Soon the glow went from dull to bright red as the stone began to melt away. Once the stone had run like a glowing syrup stopping just short of the King's feet, a lone figure appeared in the opening.

"Oy Gevalt, get your tucheses out of here! We need to find another way to kill this little pisher," Teivel said as he waved his men back from the glowing figure, calling a full retreat.

----*----

Alex crossed back over Lake Washington and into downtown from his Renton home. The early afternoon traffic was tolerable, but had gotten far worse than what he had been used to 5 years ago. He knew that was compounded with the fact that his new norm was flying horses and wooden carts on dirt track roads.

By now the U District was in full swing, with University of Washington students walking and driving everywhere. It took him several minutes to find a place to park, and even then, it was several blocks away and $25 for four hours parking. He had no idea how long he would be at The Tribal Elf and so just paid the extra.

The phone thing bothered him the whole drive in because it indicated several things. First, Kinsey was always home these days and yet someone had entered the house and placed it on the kitchen table to be easily found. While not a wolf, she was still very territorial and over protective so not likely to run from an intruder. That meant she either recognized the perpetrator or felt no threat to their presence.

In addition to that, what else might there be in the house that wasn't supposed to be found? Were they under constant surveillance now, his home riddled with microphones and cameras? He found the possibility very unsettling.

The second concern was who was so bold as to play this hand. A phone placed in his house, a package for him delivered to the Wiccans. It screamed you are being watched and followed and we don't care if you know about it. At this point he had all but given up deciding whom it was, as it hardly mattered.

If the Dark Elves had repatriated him, Elion would surely come to his aid at some point. In contrast, if the Woodland Elves felt the need to have him returned to where he came from, then wouldn't Avenstore do his best to upset that plan, sending him back. Then again, maybe both wanted him gone from A'nland, so no help should be expected.

The whole thing was giving him a headache so he pushed it aside as he reached for the door, arriving at The Tribal Elf.

"Mr. Alex," Emma said with a smile as he entered the room.

Sitting behind the counter, her smile was bright and cheery.

"Just Alex, please," he replied as he approached the counter.

"This is what I called about," she replied with a nod.

Reaching under the counter, she produced a large manila envelope with his name written across the face.

"This was attached," she added as she handed him a folded piece of paper.

Opening the paper, he read the short note, followed with a phone number. He presumed it was the one on the phone he now carried in his pocket.

Please see that this is delivered to Alex Rogers and company. May they have many safe travels.

Opening the envelope, its sealed flap still in place, he slid the contents out onto the counter. Before him lay four US passports with other assorted ID's. He found current drivers licenses for Cassie, Abrianna and Leander, the last item named Leander Rogers, apparently now his brother. Each Passport carried the same names and had photo ID's for each bearing a more than a passible likeness of each.

"Are you guys going somewhere?" Emma asked as she scanned the contents of the envelope.

"Looks like it," was Alex's reply as he scooped up the items and said his goodbyes.

Chapter 10

Alex stepped in the front door and was surprised to find all three of his companions sitting comfortably in the living room. The surprise was that all three had one of his fantasy books in hand, reading.

"This is very disturbing," Abrianna said with a frown as she waved a Gor book his way.

"I like this one," Leander added while waving a Conan the Barbarian title at him.

"This one makes no sense at all," Cassie commented in a confused voice while holding up "A Spell for Chameleon".

"Why are you reading this?" Alex asked, expecting them to be using their new-found language skill in researching on the computers.

"We thought we would read some of your books to learn what people here think of our realm," Cassie offered.

"Honey, people here don't believe any of that is real. It's all considered works of fiction, things people read to escape their dull routine lives here."

"OH, thank goodness," came Abrianna's reply as she closed her book and set it aside.

"What did you find at The Tribal Elf?" Cassie asked as she did as her cousin, setting the book aside.

Alex noted Leander had chosen to keep his book, holding it open to the page he was reading while listening to the others.

"First, we are being watched. I am not sure if the house is bugged but we are certainly being followed."

"I have seen no insects in the house?" Abrianna replied.

"Sorry, it's a term meaning there are electronic devices in the house that hear what we say and possibly even let them watch us."

"Even in our bedroom?" Cassie asked in horror.

"I don't know. I will try and sweep the place when I'm done."

"Normally I would block the scrying," Abrianna said absently.

"Yes, well, I will try some earthly magic to do exactly that. In the meantime, here is why they called."

Pulling everything from the envelope once more, Alex passed out the items inside to each of the three, keeping his own passport.

"Abrianna Griffin?"

"Yes, in my world, people usually have a first and last name. Those blue books are called passports and are required to travel from one country to another. The other items are drivers' licenses and social security cards. They are used for local proof of identity. They likely used that name knowing you are of House Griffin."

"With this we can drive, drive what?" Leander asked, holding up the small card with his picture on it.

"Cars. Here you have to take a test to prove you can operate one safely," Alex answered.

"That's a relief. I must say it did concern me that not everyone I saw appeared competent to operate their cars," Leander said with some emphasis.

"Yeah, well don't give them too much credit," Alex said with a shake of his head.

"Leander Rogers," Leander said aloud as he opened his passport.

"Apparently we are brothers," Alex explained.

"Indeed!" Leander said with a smile.

"Alex, why were we provided these documents and by whom?" Abrianna asked, bring the subject back around.

"I don't know, but it looks like someone wants us to go to England."

----*----

Ben had returned to Great Vale in time to receive a message from King Teivel of the Northern Mountain Dwarves. As a rule, the dwarves had little use for magic or wizards, finding both more trouble than they were worth, or so they claimed. As such, the message from the king was delivered the old fashion way, via messenger.

"Sire, you have guests in the audience chamber," his man informed him as he landed Shadows.

"I could get used to this," he said absently as he patted the mare before his stableman led her away.

"Lead the way," he instructed the steward.

Ben didn't need the man to show him where to go, rather it was customary that the man would announce Bens entrance upon his arrival.

"His Royal Highness, King Ben," the man bellowed as Ben entered the small chamber.

The only occupants, two broad and well armored dwarves quickly rose to their feet and bowed as he crossed over to his seat. The action set off alarms in Ben's head, as dwarves were never so deferent to anyone, even their own King.

"Please, be seated," Ben relayed after seating himself.

"Sire, it is good King Teivel's wish that we wish you well and ask for an audience in the Lord Protector's name," the first dwarf started.

"We are not here to kvetch, but things are all meshuggeneh," the second offered.

"Shmuck, let me say this," the first said to the second while striking him in the chest with a backhand. The slap on the dwarf's leather breastplate echoed in the room.

"Your pardon, Sire, my companion is not as educated as I in the ways of the court."

"Neither am I. You, vus mach's DA?" Ben said in his best Yiddish.

"Some shmegegge has the chutzpah to make our tunnels fershlugina, fershyay? Dwarves have died and it's all mishegas in the tunnels," he replied.

"Sire, King Teivel was hoping you could use magic make the shmegegge gay avek," the first added, returning to his more comfortable terms.

"Tell these men everything you know about the schmendrick and I will see what we can do to help," Ben answered, while waving in some of his officers who had been waiting just outside a side door.

"And so it begins," Ben thought to himself as he watched the two dwarves leave the chamber.

----*----

Avenstore was back in his corner office trying to catch up on things he had neglected while away. He was satisfied that the Dark Paladin was well placed and, on his way to disrupting the stability of A'nland. He was less confident that his trip to the Dragon's Teeth had paid off as good returns. He needed to keep the beasts out of the coming turmoil if he was to have the desired effects.

"Sir, Ian is here to see you," his assistant announced after a gentle tap on the door.

"Send him in Roberta," he replied with a weak smile and a wave of his hand.

"There was an issue while you were away," Ian announced after crossing the room and waiting for the door to close. He dropped a plain unmarked folder on the desk and stood waiting.

With most of their native elven names too hard to pronounce or difficult to explain to the locals, the resident members of Avenstore's people chose identities closer to their chosen appearance. Ian looked every bit the Scotsman his name implied.

"Sit," Avenstore said while sliding the folder over to himself and flipping it open.

Taking the top page, he began scanning its contents. Following suit with the next two pages he set the pile back into the folder and flipped it closed.

"A magic circle?" he asked after a moment's consideration.

"That was my thought as well, though the people on site couldn't confirm anything more than the burst of energy from within the coven walls."

"They said it was strong event, that coven isn't powerful enough for such," Avenstore commented as he indicated the folder.

"Strongest any had felt in this realm in centuries. Did you see the Wizard and his wife were there when it happened?" Ian asked.

"Where are they now?" Avenstore asked, ignoring the question.

"His house in Renton. The four of them left shortly after the magical burst. Later only the wizard returned to the shop. He stayed but a moment and carried a parcel out when he left."

"Any idea what kind of spell it was or whom it was intended for?" the King asked of his man, concern tinging the question.

"No Sire, only that one of our people swore he heard one of the Wiccans speaking in a tongue not native to this realm," the elf replied.

"Why would they waste that much magic on something like that? Teaching the Wiccans makes no sense," Avenstore pondered as he considered the possibilities.

"We have watched this group for quite some time now anyway. They make a nuisance of themselves chasing down ancient magic artifacts," the elf added for emphasis.

"We need to contain this before it gets out of hand," Avenstore finally replied.

"How?"

"If its magic they want to learn, perhaps it's time they learn not all magic is good for them."

----*----

Alex had no idea how his companions were going to take to the flight to England, but he was going to do his best to prepare them in any event.

"OK, I booked us first class seats, so at least we won't be cramped for the flight. It's a one way ticket since I have no idea how long we are going to be there," he stated as the three sat in the living room listening to him.

"For when, tomorrow? How long is the trip?" Cassie asked.

After their earlier conversation Leander had gone back to his reading while the women began quizzing Alex of England.

He had grabbed one of the unused laptops to check on flights and still answer the continuous stream of questions.

"It's a nonstop, so the flight time is just over 9 hours and no, it's a little more than a week out. We aren't ready to travel yet."

He had gathered all their documents so he had all the information he needed to get them set up with the airlines. As he entered each of them into the website, he marveled at the realism of the items. He had retrieved his expired passport and compared it to the new arrivals, finding no indications they were fake. Whomever had forged these documents was a real pro.

The thought brought back the image of his first meeting with King Elion, so long ago.

"Did you guys pull my resume or something?" Alex had blurted when the King had divulged all he knew of him.

Elion had laughed at the comment, "You might be surprised to learn that is likely. We also use private investigators as well as technological methods. Remember, our magical strengths translate there as well as your's do here."

That comment still echoed in his head. Was that how the elves dealt with the change in magic here. Rather than try and force it, they converted it to something else? Or was it a mixture of both. All the thoughts were just giving him another headache.

"We will need to be in the sky for 9 hours without landing? How is that possible?" Abrianna asked.

"It's more like riding in a bigger car than it is riding Rose and Shadows," Alex explained.

"What about personal needs?" Cassie suddenly asked before getting and heading quickly to the bathroom, closing the door behind her.

Both Alex and Abrianna shared a confused look.

"Anyone hungry?" he asked after a shrug and heading into the kitchen to start dinner.

----*----

It was the day following the magic circle event and Emma was in the back room of The Tribal Elf working. She was trying to clean up the mess left after the last visit of their four newfound sources of learning, but the excitement of yesterday had her very distracted. The coven was absolutely buzzing with exhilaration over the latest event, one magically providing them all with a new set of abilities. With so much enthusiasm, several of their members had to be pointedly reminded not to practice off premises by Abigail.

Today Emma was in charge of the shop, a newly bestowed duty, one indicating she was rising in responsibility in the coven. Not alone today, she had Aubrey watching the front counter while she did the dirty work in the back, her choice. Finishing her tidying up, she was just in time to see a newcomer enter the shop as she passed into the front room.

"Hi, I am looking for whoever is in charge here?" a young woman asked Aubrey.

Emma could see Aubrey behind the counter from where she stood. Only 18, she was still learning the ways of the coven. One of the first rules was, be wary of strangers asking questions. It was almost a regular occurrence to have someone either looking to join *the witches* under a misguided impression of learning dark magic. The opposite was also of great concern, someone looking to expose them as a deranged cult, bent on corrupting other impressionable young women.

This woman, however, looked like neither. Emma had seen her fair share of both kinds and this one was something else entirely. She was nicely dressed, her slender frame displayed in tight jeans, and a snug top with lots of cleavage. She had a waisted leather jacket over the top with thigh high boots sporting three-inch heels. The outfit said I'm casual but expensive, and I'm very sexy.

"I'm running the shop today, how can I help you?" Emma asked, dismissing Aubrey as she directed the woman over to one side of the room.

"You are not what I expected. Aren't you kind of young to be in charge?" the woman replied as she studied Emma.

Emma returned the scrutiny of the stranger, looking her up and down. She estimated the raven-haired young woman was not much older than her 23 years of life. It wasn't until she returned to the piercing green eyes studying her that she reassessed that opinion upward. She could also see a hint of mischief behind the emerald pools that seemed to draw her in.

"I'm not sure who you've been talking to but it doesn't take an advanced degree in economics to run a thrift store," Emma replied after she shook off the effects this stranger had on her.

"I'm not here about the store, silly girl. I want to speak with the Head Witch of the Coven here, or High Priestess, whichever title you prefer," the woman announced casually.

The statement immediately put Emma on guard. It was not a secret that the Coven was the group that ran the shop. It was the reference to witches that put her off.

"We are Wiccan, not witches, and Abigail is not here at the moment. May I ask why you are looking for her?" Emma probed.

"I'm not normally a joiner, you see, I tend to go solo, but I felt something around here yesterday that got my attention."

"What did you feel?" Emma asked cautiously.

"Magic," the woman replied.

The statement caused Emma to respond with an unintended gasp. The statement wasn't what surprised her, it was the fact that it was said in the language they had all just learned.

Chapter 11

Ben was sorely missing Alex's presence as he traveled north once more, this time to the base of the Northern Mountains. Not so much for his magical abilities as for his role as Ben's fixer. This would be the kind of task that Ben would assign the younger man, a role that he realized he had unconsciously created in their relationship.

Before Alex's arrival, Ben had been required to deal with all the challenges to the realm himself. Now, he had an aide that, while inexperienced, had a good head on his shoulders and was now a member of the family. Ben suspected that, whatever Elion had dropped the boy into, Alex would prefer being here as well.

Riding his personal mount for this trip, Ben had to forgo the luxury of the winged horses left behind with the disappearances. His companions, the dwarf messengers, as well as his personal guard, meant the more traditional mode of transportation was required. With a few long days of rough travel ahead of him, Ben tried to drive the loss of his family from his mind and concentrate on how he was to vanquish this latest threat.

He felt a sense of urgency in addressing this challenge to the stability of the region, a threat he was sure rooted in a Dark Elf plot.

"Sire, are you sure it is wise to push so hard?" his Captain asked.

"I intend to cut our travel time in half, better to stop this in the mountains than wait for it to come to our doorstep," Ben explained.

"But Sire, the men will need rest before battle, and so few" the man replied, concern in his voice.

"I don't think this is going to be that kind of fight," was his only reply before spurring his horse into a lazy gallop.

----*----

"Come again?" Emma replied as the dark-haired woman stood expectantly before her.

"I know you understood me, don't play dumb. I heard a couple of your members speaking it as I walked by yesterday. I passed them by while I was looking for the site of the magic I felt. They came right out that door, speaking about it," she said while pointing to the door behind her.

"What did you say your name was?" Emma asked, trying to buy herself a little time to absorb this information.

"I didn't. It's Jaenanya, but my friends just call me Joey."

"That's a very unusual name," Emma remarked.

"Not where I come from," Joey said with a dismissive tone.

"Well, I am Emma and you are looking for Abigail, who is not here at the moment. If you leave me your contact information, I will be happy to pass it along to her once she gets here," Emma said as she regained her composure.

"So, she will be here today?" Joey asked, ignoring the request.

"Eventually, Abigail usually stops by the shop at least once a day to check on things," Emma answered.

"I'll wait then," Joey said, dismissing Emma and she walked over to one of the many displays in the store.

Emma watched as she selected a small statuette, scoffing as she looked it over before placing it back on the shelf and moving on.

Emma noted the figure was one of their collection of many mythical creatures, that one was of a succubus.

----*----

The Vassal King was enjoying this new turn of events as he sat in the audience chamber. The crowd before him was made up of various lords and their retainers. The gathering was in support of the push south, into the mountains and possibly beyond into Windfall itself.

"The dwarves are in retreat you say?" one of the more ambitious Lords asked.

"Driven from their very tunnels and ours for the taking," Ailmer replied as he looked out over the gathering for the reaction of the others.

He could see the silent whispers and hear the murmuring as the men considered the news. He knew his wife, Vennala, was leading a similar gathering containing the wives and consorts of the men before him. She insisted that whispered thoughts in a man's bed-chamber carried far more weight that the commands of a king.

It was that concept that had spurred Ailmer to provide separate sleeping arrangements for himself and his wife. He had little doubt that Vennala practiced what she preached.

"So, what now?" another lord asked as the crowd settled.

"The Paladin drives straight to the heart of the southern kingdom. Once it disposes of the monarch, we sweep in," Ailmer explained.

"And if he won't do battle with the creature?" another asked.

"Then he is on the run from its advances, driven from his palace."

As Ailmer explained things to his Lords, he realized the brilliance of Avenstore's plan. Why risk the lives of himself or his men against an army, when one powerful combatant could strike at its head. No matter the numbers, only so many men could be brought to bear against one indestructible foe.

"We can't take and hold Great Vale," someone muttered.

"We don't need it all, just parts. I suggest scouts to confirm the dwarves location while you continue to gather your men. Once we are at full strength, we can march on Windfall and gain control of all west coast ports."

Ailmer was well aware, the man was right. The Vassal Lords did not have a huge number of men to draw upon for this excursion south, much less to hold the territory. Each Lord had a vast track of land to call their own, but the growing season was short here in the north. The true wealth in the lands were the herds of beasts.

Every spring the heavy coats would be shorn, providing one of the finest threading materials in all the lands. Spinning houses on both sides of the Western Sea competed for the bales of soft heavy hair. With that, a small percentage of the herds were slaughtered, providing what was considered a delicacy outside of the north.

It did not take a large number of farmers and herders to make a Lord wealthy, just enough to hold his competitors at bay.

"We won't have enough men to drive them from the city," one of the lords added as if reading Ailmer's mind.

"Once the Dark Paladin drives them from the city, we will only need enough men to hold the fortifications controlling the harbor," the Vassal King replied with a smile.

----*----

Joey scanned the shelves lining the Wiccan shop, trying to find anything to relieve the boredom she was struggling with. She had her orders and so it wasn't like she had anywhere else to be anyway. She laughed silently as she surreptitiously watched the two young women that made up part of her target group, chatting away and completely unaware of the danger they were in.

It was like they were floating on the surface of the sea with sharks circling just beneath their feet. Were it up to her, she would have seduced the pair, draining them of their life force and been done with it, but the choice was not hers to make. Like the succubus statuette she had seen earlier, she was a non-human being that lived on the edge of reality for the dominant species of this realm.

Similar to the Dark Elves that she currently served in this reality, they were either creatures that had survived the millennia known only to humans as myths, or they came here from other realms. They were commonly known as demons, vampires, shape shifters, werewolves or various other names and they all lived in the dark corners these humans feared to go. So long as they remained hidden from discovery, living only in legend, they were free to feed on the people around them.

However, every so often they were called upon to serve the dominant nonhuman species that worked to keep their existence a secret. Her mission here was to get as much information from these Wiccans as possible to determine the amount of contamination from the White Wizard. King Avenstore had brought her into their little secret circle regarding the man and his companions.

While the Wizard was fascinating, Joey was more interested in his Nymph wife. Draining a wizard could add to her own powers, but a nymph, a sexual being herself, could add so much more. The thought of seducing and draining the Nymph was absolutely titillating for her. Drawing in the native sexuality of the female would be like an exotic dessert on top of a fine meal.

Alas, the couple were not hers to take, however, as Avenstore had made that quite clear. The witches, though, were fair game depending on what they knew and how much risk there was in her actions against them.

"Abigail there is someone here waiting for you," she heard the one called Emma say as an older woman entered the shop.

"Showtime!" Joey said to herself as she returned her focus to the present and slowly crossed over to meet her victim.

----*----

Amelia was not used to providing for the needs of her current guests, though that worried her not at all. Her previous experience with the dwarves was a reversal of fortunes and it was now her chance to repay the favor. King Teivel and his entourage had arrived at her gates with a hoard of dwarves in his wake.

"Greetings Balabusta, this nebbish dwarf is honored by such a mensch as yourself."

"Can it Boychick, your flattery is bupkes. You are, nonetheless, welcome as an honored guest in Windfall," Amelia relayed with a wave of her hand before warmly embracing the Dwarf King.

"It has been a long time, mishpocha," Teivel said with a smile as she led the group into the castle walls.

"I hear there is trouble in the mountains. Your messengers reached Ben and he is on his way here now," she replied as she motioned for the staff to assist with the others.

"A pisher from the north has made a meshuggeneh of our tunnels. There is only the one, but he has resisted all our efforts. I am thankful for your hospitality,"

"Well, don't go all ver clempt, but you can stay as long as you like," Amelia replied with a warm smile.

----*----

Abigail was distracted as she entered The Tribal Elf. Since the appearance of Alex Rogers and his companions, her life and the lives of her coven had been turned upside down. Those things that she had considered myth and fantasy were suddenly real.

Besides the new language ability, the coven had been blessed with a new look on life. They also seemed to be able to perform magic at a heighten level. The few practice spells they performed had proven quite successful and the entire group was excited to see what else that could do with more practice.

"Abigail there is someone here waiting for you," she heard Emma say as she entered the shop.

"Hello, how may I help you?" Abigail asked as she considered the young woman before her.

"Is there someplace where we can speak privately," the visitor asked softly as she crossed the room.

Abigail felt two distinct and intense emotions from deep within her. The first was a desire to do whatever this raven hair beauty asked of her, a foreign attraction to her, compelling Abigail's cooperation. The second emotion was far more intense, on the other hand. It was screaming danger in her head. This was a new voice to her and she somehow associated it to Alex.

"You may speak freely here, we have no secrets," Abigail replied as she motioned to the others in the room with her.

The woman seemed confused at the response. Her facial expression changed from a pleasant smile to one of concentration as she stared into Abigail's eyes. Both sensations increased in intensity as her attraction to the young woman became desire.

"Abigail, something is wrong," she heard from Emily as she tried to look around the room.

Unable to look away from the young woman's gaze as she closed the final steps, Abigail struggled to focus on anything but her desire. Her mind raced to understand the situation, until panic set in, and she went to her *go to* response for danger.

"Defensive spell," she suddenly blurted to the two younger Wiccans.

----*----

"Demon be gone!" Joey suddenly heard from all three women at once.

The pull of unseen energies was more than she could deal with as a sudden burst of force sent her flying off her feet. Tumbling, she was tossed out the front door and onto the street by energies too powerful to block.

Joey quickly regained her feet, brushing off her clothing and injured dignity as those around her on the street looked on with a mild curiosity. Standing in front of the shop as she watched the woman inside locking the door, she pulled her phone out and hit the redial button.

"We have a big problem. Can't talk here so I'm on my way there to explain," was all she said before hanging up and walking away from The Tribal Elf.

----*----

With both men going through their morning routine, still in their particular rooms, Cassie and Abrianna were testing their cooking skills. With Alex showering and Leander dressing, the women were in the kitchen, making breakfast for the four. It wasn't that they had no experience in doing such things, quite the contrary. When they were younger, her mother had insisted that both girls become capable of fending for themselves without the expectation that there would always be someone around to cater to their needs.

It was the unfamiliar nature of everything they touched in the kitchen that was a challenge for them. Alex had been doing the majority of the cooking for the group, while doing his best to demonstrate how everything worked. Unfortunately, until recently, the running monolog he had going while cooking had been mostly unintelligible to the pair.

"Brie, can you get me the eggs?" she asked as she heated the pan on the thing Alex called a gas range.

She had marveled at the ease with which one could adjust the open flame to get the heat just right. The wood fired stoves of her world were more about working with whatever heat you got.

"Here you go," Abrianna replied as she set the bowl of liquid goo on the counter next to the heating pan.

Abrianna had been beating the eggs for something Alex called a scramble. He would mix cheese and meats into the bowl with the eggs and then cook them in the pan until firm. The precooked bacon and sausage were already diced and ready to go, as Cassie had prepared them first.

The sight of the eggs, however, set something off inside her that made her swallow hard lest she loose whatever remained in her stomach from the night before.

"Are you ok?" she heard Abrianna ask as she turned to see her cousin staring at her.

Without replying, Cassie darted from the kitchen and into the nearby bathroom, slamming the door behind her.

----*----

Abrianna had been setting the table with plates and eating utensils when her cousin asked her for the eggs she had prepared earlier. Cassie had been insistent, she wanted to cook this morning, so Abrianna had been more than happy to assume the role as a helper. She concentrated on setting everything up as the smell of bacon and sausage filled the house.

Placing the bowl of beaten eggs next to the heated pan, she had stepped back and glanced at her cousin to be sure she had used enough eggs. What she saw was Cassie's face go pale and then panic.

"I wonder?" Abrianna said to herself absently as she watched her cousin dart from the kitchen and into the nearby bathroom, the door slamming behind her.

Chapter 12

After breakfast Alex loaded his three companions into the Jeep and headed to a local shopping mall. He had frequented the Southcenter Mall many times in the distant past and was quite familiar with its shops and layout, or so he thought. He felt it made the perfect place to expose Cassie and the others to his world safely for the first time.

Before leaving the house, Abrianna had tried to warn Alex that Cassie might not be feeling too well. His wife had waved it off as too long on an empty stomach and nothing more. She declared she felt much better after eating and they dropped the subject.

"Alex, who is Wendy and why does she have so many homes?" Cassie asked as they passed the fast food restaurant.

"And the King of Burger, is that the same as Che Burger?" Leander offered as they passed the competitor.

"Yeah, those are all places to eat," he replied as he pulled into the vast parking lot of the shopping mall.

Everyone had gone quiet as they gawked at the rows of parked cars leading up to a large multistory parking structure.

"So many cars," he finally heard from Abrianna.

"And that's why we are here. Inside that big building there are all the owners of these cars. I want you all to get used to the crowds before we try and fly to England," Alex answered as he slipped the Jeep into an open parking space.

Since it was now the weekend, the place was every bit as busy as Alex had hoped it would be. He had ulterior motives in bringing them to such a crowded location. With so many people in motion his desire was that whomever was watching them would have to close in rather than risk losing them in the mass of humanity. At that point he could try and identify which of the elves was messing with them.

"What's with the hat?" Cassie asked as Alex pulled a ball cap out from under the seat and placed it on his head.

"Fashion statement," he replied with a smile before passing her a kiss.

Entering the main central doors on the south side of the vast building, even he was taken aback by the sheer mass of humanity before them. The multistory structure was far larger than he remembered it to be and had shops whose names had have never heard of.

"Everyone, stay close," he announced before leading the group into the crowds.

Before leaving the house, he had put together a list of things he intended to buy on this trip. They needed proper attire for the three A'nlanders beyond the meager purchases Alex had made the first days back. They also needed luggage for the pending trip overseas, and something Alex had only recently learned about.

Yesterday, before embarking on this adventure, Alex had excused himself, leaving the others at home once more. He needed to address his concerns over their being monitored specifically security concerns. He had little doubt that Elion was keeping an eye on them, if for no other reason than a passing curiosity about their welfare. It was the nagging suspicion that there were others out there less inclined to see him reach a ripe old age that motivated the trip.

"Hello, I'm Bill. How can I help you?" the man at the security services store had asked as he entered the shop.

Previously, Alex had done a quick search of security businesses and discovered a surprising number in the greater Seattle area. Based on the volume of competitors, he decided that this town was seriously paranoid. This place seemed to have a very diverse set of services and equipment for sale and great reviews.

"I have an embarrassing question to ask. How can I tell if I am being bugged?"

"No need to be embarrassed, it's much more likely to be true than most people realize. What makes you think you are? Are you in the tech industry, we have a lot of customers from there?" he asked.

"Something like that, yes. I can't really discuss the details, but let's just say I have a small company that writes software." Alex replied, jumping on the man's assumption.

"Nothing for the government though, it's all private sector stuff," he added, recalling his previous life. No one ever wanted to get on the bad side of the US Government.

"Are you in the Cloud?" the man asked, surprise in his tone.

"Oh no, only on prem. That's why I think they are bugging me personally, looking for information. Also, someone might be being following me," Alex replied, taking some of what he had learned when buying the laptops and putting it to good use.

He really wasn't sure what the Cloud was, but he knew it was "Off Prem" and made it easier to share information and services. That also meant that certain extra precautions were required to protect yourself there due to the greater exposure.

"Good plan," the man replied with a knowing nod.

From that point on, the two had discussed a remarkably large number of devices and services that Alex might consider to address his suspicions. In the end he purchased several items from the man and had contracted him to do a little snooping.

"What do you have for a cell?" the man had asked at one point.

"Just this," Alex replied while handing the phone in his pocket over for inspection.

"Nice. Expensive that one, but you might consider a burner for business use. Keep that one for personal calls only."

"Burner?"

"You know, a prepaid phone. Good, reliable, but easily disposed of once a month to keep anyone from tracking you or your calls."

Bill explained the process for buying the phones and recommended several brands and service providers, the mall containing more than one of them.

It was that conversation that brought Alex to this shop in the mall. It didn't take him long to locate the particular store in mind, and he made sure everyone was with him before waving to the clerk. Walking straight up to the counter, he quickly found himself face to face with the young man behind the display case.

"Excuse me, I need four prepaid phones that will work in Europe, specifically England," he asked the sales clerk in the small cellular store, their first of many stops he had planned to make

He was quickly provided four phones, all set up for use in England and paid up for voice and data for a good 30 days use. He had the sales clerk set up each of the phones for cross calls and tipped the man generously for the effort. He paid for everything in cash.

"Here," he said as he handed one to each of his companions.

"Each phone is programmed with your name and the name of the caller appears like this," he explained as he called Cassie.

"Now do this," he said as he showed her how to answer the call.

Repeating the process so each could see how to call another, all were soon up to speed.

"Much easier than a message bird," Leander commented after a test call to Alex.

"Don't lose it, and keep track of your battery life. I'll show you how to charge them later," he admonished them before waving them on to their next purchase.

Stop two was an upscale watch shop where he chose watches for each of them.

"My world runs on measured time," he explained as he passed out the specially selected purchases.

"Transportation, business and personal appointments all have specific times of operation or availability."

Alex had purposely picked models with both a digital display and analog hands to help facilitate their readability to the three. An easy choice for him and Leander as men's watches had a dizzying variety of models, the requirement proved more challenging for the ladies. In the end it left them both with high end sports watches.

Leading everyone over to one of those lounge areas set aside for the shoppers' convenience, he walked them through a short lesson on telling time. Both Cassie and Abrianna took to the digital displays while Leander much preferred the analog, its similarity to a sundial more to his liking.

"So, it is eleven twenty-eight in the morning!" Cassie announced proudly, once Alex had talked her past the AM/PM conversation.

The next stop was one that Alex had debated on, as it was completely frivolous but, in his mind, very necessary. He had researched the different stores in the mall to be sure they carried all the required items the four would need. As he did one item kept appearing over and over again.

"May I help you?" the young woman asked from behind the counter as Alex led a distracted Cassie into the store.

"Yes, we would like to look at wedding sets. We were recently married but didn't have time to choose rings," he replied.

----*----

Cassie was completely overwhelmed with the shopping trip Alex was leading them on. She had never seen so many huge shops packed so close together, with level after level inside this huge structure he called a shopping mall. The clothing in this realm was so different from that of her home world and the sheer volume was overwhelming.

The phone and the watch were magical marvels, things she could see an obvious need for. The clothing on the other hand was bright and colorful and, in many cases, not very functional. It was almost as if accenting what wasn't covered was the intent of the garment. Her thoughts went back to Alex's many book covers, and the mostly unclothed females there. She noted this store, though, was not for clothing.

"Alex, what are you doing?" Cassie asked as she scanned the sparkling contents of the showcases surrounding them.

"In my world, when a couple gets married, he gives her a ring to show his love and commitment," he replied as he motioned to the wedding sets behind the glass.

"They are beautiful," Cassie commented as the woman moved a particularly spectacular tray of rings before her.

Cassie watched as Alex slid closer to her and started scanning the selections. She didn't understand why, but there was an excitement building inside of her as he picked up one after another of the sparkling jewel encrusted bands, inspecting it closely and then setting it aside as apparently unacceptable.

"Let's try this one," he finally announced as he reached for her left hand.

Cassie could see the tremor in her hand as Alex selected a finger, gently sliding what appeared to be two bands, not one, as a matched set onto her finger. She could hear the gasp from Abrianna next to her, as Alex withdrew his hands, leaving the sparkling jewels free to dazzle on her finger.

"Excellent choice, subtle yet elegant. That is a platinum set with a 2-carat cushion cut engagement ring, jacketed in an additional 1 carat total weight in the wedding band," the sales lady explained.

By now Abrianna and Leander had moved even closer to the couple and Alex could see Cassie's cousin eyeing the contents of the tray before Cassie.

"That one is nice," she whispered into her cousin's ear as she pointed to an engagement ring siting alone.

"I like this one," Cassie replied as she admired the large central stone in the setting on her finger.

"Try it," Alex motioned for the sales lady to assist Abrianna.

"Do you like it?" Alex asked Cassie as he returned his attention to his wife.

"I have never seen anything so beautiful," She replied, not taking her eyes off the set.

"This is the one," Alex replied to the sales lady while glancing over to her as she slipped the solitaire on Abrianna's finger.

"Alex, Abrianna and Leander are not yet wedded," Cassie whispered as she glanced at her cousin's hand.

"In my world, this is betrothal and this is wed," Alex replied as he lifted one of the wedding sets still in the tray. Separating the rings, he displayed the engagement ring alone and then reunited the set.

"How does one compensate the shop keeper here for such a purchase?" Leander asked, having heard the exchange.

"By letting me take care of it for you," Alex said simply.

"I am at a loss at such generosity, however," Leander began to reply.

"My friend, you have earned my gratitude at a value far greater than the cost of that ring, please let me do this for you both as a way of saying thank you," Alex replied as he passed one of the credit cards from his wallet to the sales lady.

Cassie smiled as she watched Abrianna present her hand to Leander for inspection. She could see her cousin bursting with excitement as she moved up next to her intended. For once Leander made no move to slip away from her, rather he wrapped one arm about her as the two stood so closely together.

"A wedding band for you as well, sir?" the woman said, pausing before processing the purchases.

"A simple band that compliments hers. Sorry Leander, there is no male engagement ring," Alex replied after a moment's consideration.

It took no time at all for her to find a ring in Alex's size and style, while the ladies were far more interested in inspecting their own. Glancing at the receipt as they prepared to leave, Alex noted that they had come close to dropping six figures on the three of them. He suspected as much from the expression on the saleslady's ecstatic face, her commission likely significant.

As they were leaving the shop, Alex noted a group of teenage boys had been watching them at the jewelry counter. He thought it odd as he guessed them to be no more than seventeen or eighteen. In his experience, boy's that age rarely displayed an interest in jewelry. He quickly dismissed the thought as the group moved on in a separate direction from his.

----*----

And so it went for the rest of the afternoon, with them jumping from one shop to the next. Everyone started getting special treatment from the sales staff as the purchases piled up, the number of bags they were carrying labeling them as big spenders. Clothing for Leander was an easy fix with one stop at American Eagle for casual clothes and one at Nordstrom's for everything else. Foot Locker had sneakers for everyone and Sears the luggage.

The women, however, were a different challenge entirely. They made an easy dozen stops just before a late lunch and had a million questions.

"People actually wear that in public?" Cassie asked as the passed a lingerie display in the window of Victoria's Secret.

"No, that's called intimate wear, it's for the bedroom," he explained.

"It won't keep you very warm at night," Leander said as he appraised the mannequin.

"In my experience it usually ends up on the floor," Alex said with a wink at his wife.

A brief look of confusion was soon replaced with a stricken look, as the man realized the implication. Though Alex knew Leander to be a less than worldly man, something he was sure Ben appreciated in his future son-in-law, the presence of Abrianna seemed to magnify the behavior.

The totally hands-off relationship the two had maintained since their arrival here seemed to be wearing thin for Abrianna, in Alex's opinion. In several cases he had seen her reach out to her man in a loving fashion, only to have him sideslip the advances while glancing to see if anyone was watching. The gleam in Cassie's eyes told Alex his wife intended to address that.

"Maybe we should go inside and look, Brie," Cassie said with a smile as she grabbed Abrianna by the arm and led her towards the shop.

"Cassie, I am going to take Leander over there to Sears. Meet us there in that lounge area or call me when you are done here," he said as he produced his phone with one hand while handing her the credit card and several folded $100 bills with the other.

"Put that in your pocket," he said after she accepted the offering.

By now Alex had taught all three the use of both credit cards and cash, explaining the credit system. He had even had her sign a credit receipt for him in one of the shops, showing her how the card scanner worked. Beyond the need for clothing, he wanted to use this shopping trip as a test run should the group ever become separated. He had provided the women with money, watches and phones, all the items they might need in a pinch.

Taking Leander into Sears, they wandered over to the Tool Department, stopping at a display case.

"Pick one," Alex said while indicating the various folding knives on display case.

Alex smiled at the look of delight on Leander's face. They had the sales clerk pull several knives from the display, listening as he described the characteristics of each.

Eventually Leander selected a Cold Steel Recon 4-inch folding Tanto while he picked a 3 ½ inch SOG Banner. Both had locking blades, and could be opened with one hand without trouble. Alex demonstrated to Leander how to clip it to his pants pocket for easy recovery. His friend went through the motions several times of drawing the blade and flicking it open with one hand.

"Thank you, my friend, while I have not seen any danger, I have felt naked without a blade of some kind."

"In my world these are more of a tool than a weapon," Alex replied.

He wasn't sure how much help the folding pocket knife would be in a real fight, should it come to that, but he knew his friend felt better with it. While they had been wandering the mall, Alex had been keeping a watchful eye out for anyone that might be following them. Several times he thought he had spied a tail, only to have the subject disappear and not return.

At one point, after recovering the women outside of Sears, Alex had to set everyone down for a bite to eat while he risked a run to the Jeep to drop off their ever-growing stack of bags. He made the round trip in record time, not happy about leaving the three unattended in the food court. He had noticed a couple of teen boys eyeing the party, the same group he had seen after the jewelry purchases. They had a look about them that he took to mean trouble, but nothing he and Leander couldn't handle. He didn't consider them a direct threat, more of a nuisance should they try a snatch and run.

Moving toward the door to the parking lot, he was relieved when none chose to follow him with all the packages he was carrying. If that had been their intent, he had expected them to follow, thus leading them away from the others. Returning quickly, he was relieved to see the teens nowhere in sight and his companions right where he left them.

"Alex, can we go home now, I am exhausted." Cassie asked, drawing a look of concern from Abrianna.

"Absolutely," he replied as he led the group back out into the parking lot.

Chapter 13

Alex was leading his companions across the crowded parking lot and out to where they had left their ride. Cassie was slightly behind him and to his left while Abrianna and Leander were behind and on his right. The Jeep was easy to spot, as it stood tall over the smaller import cars parked around it. Unfortunately, Alex had been so concerned about his wife that he let his situational awareness slip.

"Yo, Bruh, what's the rush?" the largest of the four teens said as they stepped out from between the cars surrounding their destination.

Alex figured he must have been followed earlier when he made the run to the Jeep, as they had been waiting for his arrival instead of following them from the mall. The four young men were really not much of a concern in themselves, however the gun and two knives being brandished between the four was.

Standing in the traffic lane between rows of parked cars, Alex saw them appear from behind his vehicle. Stopping, he held out his arms indicating to those behind him not to advance any further and stay back. He knew the group must have planned the intercept as they approached on three sides.

"We saw you drop a wad at the jewelry store for all that bling. She's a dime and doesn't need the add," the kid with the gun said as he waved it at Cassie.

Ignoring the knives for the moment, Alex focused on the gun, doing his best to keep himself between it and those behind him. Closing the distance between himself and the leader very slowly, he could tell from the bore of the barrel and the finish of the slide, it looked to be a cheap 9mm semi-auto.

That mattered little because at this close range the kid could hardly miss if he fired it at Alex. His bigger concern was he hadn't briefed his companions on guns and feared they would underestimate the danger of the situation.

"Hand over the watches and the rings, oh and your wallet," he finished while motioning at Alex with the gun.

"Alex?" Cassie started to ask from behind on his left.

"Do what he says honey," Alex replied as he started removing his ring and went for his wallet.

Glancing over his shoulder, the confused look on her face hurt him a little, but he didn't dare risk her life for things so easily replaced. Alex put everything he had in his right hand, leaving the left free, as he slowly extended the items to the kid with the gun. The click he heard behind him on his right, however, sent his adrenaline racing.

"Hey, back off!" he heard from the kid behind as one of the other teens brandished his knife at Leander while reaching for Abrianna's ring.

Alex turned his head slightly, and exactly at that moment the kid had taken a swipe at Leander with his blade. Apparently, Leander had stepped up between the boy and Abrianna as the kid had reached for her jewelry. Far more familiar with the use of edged weapons than the teen, Leander deflected the lunge with one hand while brandishing the newly purchased pocket knife with the other.

In one smooth motion, he struck the kid squarely in the arm holding his knife, driving in all 4 inches of the blade deep into the kid's arm. The sound of his scream was clear to everyone, followed by the sound of a knife hitting the concrete as the boy dropped to his knees, crying and holding his arm.

Alex's primary fear was realized as he turned to watch the teen with the pistol shift his aim left, intent on shooting Leander. That was Alex's cue to act, as the movement brought the gun into reach. He had been moving toward the kid to pass his belongings to the boy, now he lunged.

Dropping the items in his right hand, he doubled up his fingers into a fist. Driving forward swiftly and stepping into the boy, he closed the distance until he was within striking distance. Hitting the teen with his right hand, he used his left to swat the gun away. He hit him so hard, the kid started to drop in place, his eyes rolling back in his head.

The open palm of his left hand connected solidly with the boy's gun hand, and Alex could feel it against his skin. Although the gun started to fall from his grasp, it fired as the kid tensed. The heat of the blast against his hand, gave him hope he had diverted it just enough to direct the bullet away from the group behind him, or so he thought.

Spinning in place as the kid crumpled to the ground, gun tumbling away from him, he was just in time to see Cassie grab for her left arm. He could see a small amount of red just starting to appear between her fingers. Her right arm had been out, pulling Abrianna away from Leander and her attacker. Even shot in the arm, he could now see her fending off the last kid holding a blade, protecting Abrianna by stepping in front of her. The fourth assailant was running for all he was worth, with Leander in pursuit.

Leaping to Cassie's defense, and kicking the gun away as he did so, Alex quickly stepped in to deal with the kid with the blade, but not before he had managed another slash at his wife. Cassie avoided the blade, but the blood across her upper arm flowed with the exertion.

Striking the kid square in the jaw before he could turn on Alex, he dropped as well, his head striking a nearby bumper before he hit the ground.

"Are you ok?" he asked quickly, receiving a nod from Cassie in reply as she motioned for him to deal with the attackers spread around the three.

Abrianna jumped to her cousin's side while Alex turned and collected both the gun and the knives to eliminate any further risks, setting them by Cassie. Two of the attackers were out cold while the third sat on a car hood whimpering and holding his arm where Leander had stabbed him. Dragging the unconscious bodies to where the third sat crying, Alex returned to his injured wife, picking up the gun.

"Alex, what is that thing?" Cassie asked, nodding toward the gun.

"Is she ok?" he asked her cousin, ignoring the question as he knelt next to the two women upon his return.

"Sit there!" Leander commanded as he shoved the fourth teen to the ground between the two unconscious companions. The one with the stab wound had disappeared while Alex wasn't looking, but no one cared.

"It's not terribly deep, but it's bleeding pretty good, it looks like a combination of a cut and a burn," she said as she used one of their recent purchases to temporarily patch the wound, ripping the shirt into strips for bandages.

Any further conversation was halted as both mall security and Seattle Police appeared, surrounding them, and likely drawn by the gunshot. Alex made sure he set the gun and both knives out away from the group and in clear sight of the gathering police. Before long they were awash in first responders, Cassie engulfed by Emergency Medical Tech's while Alex was running interference with the police and advising the others to say as little as possible.

"We need to take her in for treatment," the ambulance driver told the cop talking to Alex.

"Where?" Alex asked before the cop could reply.

"Valley Medical," the man replied before turning and heading back to his vehicle.

"Do you need anything else, that's my wife?" Alex asked while motioning at the ambulance they were loading Cassie into.

"No. I have your contact information. I will call if we need anything else."

They had provided the police all the identification Alex had received at the Wiccan shop. He had little doubt that the Seattle PD was running all four of them through the system now. He just hoped the ID's would stand up to the scrutiny.

Rushing over to the ambulance, he was just in time to quell the escalating argument between one of the EMT's and Abrianna.

"What do you mean I can't go with her? I am a healer and her cousin," she snapped at the woman trying to block her access to the back doors.

"Ma'am, there isn't room. You can follow us if you like, but you can't ride with her," the Tech explained.

"Are you ok?" Alex asked Cassie as he peered past the argument.

"I'll be fine," Cassie said with a weak smile.

From her expression, Alex could see a tinge of worry.

"We will be right behind you," Alex replied as he waved the rest of his party toward the Jeep.

Leander had already collected their things and loaded them in the Jeep so all the three had to do was climb in and Alex fired up the engine. They followed the Ambulance as it weaved its way free of the roadblocks caused by the excitement in the parking lot and soon, they were on the open roads leading to the hospital.

"Where are they taking her?" Abrianna asked as she stared straight ahead at the ambulance.

"Valley Medical Center is the closest hospital to the Mall. It's a place of healing," he added in Abrianna's context.

In a very short time Alex pulled in behind the ambulance as they reached the emergency entrance.

"Follow her in while I park, and don't talk to anybody," he instructed the two.

It was no use arguing with anyone about leaving the Jeep where he was, he knew the drill. Moving swiftly while he waved to Cassie as they pulled her out the back of the Ambulance, he quickly found a parking spot and rushed inside.

"Are you the husband?" a woman asked as he caught a glimpse of Cassie being wheeled into a curtained area followed by Leander and Abrianna.

"Yes," Alex replied as he looked at the clipboard the woman was passing him.

"Please fill these out and I need a copy of your insurance card," she explained in a practiced tone.

"This will cover any charges in full," Alex replied as he produced his American Express Centurion card, the same he had used earlier in the day. As far as he knew the card did not have a spending limit and the woman did a double take before accepting it.

"Thank you, sir," she replied as she waved him on to follow the others.

----*----

"What in blazes is this all about?" Avenstore hissed as his man closed the door to his office behind him.

"That wasn't our people," the man replied hastily.

"Then who in Hades was it?" the Elf King demanded as he stuffed the urgent report back in its envelope before flipping it at the minion.

"Appears to be just some local juvenile delinquents preying on unsuspecting shoppers. Sire if four teenagers can give these people that much trouble, should we even be concerned about them?" the man asked skeptically.

"Did any of the teenagers die?" Avenstore asked after a pause.

"No, Sire," the man replied, confused by the question.

"Never confuse discretion, with weakness. The last thing any of us want, we or the four of them, is the police looking too closely at any of us."

"Yes, Sire," the man replied, duly chastised.

"And our other operative?" Avenstore asked, shifting the conversation.

"Word has gone out that she is to come to meet with you immediately. Both she and the Succubus should be here soon."

"Good. Let's hope she is more discrete should things go badly there," Avenstore said as he waved his minion out of his office.

----*----

Alex entered the small curtained area to find his wife resting in one of those rolling hospital beds while two of the hospital staff were attending to her. A woman was inspecting her wound while a man was drawing blood from the other arm. On his way in, he passed another staff member, one he took for a nurse, as she had a sphygmomanometer in one hand for taking blood pressure.

"How are you doing?" Alex asked as he acknowledged Abrianna and Leander, who were sitting quietly to one side of the small space and were doing their best to stay out of the way.

"Alex, they made me get undressed," she said while emphasizing the hospital gown and nodding to her clothes pile on the nearby chair.

"Please don't move," the one taking the blood sample asked.

"Mr. Rogers? I am Doctor Joseph; I am afraid your wife will need stitches" the woman said without looking up from her work.

"I am having her blood work done as well, just as a precaution. Lord knows where that bullet had been before this," she said as she looked up at Alex.

Alex took the comment for humor, her attempt at a calming bedside manner, he was sure.

"How deep is it?" Alex asked, as the man taking blood finished up and slipped out, leaving him free to stand beside his wife.

He took Cassie's free hand in his, giving her a reassuring squeeze as she passed him a nervous smile before the doctor waved him back while she worked.

"Deep enough. No nerve damage that I can tell, but it is into the muscle a little bit. By the way, which one of you hit those kids?" She asked with a bit of a smirk on her face.

"I did actually," Alex replied while indicating Leander was innocent of any wrongdoing should there be an issue beyond self-defense.

"An awful lot of damage for one man. Well, you broke the one kid's nose. He also has a concussion and the second has a dislocated jaw. A third was caught running from the parking lot, he had a deep stab wound in the right arm?" she asked questioningly.

Alex didn't bother to explain, should there be a legal issue with using the knife. He was still unsure if the self-defense laws were as he remembered them. He had no idea how good those identity papers he had were, but an extended investigation would likely prove problematic for the three transplants.

"They are here?" Alex suddenly asked of their attackers with concern, as the doctor seemed to know a lot about his assailants.

"Separate area, under guard. I just got word from the other attending physician. Once we release them, they are headed to jail," the doctor said as a suture tray arrived with all the things she needed to stich Cassie up.

"Also, Seattle PD said to say thanks, this group has been terrorizing the mall customers for weeks."

"The stab was Leander, he was protecting Brie," Alex commented while indicating the couple, now sure the police had little interest in prosecuting the victims.

That produced a nod of acknowledgement from the doctor. While they had been talking Alex had moved back up next to his wife, taking her hand in his once more and trying to comfort her. In the back of his mind, he worried about what the blood test might come up with, he had no idea how her nymph ancestry might translate to his world.

"OK, let's numb you up first," he heard the doctor say as she started to inject Cassie.

"It's ok," Alex said after a panicked look from his wife at the needle.

Alex heard a small gasp from his wife as the needle pierced her arm, her grip on his hand tightening slightly. He watched as Abrianna stared in fascination.

"That makes the pain go away?" she asked the doctor as she watched her repeat the process near the wound.

"Yes, it masks the pain," the doctor answered while looking quizzically at Alex.

"Please excuse my cousin, she has never seen a hospital before, she comes from a small village," Alex started to explain.

"I am a healer as well, only, I rely on plants and... treatments," Abrianna said, avoiding the word *spells*.

"Ah, homeopathic medicine. I studied a little of that as well. Sometimes it helps in recovery," the doctor replied absently as she prepared the needle and sutures.

"There is a plant I know that removes the pain. You crush the roots and apply them around the wound, after a bit you can close it without pain."

"Mandrake root?" the doctor asked without looking away from her work.

"I do not know it by that name," was all Abrianna would say after catching a brief nod from Alex.

Everyone watched in silence as the doctor worked the sutures across the opening in Cassie's upper arm.

"I'll do my best not to leave a scar," she commented as she worked slowly but diligently. Once she had finished her work, the doctor placed a bandage over Cassie's wound.

"There, that should do it. I will give you written instructions on wound care for the next few days," she explained to Alex as another woman in scrubs entered the space.

"Doctor, the bloodwork results," she said as he passed a clipboard to her and then departed.

Alex watched her scan the sheet before she looked up at Cassie and then himself.

"Problem?" he asked as he tried to interpret the look on her face.

"Not unless your recent experience has put you off children. Your wife is pregnant."

Chapter 14

"Alex, those men in uniform kept my knife. I thought it best not to protest," Leander commented as the four companions rode home in the Jeep.

"I'll get you another one, how's the arm," Alex replied to Leander while checking on his wife seated next to him.

Before leaving the hospital, and after Cassie had dressed, the nurse had insisted on placing her arm in a sling. Concerned that excessive movement might pop her stitches, the doctor had demanded on its use.

"I feel stupid with this thing on," Cassie replied as she waved her arm about within the restrictions of the straps holding it in place.

"I am sorry I didn't explain about guns sooner. I didn't think we would encounter one anytime soon, if ever," he added in the form of an apology.

Alex nodded at Cassie's statement, but knew that wasn't what was on everyone's mind. After the Doctor's announcement, they had all been surprised by the disclosure, although Abrianna had a look of understanding. Both he and his beloved wife were excited, a spontaneous hug, sending the doctor into fits as Cassie wrapped her injured arm around her husband.

Since that first moment of excitement, the sobering memory of their current situation dampened their mood. The rest of the ride home was in silence, the only noises were those of the cars and trucks around them as they traveled the short distance from the hospital back to the Renton Highlands and home.

Pulling into his driveway, he need not do anything as they all had the drill down by now. Cassie opened her door, slipping from the seat easily and then, one handed, hit the seat release allowing Leander out while Abrianna exited on Alex's side.

"Is anyone hungry?" Alex asked as he led them to the front door after confirming Leander handled Cassie's door.

It had been several hours since their lunch break at the shopping mall. Between the time in the parking lot with the

Seattle PD and the hours at the hospital it was quite late in the day.

"I'll take care of that and Leander will unload the packages, you tend to Cassie," Abrianna said as she nodded toward her cousin.

Under normal circumstances, Alex would have expected his wife's cousin to insist in overseeing her care, but he suspected it wasn't the injury that needed tending. Opening the front door, he watched as the silent Cassie did not go to the right as they entered, but instead turned left down the hallway that led to their bedroom. Tossing the ball cap he had been wearing into his office so it lay next to his computer, he headed back toward the kitchen.

"Go on!" Abrianna whispered at Alex as she nodded after her cousin.

Doing as he was told, Alex quickly caught up with his wife as she entered their bedroom. He had no sooner closed the door before he found her in his arms, her head buried in his chest as her free arm wrapped itself around him.

"Alex, please take me home. I don't want to have our baby here, this place is awful," she said as her tears began to flow.

----*----

The Vassal King sat in his great hall, as the small band of scouts gave their reports to the gathered Lords. Rather than taking his seat on the raised dais at the far end of the hall, they had gathered around a large table off to one side, a place where they could lay out maps for all to see. Ailmer still took his seat at the head of the table, a reminder to all of who was in charge here.

"You are sure of this?" one of the lords asked the officer leading the scouts.

"Yes, your lordship, the dwarves have vacated the mountains and taken refuge in Windfall. We were told that with the disappearance of the Lord Protector, Lady Amelia is ruling in his place there."

"What of the King of Great Vale?" another asked, in reference to King Ben, Wizard King of Great Vale.

"I can speak of that," another man replied.

Ailmer recognized him as one of the many scout team leaders they had sent south. This particular team had a very special member. A Mage that was magically linked to her falcon. The woman had the ability to see through the bird's eyes as it flew high and far.

It was unusual for a Mage to choose military service in this fashion, and particularly a woman, but Ailmer had allowed it due to her special abilities. The woman seemed to have a particular hatred for those of Windfall and cared little that it was under a new ruler. In all the combination made her a valuable asset.

"The King rides north at a hurried pace with a small force consisting of his personal guard," the man reported.

"And his army?" the lord asked in return.

"Nowhere to be seen my lord," the officer replied.

"So, the King rides north to do battle with your champion Sire, what say you?" the first Lord said as he turned to Ailmer.

"Perhaps, but we need to insure it is so," Ailmer replied, while considering the situation.

"It gives me an idea. I want your bird to take a message to the Captain watching over my Champion," Ailmer said.

It took the Vassal King no more than a few minutes to complete his missive, passing it to the scout team leader. With this, Ailmer realized, he could do more than just take Windfall.

"I say let him come to us, so much the better!"

----*----

Avenstore sat in his office as he appraised the succubus sitting across from him. Her overt sexual display was wasted on him as the two sat waiting for the other of the Elf King's tools to appear. He suspected the woman couldn't help herself, as she knew elves would be susceptible to her charms as much as any human and he would be quite a prize.

She was testing him, probing him for weakness. He knew that draining even a fraction of his essence would give her a rush of power that even she could not imagine. That would never happen of course. Under normal circumstance he would have already slapped her down for even thinking such thoughts, but he needed her willing cooperation at the moment. For that reason alone, he let her try.

"Woah, turn it down girl!" another extremely attractive woman said as she entered the room unannounced.

"What is she doing here?" Joey hissed as the new arrival dropped into a seat next to her.

Avenstore smiled as he considered the contrast between the two women, and it was dramatic. Compared to Joey's jet-black hair and tanned complexion, the newcomer was a light blonde and fair skinned. Not nearly as provocatively dressed, the blonde still exuded an animal sexuality none the less. At no more than five-foot-tall and one hundred pounds soaking wet, she was just the right size for his plans.

"Your failure with the coven has forced me to expand our little team," Avenstore answered dismissively.

"I can handle them without the help of a bitch," Joey snapped.

"I hear they tossed you out on your ass?" the woman replied, apparently unphased by the insult.

"We now know they have power, but do they have knowledge, that's the question. Your attempt to seduce the information from them failed, so now we need to try another angle. One a little more subtle."

"Then why am I still here?' the dark temptress asked with some irritation.

"Your usefulness is not over, I have another task for you, and it is a role that I think you will enjoy very much," the Elf King said with a smile.

"Which is?" the succubus asked with renewed interest.

"The role of a home wrecker."

----*----

Elion studied the parchment in his hands for several minutes before he set it aside. The time difference between the two realms sometimes gave one the sense of disorientation as he worked out the relationship between events there and here. With every day in this realm equating to five days in Alex's world, Elion had to pay close attention to the dates and times in these reports to understand the rate of progress. As with most complex plans, timing was everything.

The incident with the Succubus at the Wiccan coven, spoke to Avenstore's telltale trait of using dark creatures to do his dirty work. It was unfortunate that the learning spell had telegraphed their activities so spectacularly. He feared the event might expose Elion's overall plan prematurely.

The excessive use of magic had Alex's hand all over it, as the boy tended to go overboard with everything he did. In this case, however, the reawakening of the latent magical abilities within the Wiccans was an unexpected windfall. Elion had always expected Alex to face overwhelming odds in his quest to return Cassie and the others to their home, but these new magical allies tipped the scales ever so slightly in his favor.

The Elvin King had resources in that realm as well as Avenstore, small groups strategically placed to watch and report. It had been Elion's people that supplied the documentation necessary to get them to England and beyond if necessary. He was satisfied they were on the right track, both in their search for the missing pages of the Elvin history and their desire to summon dragons. His end goal was, however, much, much grander.

Affairs here were not lost on the Woodland King though, as he considered the challenges before his friend Ben. The Dark Paladin summoned by Avenstore to disrupt the course of events in this realm would be beyond Ben's ability to defeat alone. There would need to be a convergence of events to provide the noble King the means to destroy that foe.

As he confirmed his thought from before, timing is everything.

----*----

It was early morning and Emma was out back behind the store, taking the trash out to the dumpster. She had just dropped the plastic bags inside the large metal bin when she was startled by a noise. The excitement of the day before, where the coven had been threatened by a demon succubus, had everyone on edge. Looking around, she quickly spotted the source of the rustling.

"Come here, don't be afraid," she said as the face of a dog appeared from behind the trash bin.

After a moment's hesitation, she watched as a beautiful Golden Retriever worked its way out of the small space.

"What a pretty dog you are," she cooed as she tried to reassure the hesitant animal.

Its head lowered in hesitation; Emma could see the tail wagging in acceptance as it slowly approached her until it reached the outstretched hand. After a quick sniff, the dog offered itself up to the strokes of the young woman as she attempted to calm the animal.

"No collar huh? Well, you must be hungry. Come with me," Emma said softly as she led the dog into the shop and closed the door behind her.

----*----

Yesterday's trip to the mall and the subsequent events at the hospital had left Cassie upset and exhausted. After consoling his pregnant wife, Alex had done everything in his power to give her a quiet evening of rest. In the time since their arrival here, all three of his companions had learned how to prepare meals in the home's kitchen. While Alex had done all the shopping, he had instructed the others on how to make a list of their dietary needs. Abrianna had cooked for the four that evening, a simple meal, but filling.

Alex had returned the favor that morning, whipping up breakfast before the others had risen. The coffee, bacon and omelets to order was well received as each emerged from their separate bedrooms, Cassie was the last to arrive at the table.

"Leander, I think it's time you and I do some shopping together," he announced after everyone had eaten and the kitchen cleaned.

"I'll go," Cassie offered.

"No, I think you should take a break today. Besides, that arm needs to rest," he said while pointing to her bandage.

She hadn't bothered to put her sling back on, having removed it at bedtime. With both he and Abrianna to chastise her movements, it didn't seem necessary for her to do so.

"You just sit there with Kinsey and Abrianna. Let me take Leander this time," Alex said while pointing to Kinsey curled up next to her on the couch.

Alex caught the slight nod from Abrianna indicating she agreed with the decision and so he waved Leander on.

"Let's go," he said as he headed to the door, Jeep key in hand.

The pair went silently out and climbed into the vehicle before either spoke.

"I wish to congratulate you. Yours is the first royal baby in my lifetime, it is quite an exciting event."

"Thanks, but I think Cassie is not as excited," Alex commented with a humorless laugh.

He piloted the Jeep out of the housing subdivision and headed up the main roadway to the local shopping center. It was his intent to increase the A'nlanders exposure to more of the community around them before their flight to London. He wanted to minimize the gawking and the shock value of the things they would be exposed to.

"Now, this is what we call a supermarket," he explained as he found a parking spot near the doors.

"You call it super, yet it is far smaller than the building yesterday? Does it go underground, perhaps?"

"No, this is it. It's only super in comparison to the small markets of the past, like in your realm," Alex explained as the two walked across the open parking lot and entered the sliding doors.

He heard the gasp from his companion as Alex grabbed a cart and began wandering the aisles.

"So much," he heard the man comment as he followed along.

"Yes, welcome to the land of copious consumption. I am told that even the poor live better here than in the rest of the world," Alex said with a tinge of embarrassment.

The two men began filling their cart as they ticked off items on the list Alex had created before leaving. As they walked, Alex explained the subtleties of the world around them, pointing out discretely, the various individuals shopping and speculating on their backgrounds.

His home squarely located in a middle-class neighborhood, it was fairly easy to identify the housewives, college students and office workers. Still early in the day and a weekday at that, he had the benefit of their dress to aid in his guesswork. He explained the comfortable casual attire of a stay at home spouse, the business casual and proper clothing of office workers and the ludicrous selections of college student's trendy choices.

"Oh, I'm sorry," Alex heard as a beautiful raven-haired young woman bumped his cart as they turned a corner between aisles. He paused as her piercing green eyes stared up at him.

A quick glance allowed Alex to see a tight fitting black sleeveless tank top covering a very shapely bustline. The equally tight-fitting blue jeans ended where the high-topped black leather riding boots started. There were just a few items in her cart, the beer, wine and snacks, giving him the impression, she was shopping for a party.

"No, my fault, sorry I wasn't paying attention," Alex replied as he maneuvered to pass the woman on the outside.

At that moment, she made the same move, causing their carts to crash once more.

"OK, that's on me, sorry," she said with a smile while trying to move the cart out of Alex's way.

All the movement gave both men a considerable show as the young woman's tank top took a noticeable plunge in front. The activity and exposed cleavage on display was confirmation that she had nothing else on under that top. Alex decided to retreat and allow her to pass before returning to his path.

"And what is she, a student?" Leander asked as they finally passed into the next aisle and out of earshot.

"That was trouble," was Alex's reply.

Chapter 15

"Mother, why are they here?" Kelby asked Amelia as the two stood watching the dwarves making themselves at home in the great hall.

At less than 100 individuals, it was decided that the great hall was the best place for them to settle in rather than the several smaller structures it would require.

"Kelby, they have been driven from their mountain homes by that demon wandering the tunnels."

"No, I get that. I mean, why are they here, in our castle?" she asked again while indicating the sprawled mass before them.

"Long ago, before Ben became King of Great Vale, we were like them. The war had taken most of my family and Ben had saved me from an Orc raid. On the run, we took refuge with these same dwarves, who took us in and protected me while Ben went off to fight in the war."

"Sorry, I did not know. So that's how you speak their tongue," Kelby added with a smile.

"Yes, they taught me a great many things while I was their guest, the most important thing was gratitude."

----*----

"My, who is this?" Abigail asked as she entered the shop and was greeted by a friendly Golden Retriever.

"I found her hiding behind the trash bin in the alley," Emma replied as she patted the friendly dog.

"Any idea who owns her?' Abigail said as she passed the dog and headed behind the counter to check the register for sales totals.

"Nope, no collar or tags. I thought I would take her to the vet to check if she's chipped, but haven't had the chance."

"Any word from our visitors? I really want to ask them about that succubus," Abigail said after scanning the room to be sure there were no customers about.

Abigail noted idly that the dog followed the pair as they walked to the back room while they talked. Although she had no pets of her own, she had nothing against having the dog around so long as it didn't make any messes.

"I saw in the news that someone stopped a robbery at Southcenter Mall. They didn't mention names, but I saw a video clip that sure looked like them as they loaded someone into an ambulance," Emma explained.

"Ambulance? Was anyone hurt?" she asked as she stopped in place, looking at the younger woman.

"They said minor injuries, but three of the four attackers had to be hospitalized."

"Strange, I didn't feel the use of magic?" Abigail said as she moved into the ceremony room.

"I get the impression that Alex and Leander wouldn't need magic to stop a mugging," Emma said with a laugh as she followed the older woman into the room.

Suddenly both women stopped and turned to the doorway. Standing there and looking about the room, the dog let out the slightest whimper as it looked pleading at the pair.

"Come on in, it's ok," Emma said as she tried to coax the Golden forward.

Instead of entering, the dog took a step back before sitting.

"I think she is afraid of something in here?" Abigail said as she scanned the room looking for something that might upset the dog.

"Maybe it's the smell of incense?" Emma said while indicating the burning ember on the alter.

"Maybe. Well, why don't you take her up front while I get to work," Abigail replied while dismissing the younger woman.

"Oh, and let me know when everyone gets here, we have a lot of practicing to do. We all need to learn how to mask our use of magic."

"Why?" Emma asked.

"Alex warned me that others will be watching us, we need to be careful."

----*----

Captain Ianas stood on the landing where the tunnel emerged on the south face of the Northern Mountains. Next to him, and uncomfortably close, was his charge, the demon warrior the Vassal King had assigned him to watch over. Protection was not actually his duty as the demon warrior seemed impervious to all forms of injury.

It was Ianas's duty to see that the devil's spawn did as he was told and no more. Considering the fact that the thing was impervious to all forms of injury, he had little idea of what he was to do should the creature go against its orders. His only hope was it stayed the course naturally.

Still high in the mountains, the small group had a commanding view of the forest below and the lands beyond. Considering that the officer he replaced had been crushed in the tunnels below as the dwarves attempted to defend their lands, Ianas was delighted to be in the open air. The men behind him seemed to share his feelings as their constant murmurings had ceased.

"Sir," the man at his side said while pointing to a bird high overhead.

He watched as the form grew until a bird of prey rather than a message bird landed nearby. He waved the man forward and watched as he removed a small parchment from the leather harness attached to the falcon. No sooner had the message been removed then the bird took flight and quickly disappeared.

Captain Ianas took the small scroll from his man and scanned its contents.

"The King of Great Vale leads a small band toward our position. We are to engage and overcome, using the Challenge of Champions" the Captain said specifically to the silent statue towering over him.

Without replying, the Paladin stepped forward onto the precarious trail leading them down from the mountain landing and into the forest below.

----*----

Cassie sat stroking Kinsey as the two listened to Abrianna.

"Now that we know you are with child, there are many things we must consider and prepare for," her cousin began as she took a seat nearby.

"Brie I do not want to have my baby here. You saw that place they took me too. How can their healer work in those conditions?"

"Yes, I did, however, we might not make it back home before the baby comes. The Doctor gave Alex medicines that are supposed to assist in the health of the baby before birth," she replied while shaking a small plastic bottle of tablets at her.

Alex had explained to Abrianna in private what each of the prenatal supplements were for as Cassie was dressing.

"Do you trust them?" Cassie asked incredulously.

"Yes, these only increase your health, they are not for correcting illness."

"Even so," Cassie replied, somewhat mollified.

"Cassie, have you considered the significance of this? The union of a Nymph and a Wizard has never been recorded in any of our histories. Should your child be a girl, she would be exceptional," Abrianna said after a pause.

"Do you think that's why we were all sent here, to this place without magic?"

The question hung in the air as both women considered the possibilities.

----*----

Ben had reached the far side of the forest, where it met the foothills of the Northern Mountains in record time. It was there they decided to make camp for the night, his men breathing a sigh of relief. Technically, they were still in the woods, at the base of the mountain range, so it gave them some concealment from above. He had little doubt that the opposing force was aware of their approach, but there was no reason to make things easy for them.

Once they were settled in with guards posted, he called a meeting at the central fire pit.

"This is a map of the area," he explained to the small gathering of men.

"We are less than a league from where the forest ends and the foothills create open spaces. Our scouts located three places, here, here and here, where trails lead down, out of the mountains, from above," Ben described as he pointed to the places on his map.

"Place men there to alert us if someone emerges, but I do not want to engage while they hold the high ground. Have the men retreat to here, should they see the enemy," Ben outlined as he pointed to a place where the attackers wouldn't hold the high ground.

As he outlined his plan, Ben again regretted that he did not have Alex here at this side.

-----*-----

Leander was helping Alex as the two men placed their shopping bags in the back of the Jeep. As he worked, Leander scanned his surroundings, not in wariness considering their last attack, but instead in curiosity. In all his years he had never seen so many wondrous things in one place. The metal wagons Alex called cars, the large structures and the crowds of people all overwhelmed the senses.

Above all, it was the constant noise that amazed him. He listened to everything going on around him and wondered how anyone could concentrate with all the distractions. Scanning the parking lot, a name he recalled from their mall adventure, he suddenly noticed the young woman they ran into inside the store.

She appeared to be opening the front of her car instead of the rear like everyone else. She also looked angry or frustrated as she stared down into the opening before her. He then saw her look up and begin to scan the area until her eyes landed on Leander, looking back in her direction. He watched as she paused and then began walking toward the pair.

"Ah, Alex, here comes Trouble," he said, recalling the name Alex had given the girl.

"Hey, can you help me?" the woman asked before Alex had a chance to reply to Leander's comment.

"What's wrong? Oh," Alex replied as he scanned the area and quickly motioned at the car with the front open behind her.

Leander suspected that it must be unusual to open the front and so that's how Alex immediately identified the woman's car.

"It won't start and I have to get home right away. Can you come take a look?" she asked pleadingly, but in a melodic tone Leander found enticing.

He noticed she was speaking to Alex but kept glancing his way. The scrutiny making him slightly uncomfortable.

"Sure," Alex replied in a neutral tone, one Leander took as guarded.

"I'm Joey by the way," she said as she offered her hand to Leander.

"I am Leander and this is Alex," he replied as the young woman held his hand in hers.

He knew shaking hands was a form of greeting here in Alex's realm, so he took the offering in his own. He was surprised, however, in the way she responded to his grip, hers being far more sensual as she slipped her hand into his and rubbed both with her free hand. He had never seen this done to Alex before and it both thrilled him and made him very uncomfortable. A quick check confirmed Alex had seen none of it as he led the way to the woman's car.

"Try and turn it over," he said to the woman as she released Leander's hand and continued around to the far side of the hunk of metal.

Leander peered into the opening as he wondered how Alex expected Joey to flip this mass of metal on its back. Instead, she climbed inside and fiddled with something that caused a clicking sound and the noise Alex's Jeep made when he started it. This car, unfortunately, didn't start, it just kept making the noise as Leander watched things inside turning around and around.

He watched as Alex poked at a few places and had the woman try several more times before he shook his head slowly.

"It's getting gas and fire, I don't see why it won't start," he announced as Joey emerged from inside the car.

Leander couldn't help but notice the display of skin as she rested on her elbows while looking down at the thing Alex had been messing with.

"I really need to get home; I have people coming over and can't leave them waiting outside. Can I hitch a ride?" she said in frustration.

"What about your car?" Alex asked as he motioned to the vehicle.

"I can have the repair shop come get it later," she replied with a smile as she looked up at the two men. Leander noticed she didn't move from her position leaning over onto the car. Her top was barely preventing her assets from spilling out for all to see. Leander looked to Alex, but if his friend was noticing the display, and how could he not, he was unphased.

"We can take you home, let's get your stuff," he replied as he waved everyone back and then slammed the lid closed on the front of the car.

Leander followed Joey to the rear where she opened another lid. Inside he could see bags similar to those he and Alex had just secured in the Jeep, just fewer in number. As he reached inside to collect what he could, he felt her slide up next to him, their bodies in close contact with one another.

"Thanks a lot for the ride," she said in a sultry voice that only he could hear.

"Hand me that," Alex said as he pointed to one of the heavier bags, startling Leander in the process.

There was something about this woman, any time she got close to him, seemingly always in close contact, he found disturbingly alluring. His love for Abrianna was unquestionable, but this wasn't love, it was pure desire.

Moving away to allow Joey to close the lid, he quickly headed to the Jeep ahead of the two, placing as much distance between himself and the woman as possible. With the rear of the Jeep filled with their own purchases, Leander had to place her bags in the back seat. As he leaned in, he could feel her pressing in behind him, passing the ones carried by others. She stroked his back with her free hand invitingly as she reached past his shoulder.

"Leander why don't you get in back so Joey doesn't have to climb in," Alex offered as he made his way around to the other door.

"I will be happy to," was all he managed to squeak out.

Pulling out of the parking lot, Leander sat quietly as Joey directed Alex to a nearby structure, he heard Alex call apartments. Every so often she would turn in her seat so she could speak to Leander, and in so doing provide him with a flash of skin from her undersized top.

"Right here?" he heard Alex ask as he stopped in front of a building.

"Yes, thank you both so much!" she said as she reached back to pad Leander's knee.

After she had climbed out, Leander followed and began pulling her bags from the rear seat. Following both her and Alex up a flight of stairs, he watched as she unlocked a door and waved them inside.

"Are you sure you can't stay, it's going to be a blast?" she asked as she rested on hand on Leander's shoulder while indicating the alcohol and snacks in the bags.

"Sorry, no can do, maybe some other time," Alex replied as he waved Leander out the door.

Leander let Alex lead the way as they returned to the Jeep and then waved goodbye to Joey as she stood on the landing.

"She seems nice," was all Leander could say.

Alex rolled his eyes in reply without a comment.

Chapter 16

Joey watched as the two men drove away while she waved enticingly at them. The Elf King had warned her not to try and use her powers while in the presence of the Wizard as he might pick up on her. The nonmagical human, her actual target, was fair game so long as she didn't get caught by the others.

For him, the secret was in physical contact. So long as she could touch some part of his body, she could impart her lustful impressions on him unnoticed by others. Avenstore had warned her that, while the wizard was a far more tempting target, the man was dangerous. This avenue was much safer for the succubus and would create as much dissension in their ranks as a direct assault.

Even so, taking a shot at getting the Wizard was appealing to her. She could feel the power within him, something even he didn't seem to appreciate. Should he unravel the Dark Elves grasp on this realm, he would indeed be a power to fear.

For now, she just needed to enjoy the beginnings of the trap she was laying. She doubted that the human's female companion would miss the telltale lipstick marks, nor her scent that she had discretely rubbed onto him. She had also placed the electronic tracker in the Jeep where it wouldn't easily be found, insuring she could increase the number of *accidental* meetings.

----*----

"I think we should try another outing tonight, but this time one that is far less exciting," Alex offered as he addressed his three companions.

Their return home from the store had been somewhat strained as Leander tried to explain the lipstick on his cheek and the smell of perfume. Alex had explained about their damsel in distress, but it did little to defuse the situation. Though far from a jealous woman, Abrianna thought it was somewhat suspicious that Alex had not received the same amount of gratitude from this mysterious young woman as had Leander.

In the end Abrianna had to accept the fact that Alex had been with her intended the entire time. He was absolute in his position that Leander had only been a gracious rescuer and nothing more.

"One that does not have the two of you unsupervised I hope?" Abrianna stated more than asked.

"I was thinking the four of us would go out for a nice dinner, it's time you see how restaurants work in my realm," came Alex's reply.

"We ate at the shopping square, isn't that the same thing?" Cassie asked.

"Besides, I do not want to go out looking like this," she added as she waved her arm about still in its sling.

"I was thinking you could forgo the sling, provided you promise to be careful and not over do things. We leave for London in a few days and it would be best if you were well healed before we travel," he replied.

The comment drew a look of concern from Abrianna, but apparently, she agreed with him as she chose not to speak on the subject. Like her, he was concerned about Cassie traveling now that all knew she was with child. In spite of those concerns, he had little stomach for the thought of leaving her behind. Besides, he was very confident he would never triumph in any campaign that suggested the four split up.

They spent the rest of the afternoon studying, reading or just resting from the previous day's excitement. As afternoon turned into early evening, Alex suggested an early dinner.

"I see now why you called that woman trouble. I would never have thought Abrianna would worry about my commitment to her," Leander said in private as the women had gone to change for their dinner adventure.

"She has never had to worry about things like that in Great Vale, where everyone knows who you both are. Here things are different. I am just glad she didn't get to see the vixen," Alex explained with a laugh.

Apparently, Leander had never given that a thought. The look of horror on his face suggested he visualized Abrianna's reaction to Joey rubbing herself up and down his side. With that, the two men went their respective ways to get changed for dinner as well. Once everyone was ready, they loaded up in the Jeep and made the short trek to one of Alex's local haunts, a place he was happy to see was still in business.

"Mr. Alex, where have you been? I haven't seen you in here for years," the man at the door greeted him.

"Mr. Lee, yes, I have been away and very busy. May I introduce my wife, Cassie," Alex said as he shook the man's hands warmly.

"Wife? My, you have been busy," Mr. Lee repeated before he bowed slightly to Cassie and then offered his hand, taking her's in his warmly.

"And this is her cousin Abrianna and her fiancé Leander," Alex finished.

"Welcome to you all, please let me get you my best table," the man said with great enthusiasm.

"Alex, you know this man?" Cassie asked quietly as she followed behind Mr. Lee.

"Yes, for years. This place has the best Chinese food in all of Seattle and I came here all the time back then. That's why we came early to avoid the rush," Alex said as he waved to the occupied tables around them.

Looking around Alex realized there wasn't an open table to be found. He knew Mr. Lee kept one table in the back open for special arrivals, usually Chinese natives sent by family or friends looking for some home cooked meals. With his popularity, Mr. Lee could afford it, as Alex had waited over an hour in years past just to be seated.

"Here you are, let me get your menus," Mr. Lee said while waving at a busboy to bring them water and tableware.

"Chopsticks?" Mr. Lee said expectantly.

"Just for me, but you might bring extra for lessons," Alex said with a wink to the man.

The comment brought a big smile to the man's face as Alex knew how much he enjoyed teaching newcomers his traditions. Once everyone was seated, there was a whirlwind of activity as menus, tableware and drinks appeared almost all at once.

"You are important here?" Leander asked after everyone had been provided for.

"I helped Mr. Lee with some improvements to his restaurant way back when. Besides doing the engineering, I helped him with some of the city paperwork and inspections. He says we are family now and I don't argue with him," Alex said with a smile as unordered appetizers appeared as if by magic.

"So, this is not normal here," Cassie asked as she waved at all the servers providing for their every need.

"Only for me," Alex said with a smile.

"I begin to see that your husband has been spoiled in the past," Abrianna said with a smile.

"Almost like royalty," Alex replied with a smile of his own.

"Alex, I fear something is wrong, I can't read most of this," Leander said as he waved the menu about.

"It's Chinese, you are not supposed to," Alex said.

The confused looks on their faces caused Alex to break into an explanation of the way things worked here.

"Look, unlike your realm where there is mostly one common language, here there are many languages. Though China is far from here, those that now live in this country take great pride in their heritage, so they print the menus in both English and Chinese."

"Have you eaten everything on here?" Abrianna asked as she flipped through the many paged menu.

"Oh, heavens no, I have eaten only a small part of what Mr. Lee offers here. I suggest you let me order if that's ok?"

"Fine by me," Leander said as he closed his menu.

"I begin to understand why you were so confused in the tavern that first time. Between this menu and that of the food square, you have a confusing amount of options" Cassie said as she continued to scan the contents of her menu.

Soon after, the waiter appeared to take their order. Alex selected some of the more popular dishes and had to explain the family style of eating as the heaping plates of food began to appear. With the food, Mr. Lee appeared to personally provide chopstick lessons for any interested party. Both Cassie and

Abrianna attempted their use, Alex already having mastered the utensils years ago. In the end, after lots of laughter, only Abrianna stuck to the choice, with Cassie joining Leander in using a fork.

Alex was so enjoying their dinner adventure, laughing with the others as they struggled with the chopsticks and discussing the many dishes before them. All at once, Leander's face went blank. Following his gaze, Alex couldn't quite believe what he saw.

"Oh shit," he uttered as he saw Joey, at the entrance and scanning the room.

No longer in the tight jeans and tank top from the market, she was now dressed in a slinky black dress, the halter top upper containing a plunging deep V between her breasts. The silky light material snugly wrapped her waist, flaring out into a skirt that ended very high on her upper thigh. Any hope that the young woman might miss them sitting there in the back evaporated as she suddenly brightened, waving as she spied Leander facing the doorway.

"How?" Leander said to Alex as he turned to watch her cross the room.

By now all four at the table were watching her as she maneuvered across the crowded room. It amazed Alex that with so much of her body in motion, nothing was accidently exposed, though it was a close call in several instances.

"So, this is why you couldn't come to my party?" she announced to the table as she made her way to stand next to Leander, wrapping one arm around his shoulders.

"Party?" Abrianna asked as she glared at Leander while looking daggers at the woman with her arm around her fiancé.

"Abrianna, Cassie, this is Joey, the young woman from the store we told you about," Alex announced while trying to divert any more comments from Abrianna.

"And which of you owns this hunk of a man?" Joey asked as she rubbed Leander's shoulders while slipping even closer to him.

"Leander is my fiancé," Abrianna announced with some edge to her voice.

"Well, he is quite a catch. You better treat him right girl or I just might try and steal him away from you," Joey said in a teasing tone.

Leander sat unmoving, his discomfort at being the center of the conversation evident to all as his face went bright red. He dared not turn to look at the woman standing next to him for fear of ending in a face full of cleavage. Alex suspected that would be a tipping point for Abrianna's self-control.

"I thought you had a party tonight?" Alex asked, trying to defuse what he thought was a building catfight.

"Oh yeah, well the repair shop called and I had to cancel. They needed my keys and I had to sign some silly papers."

"I would ask you to join us, but we were just getting ready to leave," Alex explained as he waved at Mr. Lee to bring the check.

"Oh, that's ok, I am not really all that hungry for food," she said while looking toward Leander.

"But hey, you know what, we should all go dancing. There is this awesome club nearby and I can get us past the doorman, so we won't have to wait in line," she said, more to Leander than to the rest of the table.

"I bet you can," Alex said before he realized it.

"Alex I am really tired, I think we need to go home," Cassie said before anyone else could offer an opinion.

"Maybe some other time," Alex said to Joey.

"Your loss," she said to Leander before bending at the waist and leaning in to kiss his lips, showing everyone else far more of her rear than they wanted to see.

Alex swore Abrianna was about to launch herself at the vixen before Cassie rested her hand on her cousin's arm. The action seemed to defuse the explosion and the two women just glared at the interloper as she straightened her dress. With a wave, she made her goodbye and slipped back through the crowd and out the front door.

----*----

The ride home was thankfully short and awkwardly silent. While Alex saw Leander as the victim of this unwanted attention, he was both thankful it was not himself on the receiving end and understood Abrianna did not share his opinion. The short walk from the driveway to the front door was noticeably chilly as Abrianna either ignored or rebuffed any effort by Leander to assist.

Pushing past Alex, Abrianna quickly entered the house, greeting all with the slamming of her bedroom door as they followed her inside.

"I had better go check on her," Cassie said to the two men as she moved past them and entered the hall.

"What did I do?" Leander asked Alex in a bewildered tone.

"Leander my friend, I have no idea. Best you let Cassie handle this," Alex said.

"I think I shall retire to my room then. Thank you for taking us to dinner," he added before following the others into the hallway and out of sight.

Alex heaved a heavy sigh as he bid his friend Goodnight. Looking about the house, Alex noted the normally excited Kinsey sat quietly as if she understood the turmoil. Waving the dog to him, Alex led her into his bedroom to await his wife's return.

----*----

Cassie knocked gently on Abrianna's door before trying the knob.

"Brie, can I come in?"

Peeking inside she received a nod and a wave indicating she could enter. Cassie slipped in quietly and closed the door behind her before joining her cousin, sitting on the bed.

"Cassie, why can't I be sexy?"

"What are you talking about Brie? You are stunningly beautiful!"

"But I am not sexy. You are sexy, that harlot at dinner is sexy, I can't seem to entice Leander like that. He blushes at the mere thought of me in this," she said as tears filled her eyes, while crossing the room and pulling the night gown Cassie had picked out for her from Victoria's Secret.

"Brie, Leander loves you with all his heart. I can promise you that he dreams of the night he can see you in this," Cassie answered as she took the garment from her cousin, tossing it on the bed and pulled her back to sit next to her once more.

"Then why did he let her paw at him so?" Abrianna countered, still teary eyed.

"Men are stupid sometimes. I can tell you this cousin, I did not see a man lusting for that woman. I saw a man terrified for his life," Cassie explained, before both women broke out in a teary laughter.

----*----

Thankfully, Alex did not have to wait all that long for Cassie's return.

"Alex, I have never seen Brie so close to losing control in all my life. She is very upset and angry at Leander. Who was that woman? Is that acceptable public behavior in your world? I have not seen it's like outside of a mermaid bar?" Cassie dumped on him after returning from her cousin's room.

"Things are different here. While her behavior was a bit extreme, in my realm assertive women like that are considered liberated. It's not uncommon for a woman to approach a man she finds attractive."

"Including one already betrothed to another?" Cassie asked with disgust in her voice.

"That is not the norm," Alex conceded.

The two were talking while preparing for bed. Alex had taken the liberty of fetching them both something to drink while Cassie was in consoling her cousin. Now, they were getting undressed, and Cassie was slipping into something she had purchased at the mall.

"I like that," Alex commented as she posed seductively in the transparent baby doll nightgown.

"I thought you might. Joey is not the only wicked seductress in this realm you know, that shop held many such surprises," she said as she slipped between the sheets while motioning seductively for him to follow.

The comment caught Alex in mid stride, as he was circling the bed.

"No, she's not," Alex said as he stood deep in thought.

"I'll be right back," he said as he spun in place and headed out of the bedroom.

"Alex?" Cassie called after him, but he had already closed the door.

Chapter 17

Dashing into his office, Alex grabbed the ball cap he had been wearing that day at the mall, a USB cable, and his laptop. Returning to his room, he found a confused Cassie watching him.

"What are you doing?" she asked as he climbed on the bed next to her rather than under the covers.

"Just watch," he replied as he got settled.

He could sense Cassie's eyes on him as she watched him first plug the USB cable into the laptop and then into a small port hidden in the inside of the cap.

"I got this from the guy at the security store," he explained while he worked.

Cassie slid closer next to him as he first found the video files stored in memory card on the hat and then copied them over to his computer.

"This thing has two cameras in it, one is in front and one in the back," he continued as he indicated the two points on the hat.

He knew that Cassie wouldn't really understand the reference so he then opened the first file. As the pair watched, a new window opened in his display.

"That's us," Cassie commented as she watched the three of them, she, Abrianna and Leander, wander in and out of the field of view as they crossed the parking lot and then into the mall walking behind Alex.

The couple watched quietly for several minutes before Alex stopped the video.

"There, see, those are the four kids that tried to rob us," Alex indicated as the paused video image clearly displayed the four following Alex.

Starting the video once more, it ran for barely a few seconds before he stopped it once more.

"Alex, that's her," he heard Cassie say in a whisper as they both stared at the face in the video.

They were standing near the lingerie shop where Cassie had purchased the nightgown she was wearing. Standing across the way, at Alex's back, they were able to make out Joey's face clear as day.

"She was watching us at the mall?" Cassie asked.

"It was all a set up. She is a plant sent to cause trouble," Alex explained.

"By whom?" Cassie asked.

"We will have to ask her next time we see her," Alex said with an evil smile.

"You think we will see her again?"

"You can bet on it. She has no idea we ID'd her and there's more trouble to be made I'm sure."

Setting his computer aside, Alex turned and gently took his wife in his arms, kissing her passionately. He could feel her melting next to him, her body pressing back into him.

"Alex no!" she suddenly gasped as she slowly pulled back.

"We must tell Brie and Leander right away," she explained as she slipped from the bed and headed for the door.

"You might want a robe?" Alex said with a wink, indicating the almost completely transparent outfit.

----*----

"There, that should be much better than sleeping behind a dumpster," Emma said as she spread a blanket on the floor.

Sitting nearby and watching her was the Golden Retriever she had rescued from the alley behind the Tribal Elf. Emma was sure her apartment complex had rules about pets, but she wasn't concerned, so far this girl had been very well behaved and hadn't uttered a sound much less barked. If no owner came forward, she would go to management and get her added to her lease, pet deposit and all.

After placing food and water out in the kitchen where any messes would be on the tile floor rather that the carpet, she nodded in satisfaction.

"Ok, good night," Emma said as she watched the dog curl up and close its eyes.

Heading to her bedroom to settle in for the night, Emma never saw the beautiful blonde roommate open her eyes and look down the hall as Emma closed her door.

----*----

It was very late when Avenstore arrived at the meeting place his spy had chosen for the rendezvous spot.

"About time you got here, I am freezing my ass off," the woman's voice declared from the dark shadows.

"Not your usual style," Avenstore replied as she emerged into the light, her ill-fitting clothing hanging loosely.

"I had to improvise."

"What have you found out?" he replied, cutting to the chase.

"They definitely know more than we thought. I haven't seen the wizard or the others yet, but they talk about them all the time."

"How much do they know about magic?" he asked, the concern in his tone evident.

"Too much, and they are being careful not to do anything that might draw undo attention. They spent the afternoon working on masking spells and practicing the subtle use of magic."

"How about you, any suspicions you are watching them?"

"Nothing, they haven't a clue."

"Good, ok continue watching them, but take no action unless you hear from me first," Avenstore instructed before dismissing his minion.

As he walked away from the woman, Avenstore was optimistic. Between the succubus and now this report, he had the upper hand at turning the wizard's world upside down. The thought brought a smile to his face as he thought of Joey working her frustrations out on the unsuspecting couple. Who knows, maybe he would let her feast in the end after all.

----*----

"So, she was following us?" Leander asked as the four reviewed the video clips Alex had taken the time to separate out of the entire video set.

"Yup. She and the four from the parking lot show up several times during the shopping spree," Alex replied as he walked them through the various images.

He could hardly suppress the smile as he noted Abrianna actually hanging on Leander's arm as the two watched Alex's computer display. He also did his best to completely ignore the couple as they both emerged from Abrianna's room that morning. Evidently, the jealousy generated by the incident was all the young lovers needed to close the deal, so to speak.

"So, the market and then the restaurant?" Abrianna asked as she snuggled up against Leander's arm.

"Were all staged to create discord between you two," Alex replied.

"But why them and not us?" Cassie asked aloud, almost unconsciously.

"I wondered the same thing. To be honest, if they know about the baby, now would be a perfect time to try and upset you," Alex said cautiously.

"I am well aware that being with child can affect the mother in unappealing ways," Cassie almost snapped, but then blushed as she proved the point.

"We call them hormones," Alex added with a pat and a squeeze to her hand.

"Regardless, it would make our relationship an easy target, but they chose Leander, why?"

"He is the only non-magical member of our group," Abrianna commented as she considered the question.

"My thought, as well. I think there is more at play here than just a vamp in a tight dress," Alex said as he continued flipping through the video segments.

"However, that's not my current worry, now that she is exposed," he added as a new image appeared on his screen.

In the window, all four viewers could see several segments containing two men. In each case it was clear that the two were stalking Alex and his companion, always keeping a good distance from the four, while maintaining contact.

----*----

Later that day Alex slipped out of the house on a small errand, or at least that's what he told everyone. Cassie had just settled in for a nap, the reason for her constant fatigue now evident to all, and Leander and Abrianna were sitting side by side on the couch, a shared laptop the focus of their attention. He had them researching all they could find about the Wiccan's of London and any other objects of interest.

Taking Kinsey along for company, he made a straight shot to the security store he had visited before.

"Well, who is this?" Bill asked from behind the counter as Kinsey led the two into the shop.

"Kinsey is my bodyguard," Alex said with a smile.

Alex watched as Bill tried to bribe Kinsey with a treat, but the little dog just sat there staring at the stranger.

"Best one's can't be bribed," Bill said with a smile as he tossed the treat to Alex to slip to the little black dog.

"So, any idea who this is?" Alex asked as he dropped the prints he had made from the images on his laptop.

"That hat works great, doesn't it," Bill asked as he dropped several more images on the counter taken by someone else.

"My guys caught those two and this one too," Bill added as he dropped a few shots of Joey on the stack.

Alex could see some of her from the mall, the shopping trip at the grocer, her apartment and the Chinese restaurant.

"Your guys are good, I wondered if these were them," Alex commented.

He had contracted to have someone from Bill's company follow his every move and try to identify anyone following them. Bill did have the advantage of Alex informing him every time they were intending to leave the house, but Alex had never spotted the tail.

"Nope, my people were either in place before you arrived or fell way back to see who might be following you."

"I think I know what she is up to, but these two are a mystery," Alex said as he separated the piles.

"If by that you mean, she is a trouble maker, yeah., I expect your buddy caught hell at home after her little display at the restaurant," Bill said with a laugh.

"Oh yeah, thankfully these saved his butt," Alex explained as he pulled a couple of pictures of Joey he had as well.

"Like I said, that hat is great, isn't it!"

"So, about these two," Alex asked again pointing to the unknown men.

"Yeah, well, I hate to admit it, but they gave us the slip. One moment they were there and the next, poof, gone," Bill said with a bit of embarrassment.

"Like magic?' Alex asked, suddenly suspicious as to exactly who they were.

"Yeah, like magic," Bill repeated.

Chapter 18

Alex was not particularly thrilled at what was about to transpire, but he had few options at this point. Normally he would take Kinsey with him when he traveled for extended periods of time, but this was not one of those instances. Their trip to the UK was to be short and sweet, staying only long enough to get copies of the missing pages from the Wiccan archives there and then return home. It wasn't impossible to bring her along on this trip, just an unnecessary added complication.

Instead of the normal boarding facility, like he had used in past years, he rolled the dice and called the Wiccan shop to see if they might consider watching her for the short period. They had agreed to take care of her, excited at the opportunity to help Alex out. With their flight leaving early the following morning, he had decided to get Kinsey settled in with Emma, who had offered to watch her while they were away.

For this run to town, everyone had insisted on coming along, Cassie still in her arm sling and Leander and Abrianna refusing to split up after the incident in the restaurant. Alex knew they had not seen the last of Joey and was actually looking forward to their next meeting. He suspected the vixen had some invaluable information to share once she was exposed to the light of day.

He could see the happy face of the little black dog in his rear-view mirror as they drove into downtown. She was sitting quietly between Leander and Abrianna as she scanned the activity outside the Jeep while they passed through the business district. She would let out with the occasional bark as they passed someone on the street, but mostly she sat quietly.

"Ok, we are here," Alex announced as he found a spot on the street to park near the shop.

Alex didn't bother putting Kinsey on a leash as he knew she wouldn't run off and they were very close to the front doors of the Tribal Elf as it was. He did hurry over to Cassie's side of the Jeep, but she had already opened the door. As she was struggling one handed, he made himself useful after all, helping her out. Kinsey quickly followed Cassie out the door by jumping into the vacated passenger seat and then leaping out onto the sidewalk. Next Alex worked to move the seat forward for Leander and Abrianna's easy exit.

"Kinsey, stay," Alex instructed as she pointed to Cassie's side.

The little black dog obediently trotted over to her side and sat in the place indicated. Alex grabbed the small bag from the rear with Kinsey's essentials, as Leander and Abrianna climbed out. Satisfied all was in hand, Alex led the way to the Wiccan's shop with Kinsey at his side.

"Who is this?" Alex heard from the young woman behind the counter as Kinsey led the way into the shop.

"This is Kinsey. Is Emma here, she said she could watch her while we are away," Alex explained as the girl came out from behind the counter to meet the little dog.

"Not yet," she replied as she knelt to pet the dog lovingly.

Never one to pass up a good thing, Kinsey sat taking it all in with a wag of her tail. A sound at the door caused Alex to turn. As he watched, a beautiful golden retriever entered the shop with Emma at her heels. Oblivious to Kinsey at first, the golden rushed into the shop expecting to receive a warm welcome from the staff. Instead, a snarling Kinsey leapt at the golden from behind, sinking her teeth into its hind end.

"Yipe!!" came from the golden as it dashed from the front of the room, headed to the back of the shop in an effort to escape the snapping jaws of the smaller dog.

"Kinsey!" Alex admonished as he raced after his dog with the rest of the shop in close pursuit.

The two dogs, one howling in pain while the other a snarling mass of teeth circled around the back of the shop with Alex on their heels.

"Kinsey, stop it," Cassie shouted as she stood to one side for fear of being toppled by all the activity.

Alex had never seen his dog act this way with another and had no idea what had spurred the response. His confusion was soon resolved as he watched the golden dash into the coven ceremonial room. Closing the distance to the doorway where

Kinsey had ceased her pursuit, he could see the naked form of a blonde woman lying on her side and bleeding from a bite to her upper thigh.

----*----

"Sire, you have a visitor," the soldier said as he entered the firelight of Ben's camp.

Ben had his men spread out in small groups so that the fires could be kept small. He expected that the enemy knew well their location, but no need to make it too easy for them. He was currently squatting on his haunches stirring the fire with a stick as he was deep in thought about the possible morning engagement.

"Oy vey Boychick, what has the world come to when a King cannot afford his own tent?" King Teivel asked in good humor as he and a few other dwarves entered the circle of illumination the fire created.

"You old alter cocker, you are a sight for sore eyes," Ben replied as he straightened and embraced the dwarf king with open arms.

"How is Amelia," He asked after the two separated.

"Ver clempt about her missing daughter. Had I known before that the Wizard's tchotchke was her bubbala I would have sent her home straight away."

"A lot of good that would have done you," Ben said with a laugh.

"So, what of this gonif, he has things all fershlugina," Teivel said as he indicated the mountains in the darkness to the north.

"We expect to see him tomorrow, which is why I asked you to meet me here. I need to know everything that has happened since he first appeared," Ben explained as he pointed to a nearby camp stool.

Taking a seat next to the dwarf, Ben listened intently for several hours as King Teivel outlined his interactions with the demon in great detail.

----*----

"We have a protection spell on this space, it allows us to reveal concealment magic. I must admit that until today I questioned its effectiveness," Abigail explained to the gathered group.

In its center, wrapped in a blanket and laying on her side was the silent form of the woman who had been Emma's golden retriever.

"Is she a werewolf?" asked one of the younger Wiccans.

"Please," snorted the blonde before wincing as Abrianna treated the bite with medical supplies from the Wiccans.

"She is a shape shifter, the dog was her preferred animal form I suspect," Abrianna explained as she worked.

"Shouldn't we do something so she doesn't turn into a bird and fly away or something?" another asked.

"You people are so ignorant!" the blonde snapped.

"Her ability to shift is limited to her size. The dog, perhaps a doe or a small bear is more in line with her size and weight. She can neither shed nor gain mass to her shifting so things like birds or mice are not possible," Abrianna supplied.

"She must have sensed the spell which is why she wouldn't come in here before," Emma commented to Abigail.

"So now that she is all patched up, let's get to the why," Alex said as he indicated Abrianna had completed her work on the wound.

"I have nothing to say to you people and you can't hold me here," she snapped as she tried to get up.

"Just hold up there Goldie," Alex said as he rested his hand on her shoulder just firmly enough to keep her from rising off the floor.

"Alex, she's right. No cop on the street is going to buy that she came in here disguised as a dog," Abigail said as she pointed to the woman sitting upright on the floor, the blanket still wrapped tightly around her.

"You know, since I first got dropped here from A'nland, against my will I might add, I have been told that magic no longer exists in my world," he started, not looking at their captive but to the gathered women.

"Since arriving back here, I have seen nothing but facts to the contrary. It makes me wonder that if I tried to make her a dog, permanently, it might take hold," he finished by turning and placing both hands on her blanket wrapped shoulders.

"Don't," was all she could say at first.

"Look, you have no idea of what you can and can't do here. Any attempts at magic of that kind could kill me. I haven't done you any harm," the shifter replied in earnest.

"Why are you here?" he asked in reply.

"I am just supposed to watch and report, nothing more."

"About?" Cassie asked as she slid up next to her husband.

"How much the witches have learned," she said while indicating the gathered women watching the exchange.

"Wiccans," one uttered in reply.

"Witches, Wiccans, whatever, it's all the same to me. Women who try pathetic attempts at magic, that's what you are, or were until he arrived," she said while pointing to Alex at the end of her statement.

"What do I have to do with this?"

"Avenstore will not have an untrained human wizard undo all he has achieved here," was her simple reply.

----*----

"Alex, are you sure this is safe?' Cassie asked as they sat in the waiting area of the airport.

Arriving early as recommended, the sun was just starting to light up the area outside the terminal windows, giving the four a much better view of the large metal birds sitting in well-defined rows.

"Safer than a dragon, at least it can't eat you," he said with a smile.

"Do you think she will go back to Avenstore?" Abrianna asked, referring to the spy they had released yesterday.

"Probably, I am beginning to think that my old home is actually owned by the Dark Elves."

"There does seem to be a lot more magic going on here than I believed possible from your descriptions," Cassie replied as she watched the activity increase outside the passenger terminal with an uneasy look on her face.

"Yes, I would have to agree with that. To be honest, I never even looked to see of its existence. Here people are taught at an early age, there is no such thing."

"Another Dark Elf ploy?" Abrianna asked with a raised eyebrow.

"Likely," Alex returned.

Checking Leander, Alex could see the fascination on the man's face as he watched all the activity on the ground below. They could see all the airport workers doing their designated jobs, preparing the many flights headed out.

"So, we are to climb up inside that metal tube to travel across an ocean?" he finally asked.

"Well, it's a little less challenging than that, but yes, that's the gist of it," Alex replied.

No sooner had he answered the man than the initial first-class boarding call sounded from the gate attendant. Gathering their things, Alex shepherded his charges to the line, demonstrating how to present his boarding pass and then waiting for the all clear from the gate attendant before passing down the Jetway.

"These are our seats, Leander, you and Abrianna are there," he explained as they entered the British Airways 787 Dreamliner.

"Wow," Alex added as he examined the space that was to be their home for the next 10 or so hours.

The seating on the aircraft was 4 across, with singles on the window seats and doubles running up the center. He had considered that the first-time air travelers might prefer window seats, but that would spread them out further than he felt comfortable with. By placing Leander and Abrianna in the seats before him, with Cassie at his side, he could keep an eye on everyone.

He was not prepared for the luxurious little cubicles that were now first-class seating. His last flight overseas in first class had been an extra wide seat and stellar service. This was something else entirely.

"May I help you?" a steward asked as he stepped up to the four who were blocking the aisle forward.

"Oh, I'm sorry, they are first time flyers and we were all actually amazed at these seats," Alex explained honestly.

"No problem, here, let me see that," the steward said, as he took Abrianna's ticket from her hand.

"You are here my dear," he replied, guiding her into the small cubicle like space.

"And it looks like you are on the other side," he said after glancing at the paper in Leander's hand.

As the steward led Leander around to the far side, Alex placed Cassie in the seat behind Abrianna before following the others to the far side of the center row and slipped into his own spot.

"Must we travel separated?" Abrianna asked Alex as she peered over the divider separating the rows front to back.

"Here," Alex replied as he reached forward to push down the partition separating her from Leander.

Turning, Alex could see Cassie had already lowered the barrier separating her from her husband. After verifying both Leander and Abrianna were safely buckled in, he took his seat next to his wife and began settling in for the long trip.

"Would you care for a drink?" he heard the steward ask Cassie as he caught a glance from her, she unsure of the situation.

"Any fruit juices? We just found out my wife is pregnant," Alex replied for the both of them.

"Oh, how exciting, yes, let me go check. Champagne for the rest of you?" the man said more than asked before slipping away.

"Think of this like a restaurant," Alex commented after the man was out of hearing range, explaining the setting.

"Ok, I see. Let's hope that horrid woman in black doesn't appear here as well then," Cassie said with a smile.

----*----

King Ben studied the small band of soldiers facing off against him and his men. The colors and banners of the Vassal

King were plain for all to see, but it was the towering armored knight in the center of the group that had his attention. While human-like in form, Ben could tell this was not a creature of this realm, likely something brought here by the Dark Elves.

"What is your business here," Ben asked, or rather shouted across the open space between the two groups.

He sensed King Teivel at his side, the tension and hatred in the dwarf radiating. Behind the two were over a hundred men and dwarves at arms, all brandishing weapons of war at the ready.

"The Vassal King bids you good health. He invoked the Challenge of Champions and challenges you to single combat. He asks that I present you the King's champion, the Dark Paladin."

"Does he now?" Ben replied in a tone more conversational than an actual reply to the statement.

As Ben studied his opponent, he used his magical senses to probe the armor-clad man mountain. Well, man was a bad description as whatever lay within the metal plate was anything but a man. Ben could not identify the being within, except to note is was not like anything he had ever encountered.

It had no magic he could feel in the traditional sense, which meant it was not a threat in that way. The fact that the dwarves had dropped a mountain on the thing and it still lived was not lost on him however. It was obvious to Ben that he was not going to be able to overcome this challenger by just a feat of arms, the creature had proven impervious to all previous attempts.

This was to be a battle of wits, one in which Ben was betting his life and the lives of many others.

"It is traditional for the King to present his champion in person before such a challenge is issued," Ben said aloud to the gathered men.

"My King has been otherwise detained. He prepares for his new role as your replacement in the south," the Captain said snidely.

Ben began concentrating on the challenger before him, wrapping the creature in a web of magical energy, not to contain it, but to snare it like fish in a net. Waving his hands in a series of swirls, as if he were directing a symphony, he suddenly raised both hands. As he did so, the Dark Paladin slowly left the ground, swirling in the air as it swatted at the invisible threads lifting him skyward.

Now Ben could feel the creature before him trying to fixate on him as it flailed about, some unseen force attacking his personal shields. He had taken the precaution of protecting himself in case the villain attacked while they were talking. The assaults were deflected, but Ben could tell they were very powerful and would have proven deadly.

"Now, I can't hold him there forever, but I can long enough for my men to dispatch you all," he said to the captain without ever taking his eyes off the swirling mass above them.

All eyes had been on the spinning Paladin, one sword in each hand slashing at thin air, before a sound behind Ben drew their attention back to the Wizard. With his statement, a dozen archers stepped forward, arrows nocked and pointed at the small gathering of Vassal troops.

"I will summon my King immediately," the Captain said quickly.

Chapter 19

The trip was thankfully uneventful, the lack of turbulence and troublesome vixen a welcome relief. Alex was pleased to see his wife had actually slept a good portion of the trip, the inflight meal helping, as the pregnancy was taking a toll on her energy. He had also enjoyed the relative silence as he considered their next steps once they reached London.

Though Alex had not partaken, the steward had been good to his word and provided Leander and Abrianna champagne to celebrate. He and Cassie had non-alcoholic beverages to join the toasts and it wasn't long before the other couple was slumbering nicely as well.

The Wiccans had provided him an address and letter of introduction to the place most likely to hold the documents they came for, or at least information to help them along their quest. They made no promises as to the kind of welcome they might receive, because that particular coven was not in the main stream of the belief. In support of the meeting, Alex had made copies of all the documents the Seattle Coven had in their possession and had Abrianna write a few pages of translation.

Gathering his traveling companions, he again appreciated the, *first on, first off,* flying first class bought him. Waiting patiently, as the people before them made their way out of first class, Alex made sure everyone had their passport at the ready. They passed through security without incident, but as they emerged Cassie grabbed Alex's arm.

"Alex, look," she said while pointing to two men standing, holding a sign with *Alex Rogers* in bold text.

"It's the two from the shopping square," Leander added.

Glancing about to see who else might be around, Alex noted a couple of airport security not far away.

"Stay here," he told the three as he stepped up to the men with the sign.

"Tired of hiding?" Alex said has he stopped before the two.

"King Elion sends his regards."

----*----

"This is a little direct for you guys, isn't it?" Alex asked from the middle row of the SUV Elion's men had ushered them into after retrieving their baggage.

The four had been hushed to silence in the airport terminal as they waited for their luggage, Alex suspecting that the walls had ears. Scanning the crowd as they waited, Alex half expected the raven-haired Joey to appear from nowhere. Their luck held though, as she failed to appear by the time they exited the terminal and made their way to parking.

"Avenstore isn't as active on this side of the Atlantic. He prefers the chaos of the United States over the statelier demeanor of old-world Europe," his escort replied in a proper English accent, turning in place from the front of the vehicle as he spoke.

Alex was at first surprised by the accent, considering they had first identified the pair in the US, but gathered they simply adopted the persona of their location. Also, after closer inspection, he had a feeling they were not men at all.

"That's not to say he doesn't have a presence here, the reason for caution in crowds. We spotted the Succubus following you in the mall, but were under orders not to interfere," the elf added.

"Succubus, I suspected as much. Where are we going?" Abrianna asked from the last row of the Mercedes SUV.

"We have located you a flat near your intended destination. Its discrete and should be ideal under the circumstances."

"What do you mean, intended destination?" Alex asked, not sure of the reference.

"Simply, that your goal may not be the destination you think it is," the elf replied before facing front once more.

At that point the six rode in silence as the driver worked his way deeper into downtown London. Their arrival after sunset meant that the city was alight and it was still early enough to have a considerable amount of traffic. Eventually the buildings got taller and the traffic heavier until Alex suspected they were in the heart of London.

Stopping in front of a multistory building, he could see the first floor containing shop after shop, all dark at this hour. The floors above, though, were lit up with a distinctly residential look to them.

"Your flat is on the third floor," the elf commented as he exited the passenger seat.

Alex followed the example, first helping his wife before assisting those on the far back. By the time everyone was out of the Mercedes, their luggage was on the curb and both elves were waving them to the door. It was evident to him that there was a limit to the assistance provided, as Alex grab some of the luggage and waved Leander to the other half while the elves waited at the door.

Alex took a moment to scan the area around them. It was a typical London street with only enough room for one vehicle to pass down the center of the street with parking on both sides. The buildings on either side of the street sat facing one another. They were both one long continuous structure, with shops on the first floor and living quarters for several floors above.

The door they were entering was right next to a small bookstore, still lit inside, but the sign at the door indicated they had closed for the night.

"Follow us, please," the same elf said as they began the climb up the stairwell.

Ascending the two flights of stairs, Alex was the last to arrive on the landing for the apartment. The door was already open and the rest of his party was already inside.

"It's small by your standards, but will suit well enough," the one Alex assumed as lead elf explained.

"Two bedrooms, but just the one lavatory," he added as he waved to the various doors surrounding a common room consisting of a Kitchen, Dining and Living Room.

"What about our hotel reservations?" Alex asked, suddenly remembering his previous arrangements.

"Canceled. Should anyone come looking for, your the trail goes cold there. There was no explanation given nor alternate destination provided," the other elf answered.

"So, what makes this place so perfect?" Abrianna asked, her expression suggesting the accommodations were not exactly up to her expectations.

"Your destination is three floors straight down," the elf replied while pointing at their feet.

----*----

"You can't stall forever," Ben heard his good friend Teivel comment, as the two sat by the fire, each sitting quietly deep in their own thoughts.

The fact that the Dwarf hadn't embellished the statement with some of his famous colorful additions spoke volumes to Ben. The Dwarf was as worried as he regarding their ability to defeat this challenger.

"I needed to see the creature for myself," Ben replied.

"And?" Teivel asked.

"We will not take the day with magic or force of arms. There is an invulnerability surrounding this creature that I cannot penetrate. Our only hope is to delay until I can determine the nature of this beast and thus its weakness."

"Are you sure it has one?" Teivel asked, again in a straightforward statement.

"Everything has a weakness, the challenge is to find your opponent's before he find's yours," Ben answered solemnly.

----*----

Captain Regas sat alone at a table in the Drowning Man, scanning the room looking for a friendly face. A slight smile crossed his lips as he considered the mermaids paid him scant attention as they worked the room's other victims. Word had spread very quickly in the mermaid community from Windfall and he had no fear of further larcenist attempts on him or his men.

Sea Rapier had made port in Nyland after addressing the pirate threat described by the mermaid scout and were now looking to turn them over to a local authority. Upon his arrival, he had been informed by the harbormaster of the growing hostilities between the Vassal King and Great Vale, a concern for both men.

Although under the indirect allegiance to King Ben via the Lord Protector, he and his crew were given a pass. The services rendered to the sea port were of greater value to the community than any disputes surrounding Gundor Stronghold.

Even so, Regas had selected to come alone to the tavern before permitting any shore leave. He needed to ensure that no unenlightened soldiers might assert their own interpretations of the Harbormaster's orders. In a seaport town, his word was law to the locals, their livelihoods depended on the sea.

Although the tavern was almost full, the only uniforms Regas found were four men, sitting in the rear and paying little attention to those around them.

"What's with those four?" he asked one of the young women as she passed his table.

"The Gundor soldiers? They are in town collecting provisions for a trip south with the King. None seemed too pleased with the idea either," she finished before moving on to a nearby table of sailors.

Satisfied all was well so far as the local military was concerned, Regas rose and headed to the door.

"Captain, a moment?"

Turning, Regas found himself unnervingly close to one of the young women he saw working the room earlier. Her angelic face, framed with strawberry blonde hair, peered up at him as her head barely reached shoulder height on him. His eyes continued down her slender frame, noting the generous amount of cleavage on display.

"Are you headed south, returning to Windfall?"

"Aye," he replied.

"It may be nothing, but I heard some of the Gundor guards talking a few days ago," she began as she moved even closer, her body now pressed against his.

At first, Regas's temper flared as he suspected the woman to be working to lift his coin purse. However, as he scanned the room looking for the Head Mermaid, he noted the disinterested looks from the other patrons as they glanced at the pair and then dismissed them just as quickly.

"And?" the Captain asked in a softer tone, his respect for the girl improving by the moment.

"They spoke of an Elf King visiting Gundor Stronghold. Said the Vassal King and his wife were quite upset at first and then most excited after he departed," she explained.

As she spoke, she ran one hand over his shoulder, hanging off him, while the other hand found her fingers entwined in the hair of his beard.

"King Elion?" Regas asked in surprise as he considered the implications of the Woodland Elves meddling in current affairs.

"No, the king of the Dark Elves."

"I suppose no one should be surprised at that," Regas said thoughtfully as he considered the information.

"True enough, but they also mentioned he was quite persistent in confirming that all the dragons had departed these lands for their homes in the west and elsewhere."

"Now why would he care about dragons?" Regas asked himself aloud.

"Elves are not known to dwell on trifles," she said in understanding.

"Feel free to pilfer some coin in payment," Regas said as he gave a slight nod to the pouch at his waist.

"That's ok, I honor the pact. Besides, it's been more fun stealing information than coin, the challenge is much greater!" she said with a wry smile.

"Now make a show of sending me away or you will ruin my reputation," she said with a mischievous smile.

"Away with you, you thieving wench!" Regas bellowed as he made a show of pushing the girl from his side.

His wink was rewarded with a small grin and nod before he turned to leave the tavern. Regas had no real idea of the value of the information, but suspected King Ben would.

----*----

"Alex, what did he mean, three floors down?" Cassie asked after the two elves departed.

"Yes, are we not two stories above the street?" Leander asked as he peered through the window at the roadway below.

"Normally, I would attribute it to a communications error, we being on the third floor, but I somehow doubt that's the case," Alex replied as he considered the reference.

In his mind, the elf was speaking to a floor below the one at street level, the first-floor shop actually two floors down. It was quite possible there was a basement in the building, one accessed via the storefront. The stairs they used to access the apartment emptied onto the sidewalk below, with no other flights down from the door they entered through.

"Underground?" Abrianna asked.

By now the four had found seats in the small apartment, each choosing one of the various pieces of furniture in the small open space. Cassie had been first to grab a seat, using one of the nearby overstuffed chairs more for its proximity to where she was standing that for any other reason, Alex suspected. Abrianna and Leander had been next to make themselves at home by choosing to use the couch. Seated together, both toward one end, Alex could see Leander was becoming much more comfortable in his public displays of affection.

"Possibly," Alex replied as he moved to the last unoccupied seat in the living room, a chair identical to the one Cassie was using.

"More likely just a basement space, regardless, one accessed only through the bookstore below us," he added.

"Why am I so tired?" Cassie asked, changing the subject.

"It's called jet lag and it happens to people who fly a lot. We traveled almost 5,000 miles in less than 12 hours. The sun rises 8 hours earlier here than our bodies are used to. Besides, the pregnancy will add to the circumstances."

"I am a little hungry," Leander added to the conversation.

"Look, let's whip up something to eat and then retire early. Tomorrow will come all too soon," Alex said while waving Cassie back into her seat.

"I'll get it," he said with a smile as he headed to the small kitchen to see what the elves had provided them in the way of food.

----*----

All in all, Elion was pleased to see how things were progressing. King Ben had maneuvered himself into a truce of sorts, however brief it might be, until the Vassal King arrived. The Northern Sovereign had to relocate himself from his castle stronghold to the place Ben had selected for the current standoff.

The Elven King was most familiar with the Vassal King, and was quite certain the man would suspect a trap. Therefore, he would come in force, which would delay his arrival by many days. He admired Ben's subtle manipulations of the current circumstances, stalling for the time he needed to overcome his challenger.

Alex on the other hand, was every bit as disruptive to Avenstore as Elion had hoped he would be. Hot on the trail of what they believed was a path home, the four were both much closer to discovering the solution to their problem and in ever increasing danger. While he took no pride in placing the group in mortal peril, he reminded himself that with great reward comes great risk.

Chapter 20

The following morning, Alex led his three companions down the two flights of stairs and exited through the door that dropped them out onto the street. He had verified the bookshop's hours the night before and even with the late opening time and the difference in time zones for the four travelers, they had barely gotten up before the shop opened its doors.

Alex expected to be given the run around today, likely shuffled off from one group to another. A quick breakfast and even faster grooming cycle had all four prepared for whatever the day had in store for them. Or so they thought.

"How may I help you?" a young man asked as Alex ushered everyone into the shop.

"We were told you might be able to help us locate the source of some pages we have," Alex explained while holding up the letter of introduction he had from the Seattle Wiccan Coven.

On the flight over from the US, he had wondered what type of reception that letter would receive, and what the place they were looking for would be like. His imagination took him from a gothic structure in a horror movie to a dusty archive in the recesses of London. In all his considerations, he never imagined a modern bookstore. Passing the folded sheet to the man, Alex and the others watched as he scanned the contents.

"And the pages you have?" the man asked, referring to the copies they had made of the parchments.

Abrianna passed the copies in their possession to Alex, who forwarded them to the man.

"Brooke, can you come and look at these?" the man asked as he scanned the copies.

All eyes turned as a tall, slender woman appeared from the back of the shop. Close cropped dark hair framed a slender face, a pleasant smile crossing her lips as she approached the group. Silently, the man handed the new arrival, first the letter of introduction, and then the stack of copies.

Alex watched as the smile faded from her lips after reading the first page of the copies they had provided for inspection.

"Where did you get these? Do you have the originals?" she asked pointedly, waving the stack at Alex only long enough to make her point before returning to scanning the entire stack.

"Those are copies of copies," Abrianna answered, glancing at Alex for confirmation she said it right.

"Who has the originals?" Brooke asked.

"That's what we are here to find out," Alex answered this time.

Rather than replying to Alex's statement, the woman continued to inspect the copies for several minutes. In Alex's opinion, he didn't think she was looking at the pages at all, rather she was debating some internal question.

"Call Christina," Brooke finally told the younger man standing next to her.

Without further explanation the woman led Alex and his party over to a seating area.

"Please be seated, our Director should be along momentarily," she explained.

The four sat as instructed, Alex scanning the area to be sure they were not being set up. While he had no previous indications they were being followed, this was their first time stepping out into the light so to speak. By reaching out to these people, they had announced their presence to anyone they held allegiance to, be that Dark Elf or Woodland.

In a surprisingly short time, an older woman appeared, first speaking to the pair minding the shop in hushed tones before approaching Alex's party. The woman called Brooke still held all their paperwork in hand, passing it all to the newcomer, piece by piece, as they spoke.

"Mr. Rogers?" the woman asked, from where she stood, as she had apparently retrieved Alex's name off the letter in her hand.

"Alex, please," he replied before introducing the rest of the party.

"And I am Christina. Would you all please follow me," the woman replied as she led everyone into a room in the back.

Closing the distance to her, with the others in the shop apparently returning to their duties, Alex stood, as did the rest of his group, and headed her way. With all their paperwork in hand, she pointed them at seats as she closed the door behind them all. Then taking her place behind a desk overrun with paperwork, she scanned the copes once more before speaking.

"Can any of you read these sheets," she said while holding up the parchment copies.

"I can, I provided the translations there," Abrianna replied with a nod as she pointed to one of the sheets.

With that as the introduction, Alex repeated their tale he told the Seattle Wiccans, keeping it as concise as possible. The surprise on Christina's face was evident as she scanned the group and then rose from her seat and circled her desk to stand before Abrianna, seated closest to her. Without a word, she reached out and gently placed her hands on Abrianna's cheeks.

"You have magic in you," she said in a tone that suggested she was stating the obvious.

"He has far more than me,' Abrianna replied as she indicated Alex.

Alex could see a light in her eyes and she passed over to stand before him. A look of anticipation fixed on her face as she once again closed her eyes and reached out to touch him as she had Abrianna. He opened himself to her, sensing the probing while estimating her own potential. Of those humans he had encountered since his return, she was the most powerful. He sensed her on a par with Abrianna.

"Oh, oh my," she exclaimed as she stepped back from her probing, her eyes wide as she stared at Alex.

----*----

"What is it?" Abrianna asked, the unexpected response taking her by surprise.

Rather than reply, everyone watched as their hostess moved away from Alex and stepped over to a glass doored bookcase. Removing a key from her pocket, she unlocked the door for the top shelf. Opening downward, thus making it unnecessary to hold it up, all eyes in the room followed her movements as she removed several volumes and set them aside, apparently not her goal.

Once she had removed enough to gain access to the back of the shelf, Abrianna heard something slide and she could see a hidden compartment in the back behind the books. The woman removed a leather-bound volume from the hidden space and turned to the others without returning the other books to the shelf.

Christina held the book with reverence as she gently flipped through its pages until she found what she was looking for. Crossing back to Abrianna and not Alex, she passed the book to the woman and pointed to a spot on the open pages.

"Start here," she said as she waited for Abrianna to take possession of the volume.

"This is Elven," Abrianna announced as she held the volume reverently.

Doing as instructed, Abrianna started reading where indicated. She immediately understood why she had been selected to do the reading as the words on the pages were of the same language as the parchment copies. As she worked her way down the first page and then over to the next, her heart began to race as she grasped the meaning of the contents.

"You think he is the one?" she finally asked Christina as she looked up from the book while nodding her head in Alex's direction.

"You tell me?" Christina replied with a nod of her own.

"What is it?" Cassie finally asked, the irritation in her voice evident as Abrianna suspect her patience was wearing thin.

Moving back to the first page, Abrianna began reading aloud.

"The children of the past should continue to gather as their parents and their parents before them, but only in small numbers. They must do so lest they be discovered, for the evil will continue to consume holders of free magic.

To these groups are entrusted the knowledge and traditions of the ancients, which they are to hold dear. Should their numbers become too great, cast them out like seeds in the wind so the old ways will remain safe, spread across the lands."

"That's the start of the covens, we were charged with protecting the knowledge of the ancients," Christina explained.

"Not just the Wiccans I think," Abrianna said before reading once more.

"Take many faces and names as the enemies of peace and harmony will be relentless in their desires. Only amongst yourselves, can you reveal your close ties."

Christina only nodded, acknowledging the interpretation as accurate.

Moving to the following page, Abrianna started reading again from a different section.

"When the age of dragons returns once more, there will appear one, both familiar and strange to this land. He will be one who can pull at the thread, unraveling the bindings that tether the magic. Once the unraveling begins, the age of magic will be free to return once more of its own accord."

"You think that's me?" Alex asked with disbelief.

"From your tale, you are both strange and familiar to this land."

"That's one hell of a leap isn't it?" Alex asked after they finished.

"These parchments are the pages referencing dragons. How to call one, and how to communicate with it. If you pursue this, isn't that the return of the age of dragons?" Christina replied while pointing to the stack now resting on her desk.

"Alex can already talk to dragons," Leander said for the first time.

"You've found a dragon?" Christina asked excitedly.

"Not here," Alex replied curtly, not wanting to sidetrack the conversation.

"Alex freed the dragons from slavery in our realm," Cassie declared with pride.

"Perhaps he can do so here as well?"

"I very much doubt Heathrow is prepared to deal with dragons in the flight pattern," Alex snapped.

"The book doesn't say anything about freeing dragons, it just relays the return of the age of dragons as a point in time. For all we know the reference could in fact mean what happened in A'nland," Abrianna explained as she continued to scan the pages in the book.

"King Elion did refer to the fact that the elves resided in all the realms at once, not just here or there," Cassie added.

"You know an Elf King, have actually been in his presence?" Christina said in awe.

"Trust me, it's not all it's cracked up to be," Alex cautioned.

"What else does the book say?" Leander asked.

All eyes turned to Abrianna at the question, and as she continued to scan the pages, they sat quietly, if not patiently. Abrianna could sense the tension in the room as everyone present had their own questions in mind, she was sure.

"Just references to the binding of magic," she added slowly.

"Do you not see it?" Christina asked the four.

Christina moved back over to stand before Alex.

"Look for the magical energy around you in your mind. Look for twisted streams."

----*----

Alex did as the woman instructed and closed his eyes, allowing his other senses to reach out around him. Try as he might, all he could envision was a swirling mass of black and gray, no clear streams of bright magical energy, like he would see in A'nland.

"I don't see it," he said in frustration.

"Here, let me help," he heard her say as he felt her fingertip touch the sides of his head.

He could feel her touch his mind, a gentle nudge as she tried to get him to focus on just one small portion of the black and gray around him. He allowed her to lead him into smaller and smaller views of the chaos until all he saw was one single strand of black and gray.

As he concentrated on the single tiny cloud, he began to see what she had described. There, in his mind, he could see the magical wisp of bright energy, entwined with a black binding that wrapped itself around it, neutralizing it.

"I see it, just as you described," he said in wonder.

"Yes, and that's why we are unable to use the magic of our ancestors. The bindings keep us from drawing on more than small bits of power, bits too small to do more than mere parlor tricks."

Alex opened his eyes to see Abrianna repeating the exercise Christina had just walked him through. With her eyes still closed, he could see the subtle nod of her head as she identified the knotted energy bundles he had just witnessed. As he watched her, he could see her brow furl as she worked the problem before her.

"It won't come apart," she announced to the room.

"Yes, we have tried many things over the generations to undo the lock to no avail. We steal what little magic we can from the mismatched bindings. As of yet no one has been able to do more. Many have braved the catacombs looking for the Archives of the Ancients in hopes of finding the answers."

"Catacombs?" Leander asked, causing Abrianna to wince at the tinge of excitement in his voice.

Taking the book from Abrianna and returning it in its secure location, she waved the others to follow her after locking up. An adjacent stairwell to her office led the gathered individuals to the floor below the shop.

"Three floors down," Cassie said absently as they descended, repeating the elf's comment the day before about their goal.

Alex watched as the woman led them across a large open room, one he suspected was used for meeting and ceremonies, like the coven in Seattle. The wall opposite the entrance had several feet of built in bookcases, all packed with rows and rows of various sized volumes. He suspected the contents to be the overstock from the floor above, as it was an eclectic collection.

He watched as she reached into one the bookcases, and fumbled about with the trim on one side. A distinct click sounded as she found what she was looking for and she quickly pulled her hand away as the bookcase swung free from the wall. A section of the recessed shelving swung inward creating a gap about three feet wide. Beyond, he could make out the stone walls of a tunnel, although the light from the room only illuminated the first few feet beyond the opening.

"This is the way into the tunnels below the city, the catacombs," Christina explained.

"The book says somewhere in these tunnels is the answer to our questions. It refers to the Archive of the Ancients, where the elders stored the knowledge of our past."

"Including the missing pages?" Cassie asked.

"That would be my guess," Christina replied with a nod.

"I don't suppose there is a map?" Alex asked as he tried to peer past her into the darkness.

"There have been many attempts to chart the catacombs over the millennium, but it's as if the passages are ever changing. I myself have ventured into the darkness several times, taking great care in charting my course, only to discover my notes and drawings to be in error as I made my way out once more."

"How did you find your way back?" Abrianna asked, the question crossing Alex's mind as well.

The question caused Christina to blush a bit before her reply.

"I am an academic, not an adventurer. I used a lifeline in my attempts at unraveling the puzzle of the catacombs."

As she spoke, she crossed over to a chest of drawers. Opening the bottom drawer, she produced a plastic pipe, with a vast amount of string wrapped around its length.

"I would trail the string behind me, one end securely fastened to the bookcase. Following the string always returned me here safely, but my recorded steps and turns never matched those I document on the way in. Lefts and rights, ups and downs all contradicted themselves."

"How is that possible?" Alex asked, his conviction about no magic in his old home all but gone by now.

"Magic protections left in place long ago to preserve the old ways."

"So, there is magic in there?" Abrianna asked with hope in her voice.

"Yes, the magic of the tunnels is uncorrupted, but no one so far has been able to harness it for their own use. One might propose that the magic is there for its protection."

"Magical wards and deception spells," Abrianna commented.

"Perhaps, but I think there is more to it. Some, like myself, have ventured forth and were able to return unharmed. Others have emerged in differing parts of the city, places both known and unknown to be connected to the underground labyrinth. Finally, there are those that are never seen again."

"So, you don't guard the only access?" Leander asked, concern in his voice.

"It isn't known how many access points actually exist, but there are over a score of known portals."

"You were referring to those who never returned?" Alex asked, returning to her original thought.

"Yes, so I was. There have been some, people of questionable intent, that were never seen again. The Archive is considered by most to be of extreme value, not just for its knowledge, but private collectors would pay handsomely for the magical tomes. The volumes are considered the oldest of all recorded histories."

"Could they even read them?" Abrianna asked in surprise.

"Likely not. So it is with most without the heritage, it would be unintelligible to them, but as you know, the magic protecting them would make the volumes indestructible. Several times I have been offered a vast sum for the book upstairs, each offer outdoing the last and all declined. There have also been several attempts at stealing it."

That explained the hiding place, Alex thought to himself.

"But should the Archive be discovered; the books within would be lost forever in the illicit trade of sales to private collectors," She said with a sigh as she finished her thought.

"Leander and I will go in alone, its best you two should wait for us here," Alex started as he indicated his pregnant wife and her cousin.

"I think not!" Cassie snapped with an incensed Abrianna nodding in agreement.

"You may be the more powerful of us all, but your knowledge of all things magical is greatly lacking," Abrianna added in the way of justification.

"Besides, should you find the Archive, who will translate for you?" Cassie added, piling on.

Alex scanned the pair looking for the slightest bit of hesitation on either's part. He decided he might as well give in now as neither woman showed the slightest bit of indecision.

"Ok, but at the first sign of trouble we are retreating," he replied with a sigh.

"As you say," Cassie replied while turning to their hostess.

"You will need these," she commented as she passed both flashlights and candles to the four.

Next, she offered several water bottles, matches and a small sack to carry it all. Alex watched as Leander placed the candles in with the water bottles and then tied it to his belt to free his hands.

"Your flashlights will stop working once you reach the zone where the ancient magic still reigns," she explained.

Scanning his party, Alex could see four people dressed in t-shirts, jeans and sneakers, himself included. They looked more a group of college Dungeons and Dragons players than a serious expedition into the tunnels beyond.

Chapter 21

By now the small camp at the base of the Northern Mountains had grown to several times its original size as troops came in from Windfall. Kings Ben and Teivel had little use for the additional men, but the constant movement to and from Windfall had permitted the pair to travel secretly to and from the bastion at the sea.

The trip to Windfall allowed Ben to scour the archives there in search of information on his enigmatic foe.

"I'm thinking Renfeld was not much for academics," Ben commented absently as he scanned another shelf of volumes.

"It appears no one has been in here in years," Amelia answered in agreement as she helped with the research.

"Oy Vey, what nudnik organized these shelves? Nothing makes any sense," Teivel added as his eyes darted from one shelf to the next.

"Look for anything of Elven origin, I doubt our visitor is known to any human authors," Ben advised, playing a hunch.

With that, the three continued in silence, the occasional complaint from Teivel notwithstanding.

----*----

Alex led the way as the four entered the tunnels from the opening created by the swinging bookcase door. The passage before him was lined with tightly interlocking cut stone, and just wide and tall enough for two people to walk side by side without ducking. Flashlight in hand, he slowly worked his way into the darkness before him, the occasional light beam from someone behind him lighting up a separate section of the tunnel than his own flashlight provided.

"Stay close, I don't want to get separated down here. If what Christina says is true, we might not be able to find one another again."

Alex heard faint acknowledgments from those behind him as he continued his slow but steady pace. He didn't bother looking behind him as the first time he had tried that all he saw was three blinding white lights. Those same lights did give him the ability to study the walls and ceiling of their passage as they traveled. He could see the regular sized stone blocks stacked so tight the seams were mere lines in the walls and ceiling.

He wasn't particularly thrilled at this turn of events, force to take the mother of his child on a possibly dangerous excursion beneath the streets of London. Unfortunately, he recognized that sitting around talking about the only possible option open to them was fruitless. Better to strike out as a team and stay together than risk Cassie and Abrianna wandering out on their own after he and Leander departed.

"These walls are different," he heard Abrianna mutter behind him.

He had noted that as well, as the stone about them had a different feel about it. Slightly darker and less smooth, he attributed the change to an older section of tunnels where the stone had stood the test of time. His assumption was soon confirmed as they came upon the telltale pockets in the walls, each holding human remains.

"We are in the catacombs now," he said in reply.

He mentally acknowledged the difference in that catacombs were technically ancient underground cemeteries consisting of subterranean galleries with recesses for tombs. In comparison, the tunnels were simply the passages used to get there. They paused here long enough to be sure there were no other tunnels leading out before resuming their trek.

Passing through the area quickly, they soon left the burial space and returned to bare stone walls of the tunnel system. So far, the group had traveled in relative silence, none wanting to risk delaying the others with unnecessary questions. By the time a good 30 minutes had passed in their adventure, his wife finally broke the silence.

"Have you noticed there aren't any intersections in this tunnel?" Cassie asked, referring to the lack of optional side passages for them to consider.

"Not even in the catacombs, just one way in and out?" Leander added.

"And that we keep going down?" Abrianna said.

So far in their exploration, they had encountered small flights of stairs every so often, always going down and never up. In addition, as Cassie had mentioned, while their trek had not been linear, with the almost regular bends and turns, not once had they encountered an intersecting tunnel providing an option to go right or left of their current path.

"At least we haven't had any issues with the flashlights," Alex responded optimistically.

"You say that like it's a good thing, Christina says it's a sign we are close to magic when they go out," Abrianna said somewhat depressingly.

"I just wish we would get there already," Abrianna lamented.

Before Alex could respond, the four turned a ninety-degree bend in the tunnel. All at once, their flashlights went black.

"Grab someone and follow me," Alex said as he felt what he thought was Cassie take his free hand.

Cursing the now failed flashlights, Alex passed a fleeting wish they would come back to life before someone got hurt in the darkness. They had taken no more than a few steps when the lights came back on once more.

"What was that?" Leander asked, casting his beam about him in all directions.

With the few steps they had taken in the darkness they had emerged into a large open space that rose several stories above them. With each of the four pointing their now functioning lights in a different direction, they could make out that the chamber had a squarish shape with four distinct walls and multiple openings in every wall. The apertures were not just on the same level as Alex and his companions, the walls went up a good three stories with more tunnels on each level.

"There must be a hundred of them," Cassie said in frustration as she moved her light from one tunnel opening to the next.

"Maybe more," Leander offered, only to receive a sharp backhand to the bicep from his intended.

"Let's take a break," Alex said with a sigh as he led the group to some larger stones stacked in the center of the space.

"I thought this was all going too easy," Abrianna said as Alex made sure his wife found a reasonably comfortable spot to rest.

"Alex, this is hopeless," Cassie said, shaking her head as she motioned to all the openings around them.

"Strange that Christina never mentioned this place?" he replied as he considered their situation.

"How so?" Abrianna asked, her curiosity overcoming the despondent look on her face.

"That roll of string she showed us, it had more than enough on it to reach this far into the tunnels."

"You think she never made it this far?" Leander asked.

"I think there is more here than meets the eye," Alex replied before standing once more and slowly circling the room as he examined the walls around him.

He could feel the eyes of his companions on him as he considered each wall, looking for anything that might give them a clue to the right path to take. At one point, Alex picked a tunnel and entered slowly, as if expecting some sort of trap. Instead of some calamitous event, he found a wall before him after only a few short steps.

Retreating from his first choice, he selected the neighboring tunnel and entered that mouth. Once more he found his way blocked by smooth, tight fitting stone, no hint of any hidden door. Alex repeated the actions several more times, his companions watching him in silence as he jumped from one to another of the openings.

"Alex, what are you doing?" Cassie finally asked in irritation, her patience wearing thin at his hopping from one tunnel to the next.

"None of these go anywhere," he answered as he slowly made his way back to the three.

"What do you mean?" Abrianna asked.

"All these tunnels only go back a few paces, and then end in a stone wall," he explained.

He could see his explanation triggered something in Abrianna's mind as a look of consideration appeared on her face. Apparently, it was no more than that, however, as she remained silent. She got up from her seat and now it was his turn to watch as she crossed over to the mouth of the tunnel they had entered the room through.

"Same here," came the announcement from inside.

"What do you mean same here?" Alex asked as he quickly followed Abrianna's path only to meet her at the opening.

"See for yourself, this tunnel stops there," she explained while pointing into the darkness.

"How can that be, we just passed through there?" Cassie asked, retaining her seat.

"I'm not exactly sure," Abrianna said slowly.

Alex followed Abrianna across the floor until both had returned to the spot in the center of the room.

"Why is there no tunnel there" Alex asked aloud, not directing the question to anyone in particular.

"What are you talking about?" Cassie asked as she considered her husband's question.

"Look all around," he replied as he pointed to all four walls.

"The openings are consistent, almost symmetrical, on all four walls except there," he replied as he indicated the one spot on the far wall where the two came together into one of the four corners.

"Are you proposing we go the only way we can't?" Abrianna asked in surprise.

"It would appear we have no way out," Leander clarified, referring to all the blocked tunnels.

"Think like an Elf for a moment. Humans would assume only the openings offer a path to their goal, and particularly humans who don't believe in magic," Alex reasoned.

"An Elf would know better than that. They would assume there was concealment magic involved," Abrianna replied in agreement.

"And magic means even solid stone is no obstacle," Cassie added, joining in the conversation.

With that, all four crossed over to the corner they had been discussing and watched as Alex approached the blank space. Alex slowly ran his hands over the smooth stones in the wall before him, as he let his mind wander into the solid mass and beyond. He could sense that there was something there, hidden behind the wall and buried deep into the earth beyond, and it was alive! A sudden wave of emotion and dizziness swept over him as he realized there was something familiar there, drawing him in. He felt a combination of fear and joy that confused him.

"Alex?" he heard absently from his side, as his wife stepped forward and placed her hand on his shoulder, her question unspoken.

"I'm fine. There is something there, look, this stone is slightly different. It's like the tunnel was covered up." he added, pointing to the stone as he stepped back and examined the wall itself.

"Behind the wall?" Leander asked as he came forward to inspect the stone as well.

"Yes, you can see the outline of new and old stone. I can feel something there behind the wall, but much farther back. I can feel……something back there."

"So how do we get in there?" Abrianna asked as she too scrutinized the stone, brick by brick, testing each for movement as she did so.

"I doubt it's as easy as a hidden door," Cassie offered as she let the others poke at the stone blocks.

"I could try blasting the stone, but I detect solid earth beyond. I have a feeling that whatever magic works this room also provides access to what lies beyond."

"I doubt that would help," Abrianna responded, referring to his offer.

"Well, what then?" Cassie asked.

"Good question," Alex said in bewilderment as he considered the stone once more.

----*----

Captain Regas sat in his cabin as he considered the information that had been provided to him at the bar. The mermaid had been concerned enough about its source and content to seek him out personally rather than just passing it along the usual channels. His mind made up, he reached into the drawer of his small desk and retrieved a small strip of parchment.

Taking great care in crafting his note to convey as much information as he could in the small space, he finally set his quill down and surveyed his handiwork. Satisfied with the contents, he pulled one of the rare acorns he had been provided for such circumstances and wrapped the strip around it.

He paused at that point trying to decide who should receive the missive. Under normal circumstances, he would send it directly to the Lord Protector, that noteworthy his sovereign and commander of all Windfall forces. After several moments of consideration, he decided to cut out the intermediaries and envisioned the one person, not likely to defer the information's use to others.

----*----

The four sat in the light of a single candle as they discussed their next move. Saving the flashlights for later as they provided a more intense beam for searching, they talked through the challenge before them.

"So, I think it's fair to assume these tunnels still hold an enchantment from ancient times," Abrianna offered, referencing the now blocked entrance.

"And the tunnel from the bookstore to this chamber only works for some, but not all, in reaching this place," Cassie added.

"I can't imagine Christina wouldn't have mentioned it had she made it this far," Alex agreed.

"So why are we different?" Leander asked his companions.

"There are several factors at play here, but I do believe it is as Christina's book described. I believe Alex is the one in the prophecy," Abrianna supplied.

"So do we," a voice in the darkness offered, causing Cassie to start.

As the group watched, three men stepped out of a tunnel across the room and into the candlelight. It was then Alex noted the gun in the hand of the one in front of the other two.

----*----

Ben had returned to the base of the Northern Mountains in time to see the morning sunrise. Leaving King Teivel behind with his sister, Amelia, to continue their research, he had hastened to return before Ailmer's men started their day. All had agreed that Ben's absence from the camp would be a bad thing should the Northerners come calling unexpectedly.

He had just turned his mount over to one of the camp guards when a message bird suddenly appeared, flitting about until he held out his hand palm up for it to land. Once the smoke had cleared, he quickly unrolled the parchment and held it into the light of the morning sun to read.

Avenstore extremely concerned dragons all gone from the east. Confirmation he is behind aggression from the north. Vassal King headed south in force.

Regas

Ben reread the message before tucking it away in his belt pouch. Turning quickly, he headed for his tent where a small field command center had been set up as well. Pulling a strip of parchment identical to the one he had just read, he made his own missive and quickly sent it on its way.

"Dragons huh?" he said to himself with a smile.

----*----

"Who are you?" Abrianna asked before anyone else could challenge the three.

"You might say we are the keepers of the status quo," the one holding the gun replied after a moment's consideration.

"And the reason some have never made it out of here alive?" Leander asked pointedly.

"No one has ever made it this far, but yes, we have been known to let the reputation of these tunnels cover the expedient removal of the more troublesome over the ages," the leader answered, his gun centered on Alex's chest.

The response gave Alex more information than was intended, he was sure. The fact that they had reached deeper into the tunnels had caused these three to feel the need to take direct action. He also expected that they had not been lying in wait, but rather had rushed here to intercept the four before they got any further. He expected that he, Cassie and the others of his party had tripped some magical ward set to give off such an alarm.

"So, what now?" Cassie asked the three.

"Fortunately for you, we are under explicit orders not to kill you if we can avoid it, only to prevent you from undoing all our hard work here."

"That's generous of you," Alex replied sarcastically.

While speaking, Alex detected a subtle movement to his right as Leander shifted his position slightly away from Abrianna.

"That doesn't mean we can't kill you, just that we shouldn't," the man added as he gently shifted the revolver in Leander's direction, halting his movement, before returning it to Alex.

Alex motioned for Leander to back off, while he stepped forward.

"So now what?" he asked in a demanding tone.

"You come with us," the leader replied as he waved one of his minions toward a tunnel opening opposite the wall the three had entered from.

Alex turned and helped Cassie up from where she had been sitting, the stone block the only reasonable place for her to sit.

"I'll get that," the other minion said as he waved Alex away from collecting their things.

At this point, the villainous three had the four explorers surrounded, the one with the gun waving the captives toward the first, now standing by a tunnel opening. All this while his companion collected the loose items on the stone Cassie had been using as a seat. Before they snuffed the candle, the one with the gun snapped his fingers, creating a soft blue glow that dimly lit the entire space.

"Wouldn't want you getting any ideas," he said with a smile to Alex.

Unfortunately, that had been Alex's intent. Once the candle went out, he had positioned himself to launch at the leader, hoping to catch him off guard. However, the action did confirm that at least the leader was an elf.

"That way," the elf said as he pointed to the one waiting at the tunnel's mouth.

Taking Cassie by the hand, Alex dismissed any more thoughts of escape for the moment, curious as to what the elf and his companions had in mind for them. With Leander and Abrianna before them, the four entered the tunnel, two abreast, with the gunman and the one holding their meager supplies taking up the rear. The group of seven had traveled no more than a few feet up the tunnel before it abruptly ended in a blank stone wall, like all the others.

"Boss?" the man leading the group said as he turned, looking to the elf with the gun for assistance.

Before Alex could turn to see what was being asked, the saw the stone wall begin to shimmer in the pale blue light that surrounded them. Slowly the shimmering stone disappeared, giving way to a lighted space beyond, the candle light inside flooding the tunnel with a yellowish hue.

"It's a magic portal," Abrianna said as she offered for Alex to inspect a part of the wall she had just been reviewing while they waited.

At that moment, Alex wondered if something similar had happened to them when the flashlights went dark before entering the chamber. With no light on the other side of the portal, they would have passed from one dark spot to another, without noticing. Once the flashlights returned to use, they had already passed through.

"No time for that. Inside," the leader said from behind the four, as the man in the lead stepped into the room ahead of the group.

Alex heard an audible gasp from Abrianna as she entered before him.

"By all the gods!" she whispered in awe as she looked about.

Chapter 22

"Here is another one," Kelby announced as she pulled the tome from the shelf.

"Set it with the others," Amelia replied in a less than joyous tone.

Kelby knew her new mother was slightly irritated, but not at her or her sister. Since receiving the message from Uncle Ben, it had been all hands on deck, searching the castle libraries for anything related to dragons. Since no one knew what they were looking for, there had been no boundaries set and all references were fair game. So far, they had well over one hundred volumes of various sizes stacked up in the dining room, as it held the only table large enough.

There, Amelia had recruited local scholars from the Guilds of magic users to help scour the contents. A rare opportunity of access to the castle archives, they had all jumped at the chance, no matter what the subject was.

"Found another one," Leena declared as she stepped out from between two towering bookcases.

Kelby saw her mother wave her sister toward the stack of books by the door, not even bothering to speak as she continued to scan the shelf before her.

----*----

"Be careful with her," Alex snarled as he watched his wife being shoved into a cage.

The slam of the metal against metal was all he got in reply as the man didn't even bother to turn in his direction while he locked the door in place, pocketing the key. Unlike the squared-out cube of an animal cage, this metal prison was cylindrical with the vertical bars coming together as points at the top and bottom of the cage. The horizontal counterparts were unevenly spaced and ran at various irregular angles, securing the vertical rod spacing and making the entire structure more like artwork than a prison.

Inside, a circular wooden disk at its base, and just before the verticals turned into a point at the bottom, made the containment tolerable. Alex watched as Cassie slip her legs between the bars to sit on the wooden disk, her back leaning against the rods opposite the door for support. Grasping vertical bars in each hand to brace herself, she glared back at her captors as the cage began to rise.

"Down right medieval, isn't it?" the leader asked as he watched the cage being hoisted to just over head height.

Alex tended to agree with the statement as he and Leander stood against one stone wall, both hands manacled over their heads. Before him, both Cassie and Abrianna had been placed in identical cages, designed to hold only one, and suspended from the ceiling by a heavy linked chain. On the plus side both had discovered they could sit in their prison, while Alex and Leander had no such option.

"You see, I am not so cruel as to make the women stand in your presence," The elf commented as if reading his mind.

"Royalty you are," Leander replied with sarcasm, implying a chivalrous choice had been made.

"Rejoice, you are the first humans in maybe a thousand years to find the Elven Archive alive. This is the place you seek," the Elf explained as he waved both hands about him theatrically.

"I expected it to be a tad cleaner," Alex replied.

"Oh, this?" the Elf said as he tipped a metal helmet by his foot with his toe.

"Remnants of long forgotten trespassers. We can't leave bodies lying about in the tunnels or it might inspire others to continue searching. Humans have a bizarre sense of morbid curiosity."

"The ossuary!" Alex burst out as he remembered the place on their way in with all the bones.

"So, you understand?"

"I do not," Leander said in confusion.

"Those who die in the tunnels are stripped of their bodily goods and the bodies are placed in the ossuary to hide the evidence," Alex explained.

"And us?" Cassie asked, redirecting the conversation to the situation at hand.

"That is not for me to decide. For now, I have followed my orders and you are no longer a threat, but I fear for you that the next time we meet my shackles on your wellbeing will have been removed. Farewell," the Elf said as he waved his companions back out the way they came.

Heading toward the darkened portal, one of the men reached down and picked up a discarded flashlight, one of the four carried by Alex and his companions. The man triggered the on/off switch several times without success.

"Bloody thing doesn't work," he muttered as he tossed it back onto the pile it came from.

With the elf supplying the light as before, the three exited, disappearing into darkness. Scanning the room after the three had departed, he noted their entry was now gone, a shimmering mirror blocking the portal.

All around them, he could see a dizzying collection of artifacts, some he suspected where hundreds, if not thousands of years old. Helmets, shields, swords and spears were deposited about, in no particular order. Mixed in around them were an assortment of leather, mail and plate armor pieces. If he had to guess, he would say they had been tossed aside and simply left to lie where they dropped.

The walls of the chamber were lined with shelves, containing hundreds of volumes of varying types. He saw bound books and rolled scrolls, even stacks of unbound sheets, piled between the tomes.

"So, what now?" Cassie asked in irritation.

"There is something not quite right about all this," Alex replied as he continued to scan the room about them.

"Where would you like to start?" Abrianna replied sarcastically.

"No, I mean think about it. We come down here searching for the Elvin Archives and they find us at the opposite end of the room, intent on heading the other way," Alex explained.

"Were they intent on preventing us from reaching the archive, it would seem sensible to let us continue on our path and merely observe, or at least hold use elsewhere," Lander reasoned.

"Exactly, it's like they could care less if we found this place. They are protecting something else," Alex confirmed.

Alex had been inspecting his shackles as they talked, the metal bands about his wrists seamless as was the chain attached to them. Looped through a ring set in the stone wall above him, he inspected the one above Leander's head as it gave him a better angle to view.

"It's no use, they are all magically fused, as are the doors to these cages," Abrianna supplied as she watched Alex from above.

"And they presume we have no magic to free ourselves," Alex said absently as he studied the discarded flashlight by the portal, deep in thought.

----*----

Avenstore had finished his daily routine and was preparing to leave for the day when his private phone rang. His cell phone was of the latest technology and incorporated all the best security features available. That didn't prevent him from exercising caution as he recognized the incoming caller.

"Yes?"

"We were forced to intercede. All parties involved are guests of the library," the voice on the other side explained.

"Understood. Let me think of this and I will get back to you," Avenstore replied and then hung up.

"What to do, what to do," he mused to himself as he set the phone down on his desk and leaned back in his chair.

The four had reached deep enough into the catacombs to find the master portal chamber, a feat worth note. It also meant they were in a position to undo over a millennia's worth of work, if they were clever enough to unravel the mystery of the chamber.

Their deaths were the simple solution to the dilemma, however Avenstore was aware of Elion's fondness for the boy and his wife. Their unborn child complicated matters even more as it represented a greater threat, or opportunity, than anyone completely understood.

Fortunately, since none of their party should be able read the Elvin script the entire library was written in, there was little danger should they break free of their chains.

----*----

The four had been imprisoned for several hours as they discussed the possibility of escape. Both he and Leander had reverted to leaning into the cold stone wall rather than standing, the position allowing for some relief. Both women had relayed their discomfort as well, the cages offering very little additional space for them to move about.

"We need to find a way out of here before they get back," Cassie said from her perch high above the floor.

"How long do you think they will keep us here?" Leander asked no one in particular.

"My guess is no more than a day or two if they plan on keeping us alive," Alex replied, concerned about his pregnant wife without water.

"And if they don't?" Abrianna asked in return.

"Then we have all the time in the world."

Alex was mentally kicking himself as he tried to examine the manacles around his wrists, chained above his head. He had been so fixated on Cassie's manhandling that he had completely ignored the Elf as he secured himself and Leander to the wall.

"Can you tell how they open?" Cassie asked, her movements causing the cage to swing slightly above him.

"No, they appear solid, as if cast as one piece," he replied in frustration.

"Can you slip out of them?" Abrianna asked in return.

"Unlikely my love, they are quite tight," Leander replied to his betrothed as he worked his wrist in the circle of metal as well.

"Yes, they are, aren't they," Alex added as he considered there was no way his hand was slipped inside the tight circlet.

Testing the fit once more he found it was so tight, he couldn't even slip a finger of his other hand between the metal and skin without digging into his own flesh.

"Think like an Elf," he muttered to himself as he closed his eyes.

By now it was becoming very obvious that the source of magic was nearby. His abilities were returning to him as he could draw from the less corrupted magical energy around him. Letting his senses flow over the metal ring, he could see the uniformity of it, no breaks or seams where it might have come apart. Acknowledging it was unlike a traditional manacle, he considered what he knew about metals. Unsure if this was really iron or some other more exotic blend, he started with the basics.

"It expands when it gets hot!' he blurted.

"Pardon?" Leander asked, surprised by the outburst.

Without taking the time to explain, Alex wrapped one hand around its opposite's manacle and began adding heat to it. As the metal warmed, he could feel its grip around his wrist begin to loosen. Excited at his progress, he added more energy until the warm sensation turned painful.

"Ah, hot, hot, hot," he burst out, as he quickly tried to cool the spot on the ring where he added a little too much heat.

Fortunately, his hand slipped free of the ring at the same moment, adding to his mobility. Repeating the process, more carefully this time, on his other wrist. Once free of his own restraints, Alex repeated the process on Leander's until both men were freed of their shackles.

"Get us down," Cassie declared as she indicated the winch wheels wrapped in chains.

Indicating Leander should go to the wheel controlling Abrianna's prison, he quickly crossed over to the one holding Cassie in place. Carefully releasing the lock as his other hand firmly held the wheel in place, he gently turned the hoist, unraveling the coiled chain and lowering the cage.

"How do we get these opened?" Cassie asked as Alex replaced the wheel lock when the tip of the cage touched the stone floor.

"This is just a lock," Alex replied after a brief inspection.

"There is a key hanging over there," Abrianna said as she pointed to the wall near the mirror.

Alex hadn't seen the man hang it there as he left, but then again, he wasn't watching that, his attention on his wife dangling overhead and the other with the flashlight. Leander crossed over to the spot Abrianna indicated and returned to her cage, testing the key.

"There!" he announced as the door swung free and he scooped his intended from her place inside.

Tossing the key as he swung Abrianna free of the enclosure, Alex snatched the object out of the air and repeated the performance.

"About time," Cassie declared before putting him in a lip lock, her passionate kiss firm as she wrapped her arms about his neck while he lifted her free of her cage.

"Now what?" Leander asked as he placed Abrianna on the ground, but holding on to her as her feet appeared slightly unsteady beneath her.

"Whoa," she muttered as she wobbled in place ever so slightly.

"Yes, my legs went to sleep on me as well. The hard-wooden seat did little to help with circulation," Cassie explained as she continued to hold Alex tightly.

"Help me over there," Abrianna asked Leander as she indicated one of the overstuffed bookshelves that surrounded the four.

Alex and Cassie watched as the pair made their way across the room, stopping just long enough to retrieve the discarded flashlight.

"I don't think that works here...." Cassie started to say as Adrianna flipped the switch and a beam of white light spears the books before her.

"I swore I saw..." she started once more.

"You did," Alex confirmed.

"You saw the human with the elf try and use the flashlight with no success. I saw it too," Alex explained.

"Then why?" Cassie asked while pointing at Abrianna.

The same reason I could get Leander and I free, magic," he said with a smile as Abrianna scanned the shelves before her.

"Only a magic user can block whatever inhibits technology here," Abrianna explained.

"That's why we never experienced its effects, even as close as we were," Alex added.

"And that's why no one had ever reached that room before," Abrianna added without additional explanation.

By now both Abrianna and Cassie were standing on their own, the former now wandering freely about the room, scanning one shelf after another in her quest for the book containing the originals of their copied pages.

"You might as well make yourselves comfortable as this is going to take a while," she commented while motioning to all the filled shelves surrounding the four.

As no other could read the elven script, no one challenged the comment.

----*----

"Any progress?" Ben asked of his sister as he scanned the room full of scholars and piles of books and scrolls.

"We have collected every piece of written word in this castle with references to dragons," she replied with a flourish of one hand as it swept across the room.

Ben had managed to secret himself from his camp at the base of the Northern Mountains once more, but on the trip to Windfall, he had received word that the Northern King was no more than a day's travel away. His delay had given him time, but that was running out.

"The Paladin's weakness must be tied to dragons in some fashion, else Avenstore wouldn't have gone to such extremes to ensure their absence from these lands," Ben said thoughtfully.

In the time from the first report provided by the good Captain Regas, Ben had learned of Avenstore's trip to the west. That bit of trivia had been delivered by a servant of Elion and it accompanied a note containing a list. The parchment held only three lines and it took Ben a few minutes before he realized what they were. They were titles of books.

"Have them look for these tomes, and scour them first," Ben explained as he passed the note to Amelia.

Snatching the paper from his hand, she quickly gathered the others in search of the named volumes.

"A Meshugener's errand for sure," King Teivel commented at Ben's side.

"Let us hope not, I'm running out of time," was Ben's solemn reply.

"Why would the nudnik Elvin King pass you a note to find something you don't have here?"

Ben thought about Teivel's question for several minutes before he suddenly brightened.

"Why indeed, boy bring me Shadows!" he shouted at one of the stewards standing nearby.

Chapter 23

Cassie was sleeping fitfully at his side as Alex tried to do the same, her head resting on his shoulder with his arm wrapped about her. They had gathered anything resembling soft materials to avoid her resting on the stone floor. The subdued candlelight that continuously lit the room provided a soft glow that aided in sleep.

Alex chaffed that Leander would not accept his offer of taking turns watching over Abrianna as she searched. He could hardly fault the man as he would have declined just as emphatically had the roles been reversed, however there was no resting on Alex's part anyway. Even with his eyes closed, he could visualize the couple's movements from the sounds reaching his ears.

There would be a shuffle of feet as the pair moved from one spot to the next. Then there would be a silent pause as Abrianna scanned the contents of the shelf, possibly including a scraping as she removed an overly large book for inspection, before replacing it where she found it. Every so often he would hear her puff out bursts of air as she blew the accumulated dust of centuries off a particular selection.

"This is it," he heard Abrianna declare just as he was finally drifting off.

Alex opened his eyes, but dared not move for fear of waking his wife as he watched Abrianna and Leander move to a place more comfortable. He felt Cassie's regular breathing as she had drifted off into a deep restful sleep. From where he lay, he could see Leander doing his best to assist his intended, moving to a position slightly behind her where he could hold the light for her while she used both hands to flip through the paged of the rather large volume.

Stopping at one particular place, he saw her become more focused as she mouthed the words she was reading as she followed along with a finger. She kept on that way for several pages before she began flipping through the pages once more. She kept on this way for quite a long time before she finally reached the end of the tome before her.

"Hmm," was all she said as she looked up from her work and stared off into space.

"What?" Alex asked softly.

Returning her gaze back to Alex and acknowledging the sleeping form of her cousin, Abrianna appeared thoughtful.

"Well, the missing pages are here, but not an answer," she replied cryptically.

"That is not helpful," Leander replied before realizing the words were spoken aloud.

"No, it's not," Abrianna snapped in irritation, before touching his cheek in apology.

"I don't understand?" Alex added.

"The book contains all we need about the nature of dragons, how to communicate with one and even how to summon one. However, interlaced throughout the explanations were caveats as to their future effectiveness, almost as if the writer knew of the impending loss of magic," she explained.

"Are you saying that we need to restore magic here before we can leave?" Alex asked in astonishment.

"It would appear so," came the reply from Cassie, her eyes still closed as she lay by Alex's side.

----*----

"Sire we are nearing the city of Windfall," the scout leader reported as he rode the length of the column of troops to the king's location in its middle.

Unlike King Ben, a fighting soldier made King, Ailmer had been born to the position. His father and grandfather before him had held the title and all had ruled from on high in Gundor Stronghold. It was a family tradition to let others fight in their name. It was for that reason he did not lead the column of troops as an invading army commander, rather he rode in the middle as if in need of an overly large personal guard.

"And the enemy camp?" Ailmer asked the man as he rode beside him.

"No more than half a day's ride beyond, at the base of the mountains."

Ailmer pulled a rolled map out from a pouch at his side. Reviewing the details inscribed there, he located both the city and the location of Ben's encampment as described by the scout.

"Lord Umbral, take our troops here and make camp until you get further instructions," the Vassal King said to the man riding beside him as he indicated a spot on the map he was holding.

"Yes Sire," the Lord replied.

Ailmer had chosen the man for the position as he had no particular talent for planning nor leading men. Unlikely to become inspired to conspire against his king, the Lord beside him was the ideal candidate to run things in his absence as he would do as he was told without question and no more.

"Has the number of Great Vale troops changed?" Ailmer asked suddenly, holding up one hand to halt Umberal's departure.

"No Sire, they have not changed, their numbers are as first reported," the scout replied, confirming the last count of no more than 300.

"Go, we will camp tonight and then push forward tomorrow morning to meet my Champion."

----*----

"So, let me get this straight. To summon a dragon and fly us all back home, we first need to restore magic here?" Alex repeated once more as the four sat close together on the floor of the Elven Archive.

By now Alex had determined the constantly burning candles never went out. On that note, they never burned down either, all still the exact same length they were when the four were first imprisoned here. Before gathering to talk, Leander had retrieved their supplies, passing out water before seating himself next to Abrianna.

"And how are we to do that?" Cassie asked in irritation.

"I believe the answer to the question lies in these pages around us. This book implies the diminishing magic was well known," Abrianna replied as she waved her hand about the room.

"Do we have the time for that? Shouldn't we be more concerned with escape?" Leander asked as he gazed at his fiancé with concern written all over his face.

"It's been the better part of a day since they trussed us up in here. I honestly expected them back long ago were they concerned about our future," Alex explained, trying not to sound too morbid.

"So, we should have some time then?" Cassie offered optimistically.

"But only you can read these books," Leander stated solemnly.

"Yes, I have considered that. I know a spell that might give one of you the same ability."

"Only one of us?" Alex asked suspiciously.

"Remember in the magic circle, I told the Wiccan's that they couldn't get Elven from the learning spell?"

"Yes, you said it was a different kind of spell I think?" Cassie replied.

"Yes. And it's very dangerous and involves trading…." She explained, her words fading off.

"Trading what?" Alex asked, the edge to his voice betraying his concern.

"Memories, talents, capabilities, which ever you want to call it. I pass along my ability to speak, read and write in the Elvin tongue and the recipient bestows me something I want that they have or can do."

"How is this different than the learning spell?" Cassie asked.

"I did not learn Elvin; it is a very rare thing for a human to know, I am told only a handful can in all the realms. It was bestowed upon me by King Elion in secret. As heir to the throne, it was a gift to me when I came of age, something he did for my father before me."

"So that's the final joke on humanity, even if they find this chamber no one can read its contents?" Alex asked in disbelief.

"Apparently so," Abrianna answered.

"When was that, when did you learn it?" Cassie asked, her curiosity getting the better of her.

"About the same time you discovered sexy," she replied with a blush.

Both women fell silent at that, each deep in her own thoughts of the time long past when both passed from childhood into young adult.

"How do we do this?" Alex asked as he moved over to Abrianna's side in preparation.

"Not you, Cassie," Abrianna replied.

"Why me?" Cassie asked almost immediately.

"As I said, this is a dangerous spell and the differences between the human participants increases the risk of failure."

"What kind of risks?" Alex and Leander asked simultaneously.

"Well, best case I lose the gift myself with no effect on you," Abrianna said to Cassie specifically.

"And worst case?" Alex asked.

"We are both damaged in the exchange, the gifts collide in such a way as to destroy the transfer, damaging the participants."

"What kind of damage?" Cassie asked before Alex had a chance.

"Loss of memory, talent, or in some cases, life."

"I am uncomfortable with this," Leander said firmly, taking everyone by surprise.

Alex realized he had never heard his friend so much as imply he disagreed with the others until now. He knew his love for Abrianna had overridden his cultural upbringing, ingrained deference to royalty. Alex himself was struggling with the suggestion that Abrianna risk something with him that he wouldn't allow Cassie to undergo, as if she would concede to his wish or will.

"What's so funny?" Cassie asked, breaking his train of thought.

"Sorry, I was just imagining the fallout should I tell you no, you can't do it," he said with a smile.

"Damn straight!" Cassie replied firmly, making Alex laugh as she had to have picked that up from him at some point.

"So why is she the best candidate?" Alex directed to Abrianna, changing the subject.

"Well, there are many factors in the exchange to be considered, the first of which, is there even enough magic here to perform the spell."

Pausing from the conversation, Alex stopped to allow his senses to reach out around him. He found a surprising amount of free energy about, all masked to be invisible to those not actively seeking it. Expanding his mental view, he could see the waves of light and dark energy radiating from one side of the room. He could see the two binding as one, like he discerned in the bookstore, as they crossed the room. By the time it departed the space, it was bound in the dark, twisted form he identified above.

"We are near the source of magic, aren't we?" Alex asked Abrianna.

"I think so. While you were concentrating on getting free, I was tracing the magical waves passing through the room. I think there are actually two sources nearby, one the natural source of magical power, the other the corruption that makes it unusable. I think that's what you were sensing behind the wall before we were discovered. We were so close there to the source we could have pulled from the uncorrupted strands."

"Which was why we could still use the flashlights when others could not?" Leander asked the pair.

"Yes, Alex and I subconsciously pulled in the clean energy and blocking the bad. We do it naturally back home without thought, drawing on what's available."

"Which is why you think you can do this spell?" Cassie asked her cousin.

"Yes, the fact that we are both female, magical and share a common bloodline makes it far safer for us than should Alex and I attempt the exchange. Besides, there are more… personal reasons for it to be you and not him," Abrianna added after a moment's hesitation.

Alex did not key on that comment, however, as he was focused on her previous statement. Cassie and Abrianna did not in fact share a common bloodline at all. As Ben was Amelia's adopted brother, an argument could be made that he had more in common with Abrianna's father than Cassie ever did. Having long ago committed to keeping Ben's secret, he couldn't actually recall if the truth had come out with Amelia's rescue. As such, he trod carefully with his next question.

"Ah, how important is the common blood part?" Alex asked cautiously.

"It's not an absolute requirement, but it does aid in aligning the exchange," Abrianna asked, confused at the question.

"So, let's say you two were not blood relations, would she still be a better candidate than me?"

"Alex why would you ask such a thing?" Cassie asked in a demanding tone.

"Yes, considering all the other common factors, she would still be the best choice. The greatest consideration is the desire of the trait to be exchanged. She must truly desire what I am offering and I the…. ability she can provide me."

"What is that?" Cassie asked.

"For that we must speak in private," Abrianna replied and she rose to her feet, extending a hand to her cousin.

Alex watched as the two women crossed over to the far side of the room where they began to speak in hushed tones. He was struggling with the question of revealing Ben's true origins when he heard an outburst from his wife.

"NO!" Cassie said, her head shaking firmly in the negative.

From that point Alex suspected that Abrianna had placed a privacy spell on the two of them as he could see the conversation become much more heated. Try as he might though he could not make out a word in the exchange.

After what Alex took to be a heated exchange bordering on argument, the cousins eventually made their way back to their companions.

"It is decided," Abrianna explained as the women took their seats once more.

"You said the exchange needs to be agreeable between you two to be safe and I know that look," Alex said while pointing to his wife's face.

He was well aware of her, "I don't like this, but am going along anyway" look.

"We will give her time to think about it more before we make the attempt," Abrianna answered sternly.

"You do not truly understand what you are asking for," came Cassie's explanation.

It was plain to all that Abrianna had asked for something Cassie deemed undesirable or at a minimum unworthy of her cousin's desire.

"That may be so, however, it is what I want," was all Abrianna would provide in response.

"So how do we do this?' Alex asked after several moments passed.

"We can do this seated, and as we might pass out at its completion that might be a good idea," Abrianna began as instruction.

Alex watched as the two women shifted position so that they could face each other and interlocked arms.

"Let us begin" Abrianna said aloud.

----*----

Cassie was fighting an internal battle to control her emotions as she worked with her cousin to perform the spell. What Abrianna asked of her in exchange for the Elvin abilities was not something she understood to be desirable. Abrianna had explained that neither would lose the skill or trait they were offering to the other, rather that same ability would be duplicated in total inside the recipient. She said this as if Cassie was afraid, concerned she would be losing this ability?

Abrianna had no concept of the pain Cassie had been caused by the thing she appeared to desire more than anything else Cassie had to offer. That was what was really disturbing Cassie deep inside. Was this one thing, how Abrianna perceived her cousin. Was she defined in her cousin's eyes by the ability she was now going to pass to her as well?

"Cassie, focus!" Abrianna admonished her.

"Sorry. So, you really want this from me, nothing else?" She asked for the last time.

"Yes, Cassie, I do, more than anything else," came the soft reply.

"Well, at least you can always come to me for advice," she said with a weak smile as she grasped her cousin more firmly.

With that, Abrianna began to chant as the room seemed to swim around her. Abruptly, there was an explosive electric charge between the two and then the room went black.

----*----

King Ben touched down lightly in the palace courtyard in Great Vale as he sat astride Shadows. Again, he marveled at the speed with which the winged horse could traverse the countryside, gaining him precious time.

"To the stables Sire?" a groomsman queried as he took the reins from his King.

"I won't be staying. Just water and grain, don't bother to unsaddle her," Ben shouted behind him as he rushed up the steps and passed through the double doors to his keep.

List in hand, Ben headed to his private library, the one where he kept all the most important tomes. Everything he had ever received from his Elvin allies were stored on these shelves.

"Got ya!' Ben announced aloud as he pulled the first of the three titles off is resting place.

In short order he had all three tucked safely inside a pouch, its strap diagonally across his chest as he winged his way back to Windfall.

Chapter 24

Avenstore started his morning routine by reviewing the status reports from around the world. These were the ones provided in hard copy, the contents too sensitive to be stored electronically. Transmitted in code, one only the elves themselves could decipher, they were transcribed, reviewed by the recipient and then destroyed.

He flipped through the pages until he found what he was looking for. London was still a dilemma that hung over his head like a dark cloud. He debated sending one of his people in with supplies for the captives, extending the time he could use to determine their final fate.

"Ian, when were our guests moved to the library. How long have they been there?" he asked over the intercom on his desk.

"About 24 hours Sire," came the reply after a few seconds.

"Good," Avenstore replied before cutting the connection.

"Humans were resilient, they could wait another day," he told himself.

"Besides, nothing like a good scare to get someone's attention," he added with a smile.

----*----

Alex and Leander sat staring at the two women as they scoured the bookshelves looking for anything that might answer the riddle of the interlocking magic. Once both had awoken from the transfer, neither had spoken about the exchange beyond Cassie's new ability to read Elvin script. Whatever it was that Abrianna had received in the exchange, it apparently was to remain a secret between the two cousins, at least for now as no words were exchanged on the subject.

The waiting gave Alex time to consider their situation, he was beginning to become concerned as the last of their water was gone and no one had eaten in over a day. While he and Leander were at no risk, Cassie was with child and Abrianna not used to such hardships. Deciding he needed to make himself useful rather than dwell on the circumstances he could not control, he rose and crossed over to the mirror that would be their exit at some point.

Running his hand over the shimmering reflective surface, it felt soft and cool to the touch. Unlike the hard glass exterior he expected to find, this was more like a heavy clear plastic sheet over water. Pressing hard with his palm he could feel the surface give way slightly, the return force increasing as he stepped up his own pressure until they reached a stalemate.

"It's a portal," Abrianna explained while never taking her eyes away from the shelves before her.

"Meaning?" he asked in return.

"Meaning it's not actually on the other side of the wall we saw in the tunnel. The two points are connected and by passing through you travel from one place to another. That's what I missed in the chamber, it's not a room of tunnels, it's a room of portals. I didn't recognize it for what it was as I had never seen one constructed as such. It also explains why only a magic user can reach that room. You and I must have powered the transfer unknowingly."

Alex recalled the time he had used a portal to travel from E'anbel to A'asari. That portal had been an open arch, very different from this one.

"Just point to point?" Alex asked, a sudden idea forming in his head.

"No, portals can be associated in many ways so long as there is magic to power them."

"I am going to guess that this room is not horribly far from the chamber, then, which is why the magic still works here, it's not being blocked" Alex surmised.

"A good guess," she replied, clearly distracted by her searching.

"So, what if that's the secret? What if someone put something in front of the source of magic, blocking or controlling what gets through to the world beyond?"

"Why is this relevant?" Abrianna asked, somewhat irritated, finally stopping her search to face Alex directly.

"Maybe we are looking for the wrong thing. We are looking for the source of magic, maybe we should be looking for whatever is blocking it. The thing corrupting the free flow of magic to the world beyond."

He could see the irritation leave Abrianna's face as she considered the question.

"So, we should look for books that talk about the manipulation of magic itself," she murmured to herself.

"Exactly."

"That actually makes more sense as most of this library is theoretical studies of magical places, beings and the properties thereof."

"Here!" Cassie suddenly declared from across the room.

Holding up a rather large volume, she read from its cover.

"Practical Applications of Magical Disruption or Infusion."

"You were listening to us?" Alex asked.

"It's not like the two of you were whispering or anything," she replied with a smile.

With that, everyone gathered near a table as Alex cleared its contents to make room for Cassie's book. Stepping back, he waved the two women forward as they were the only ones who could interpret the scribbles Alex knew where Elvin script.

It was a long while before Cassie commented, breaking the silence.

"Do you believe this?" she said as she pointed to one section of the book.

The two women had been flipping through the pages, each taking one page to help speed up the process. Alex watched as Abrianna scanned the section Cassie indicated before both moved to the next page and then the one beyond that.

"You have got to be kidding me," Abrianna said in disbelief.

"Care to share with us illiterates?" Alex asked.

"We are looking for a dragon," Abrianna explained.

----*----

Ben sat in his tent, scanning the pages of one of the three books retrieved from Great Vale. With him, Amelia and King Teivel sat quietly, each a copy in concentration as they mimicked Ben's actions.

"Here is another one," Amelia announced before reading the section aloud.

"As creatures of magic, dragons are a source of powerful armament. Scales make impenetrable shields, talons form razor sharp blades that cut through the thickest armor and dragon fire that can reduce anything in its path to ash or molten slag. The last is of little use without a live dragon, as to date, there has never been a practical way of capturing, containing or reproducing dragon fire."

"We are running out of time. My scouts tell me Ailmer is camped north of Windfall and less than a day's ride from here."

"The Chaim Yankel will not dare appear without a sizeable escort lest he place himself in danger," Teivel said with disgust.

"That gives us a day to a day and a half to find out which of these can overcome the Paladin?" Amelia said aloud as she was deep in thought.

"Seems to me we need them all. We need a dragon as your champion," Teivel said simply.

----*----

"We always seem to end up back at the same place," Alex commented as Abrianna read the passages from the book.

"The book explains that dragons are probably the single strongest source of magic in all the realms. Made of magic themselves, they are said to be as pure as the day they came to be. Cassie, Kelby, me, you, my father, we all have magical abilities that are tainted by human or other interactions, thus reducing our magical purity. Even the Elves have some degradation in their lineage, although they do their best to downplay its existence. Only dragons have been true to themselves throughout time, thus retaining their magical strength."

"You are saying that at some point, long ago, a dragon has been placed near the source of magic here, absorbing it or canceling it out?" Alex asked, extrapolating the information.

"I think so, two very strong magic sources, possibly incompatible to each other, would generate a magical null space. That would also explain how they were able to trap the dragon, if that's the case, the cancelation of its magic, making it susceptible to capture."

"Maybe that's why that portal entrance was covered over. Once the dragon was trapped they sealed it in," Leander asked the others.

"If that is true, I can't imagine it's in a very good mood. Remember Tantalus and his captive dragons, they were only enslaved for a few hundred years and they were plenty pissed," Alex said with a shake of his head.

"Yes, but remember how happy they were once you freed them," Cassie added to her husband's observation.

"How does one snare a dragon?" Leander asked.

"Like Tantalus, I suppose they grabbed her eggs and placed them where they knew she could be imprisoned?" Abrianna speculated.

"We might be assuming too much. It is possible a dragon simply made its lair too close to the source and trapped itself?" Cassie offered.

"Not likely, dragons of the type we are thinking do prefer mountainous volcanic locations," Abrianna replied.

"I'm no geologist, but I am fairly sure any volcanic activity in England, died out long before dragons came into existence. I mean we are talking millions of years ago," Alex answered.

"Tricked and trapped it is, held against its will," Leander stated.

"I am thinking that the reason no one has found these chambers is because they can only be reached by magic. It's the portals that connect them, not tunnels," Alex finished as he pointed to the mirrors gateway.

"That's reasonable. I mean the assumption has always been that only the descendants of elves could reach this place. That would mean only people capable us using magic," Abrianna said, expanding on Alex's thought.

"If that is the case, then only a magic user could reach the chamber holding the dragon, and free it," Cassie said with concern in her voice.

"Yup, so my plan is for you all to stay here while I go through the portal and free the dragon, getting us a ride home in the process," Alex said with pride.

"I don't like this plan at all," Cassie protested.

"Alex is right, if we are correct and there is a dragon involved, the fewer people involved in trying to free it the better. Besides, he is the only one able to communicate with the creature on an equal footing anyway."

"And if it attacks him?" Cassie asked in defiance.

"Not likely, remember Alex will hopefully be right next to the absolute source of magic in this realm. At no other place in his world will he be able to draw in all the magical energy he needs. If our assumptions are correct, the dragon will be neutralized, able to sustain itself, but limited in strength."

"I still don't like it," Cassie said in a bit of a pout.

Alex hugged his wife, trying to reassure her before the two finally separated after a quick kiss.

"Tell me everything I need to know about portals, I mean I go back to the room we were in before, but how do I find the right one," Alex asked Abrianna as the four stood around the table.

"That is not necessarily correct," Abrianna started.

"Portals can be point to point, in which case the magic is fixed. I think that's how the portal from the bookstore tunnel works, dropping all travelers into the portal chamber. Other portals are flexible and depend on the magic user to determine the destination."

For the next several minutes, Abrianna walked him through portal magic theory, describing all she knew about their operation and manipulation. Nodding his head in understanding, he took a deep breath and headed to his destination. Alex made his way to the portal in the library, his companions all standing to one side as he considered his next move.

"I am pretty sure this portal will take you wherever you want to go. Remember, the portal acts on the mental image you have about your destination. If we are right, you should conjure the mental image of a large dragon and the source of magic. There can't be many places matching that description," Abrianna explained.

"Pretty sure?" he repeated as he stepped up to the mirrored surface.

Pausing a moment, Alex turned and faced the woman.

"And what exactly does the source of magic look like?"

Now it was Abrianna's turn to pause in thought.

"Magic can take many forms. Liquid, vapor, solid and the invisible energy we draw from are all possible. I would envision a beam of light emanating from deep within the earth, or perhaps a bubbling spring. It could even be a simple as a constant breeze, but all originate from deep underground, where the elements of nature combine to create a concentrated power, feeding all life."

Trying to make an image out of Abrianna's descriptions, Alex imagined a stone room not unlike the one they currently occupied. In its center was a circular well, a glowing beam of light streaming up out of its center, delivering the flowing energy he was so familiar with. To one side, he saw a dragon curled up and sleeping peacefully as it endured its captivity.

Stepping forward, he continued that image as he reached out to the portal and touched the surface lightly. Unlike last time where the shimmering image pushed back, this time his hand passed lightly through, followed by the rest of his body as he stepped forward. Continuing through, he found himself in total darkness. Turning in place, he could feel the cold stone of a block wall where his portal had once been.

"Well, this is not what I imaged at all," was all he could say.

----*----

Avenstore was beginning to question himself and how he had played his hand regarding the wizard and his companions. He had this growing dread, building in the back of his mind as he worked through the day, that something was amiss. So far things had gone rather well, but the feeling would not go away. His subconscious kept reminding him that this was the Wizard that freed the dragons in A'nland.

Grabbing his phone from its cradle on his desk, he quickly dialed an international call and waited impatiently as it rang on the far end.

"Yes?" came the reply once the ringing ceased.

"I want you to go check on our guests. Nothing more, understand?" Avenstore instructed.

"I understand," was the reply before the connection dropped.

Pausing a moment more before replacing the phone in its cradle, Avenstore hit the intercom button.

"Roberta, please have my plane readied. Tell the pilot, we are going to London."

"Right away, sir," his assistant replied.

Chapter 25

Alex moved forward cautiously, trying to be as quiet as possible, as he waited for his eyes to become more accustomed to the darkness. He had no idea what awaited him up ahead, but odds were, it wasn't going to be boring. So far, their trip underground had been injury free and he wanted to keep it that way.

He might have tried an illumination spell, but didn't want to alert anyone or anything that might be waiting for him ahead. By touch, he could tell the tunnel he was following was no longer lined in stone block and smooth to the touch as it had been in the beginning. He could feel it was now rather rough-hewn, chipped from the earth itself. It was still comfortably tall and wide, allowing him to move freely as he continued forward. The blackness around him was not complete, thankfully, as a soft glow outlining the tunnel mouth far ahead grew in intensity with each step forward.

Reaching its end, the tunnel spilled out into a massive cavern, the ceiling so high above his head it was lost in darkness. Looking in either direction, the walls ran off into a blackness of their own, giving him no real sense of the size of the space. Stopping there at the mouth, Alex could see the source of the glow, a pool of water in the open area before him.

The water shown aqua, with its own sparkling highlights as the bubbling mound in its center spilled over upon itself in a constantly cascading flow. Even with so much water flowing, it never seemed to be in danger of overrunning its banks. The aqua glow illuminated a huge pile of stone to his right, the result of some ancient ceiling collapse, he suspected.

"You are no rat?' Alex heard in his head, the statement startling him over the soft sounds of burbling from the glowing spring.

"Ah, no," he replied, recognizing the speaker for what it was but unable to see it in the darkness beyond the rockpile.

"With all that commotion in the tunnel, I assumed you were a rat. Elves are usually much quieter," the voice explained, still hidden from view.

"I am not an elf either," Alex added.

"Well then, what are you?" Alex heard as an eye appeared in the rock pile on the far side of the glowing pool of water.

"I'm human," he answered as he realized the huge mass was not rock at all.

"Human? I haven't seen a human in a millennium, and never here, in this chamber," the dragon stated as it moved its head slightly to get a better look at him.

Alex worked to calm himself as he attempted to estimate the creature's size. Even in this poor light, he had to believe that the thing was far larger than any dragon he had ever seen.

"Is that the source of magic?" Alex asked as he pointed to the bubbling spring between them, pulling his focus away from the behemoth and calming himself.

"You do not fear me? Why are you not afraid of this fearsome dragon before you?" the creature said, ignoring the question as it raised its head slightly to better tower over him.

It needn't bothered, as the horns on its head had already disappeared into the blackness above them.

"You are not my first dragon," Alex explained calmly.

"Not your first you say? I thought I was the last of my kind, trapped here as a novelty?"

"Maybe here, but not where I come from. I know of several."

"Name one!" the dragon bellowed in Alex's brain, causing him to cringe in pain.

By now Alex had moved forward to the edge of the spring, investigating the glowing pool as he kept one eye on the towering dragon's head.

With better light, he confirmed this was by far the largest dragon Alex had ever seen. Its head was easily as big as the Red Dragon's body. With that thought, a name popped into his head.

"Well, I only know Naga by name, the others I didn't spend a lot of time talking to," Alex replied while studying the pool.

He could feel the surging magical energy radiating from the water source. He could only imagine Cassie's nymphly delight at submerging herself in such a pool. He could feel himself drawing from its magical waters, invigorating him without even touching it.

"Naga? Naga? I recall a lovely Red Dragon by that name. Small for her size, but hey, size isn't everything!"

Alex could swear he heard the dragon chuckle at its own joke.

"You are a male!" he suddenly burst out.

"Are all humans as obtuse as you? Of course I am male. Now that you mention it, I don't believe I have ever spoken to a human before, perhaps this is why," the dragon replied snidely.

"It's just that I was under the impression all dragons were female," Alex explained.

Before replying to Alex, the dragon shifted its position. As it did so, he got a better impression of its size and heard the telltale sound of rattling chains. It was then he noticed the metal band about the dragon's neck and the links, trailing off into the darkness of the cavern.

"A popular misconception among the uninformed," the dragon replied with a sniff of indignation.

"It is true that females are blessed early in their lives with a limited number of fertilized eggs and these eggs always produce female offspring," the dragon began.

"A lesser known fact is that mating between males and females is possible and can also produce offspring. These unions are less predictable, however, but often resulting in males."

"I don't understand, why the difference?"

"In the times before the proliferation of lesser lifeforms, dragons were free to roam the skies and mate at will. As the world became more crowded, and dragons were persecuted for the damage they caused mating, such activity was curtailed. Magic will always find a way and thus females are gifted eggs to insure our existence."

"What damage?" Alex asked, being drawn into to the tale.

"I believe the last time a mating occurred, several human cities were destroyed," the dragon answered with a chuckle.

"What cities?" Alex asked, unable to control his curiosity.

"Ah, so long ago……let me think. Pompeii was one, I believe?"

"That city was destroyed in a volcanic eruption from Mount Vesuvius," Alex corrected.

"A common mistake, many dragon mating's appear to be volcanic eruptions to the uninformed. We do tend to prefer volcanic lairs after all," the dragon said in a matter of fact tone.

Alex recalled the volcanic vents under Gundor Stronghold and the dragon's lair there.

"This is all very fascinating, but why are you here?" Alex asked, cutting to the root of his presence there.

"I am imprisoned here," the dragon replied just as directly.

"For destroying Pompeii?" Alex asked, trying to relate the two.

"Hardly. I am here because that spring behaves like a female dragon."

"I don't understand," Alex replied as he studied the dragon.

"You understand the concept of opposites attract?" the dragon asked.

"Yes."

"Well the same principle applies to myself and that bubbling puddle beside you."

The look on Alex's face must have betrayed his confusion as the dragon continued his explanation.

"I am sure by now you have noticed that though the spring continues to flow, it never ever runs its banks. That is because the magic transforms from liquid to vapor to energy as it leaves this chamber."

"And you make that happen?" Alex asked, unsure of the dragon's role in all this.

"You have survived this long on your own, without anyone's help? No, I do not make that happen. The elves placed me here long ago because my natural magical energy is the opposite to that of the spring. The two become one, entwined and balanced, and thus neutralized, as in mating."

"So you are the reason magic is bound, or rather it is your magic that is the binding."

"I was tricked into this chamber by the demon elves and with the nullifying magical effects of the spring, have been bound here ever since. They sealed the portal, or so I was told, but how did you get here?"

"There are other portals, apparently," he responded, unsure himself.

By now Alex was getting the entire picture. It was apparent that the magic emitted from the spring had a polarity, for lack of a better word, opposite to the male dragon. Chained in such close proximity, he neutralized a good portion of the magical energy radiating from the spring, removing most but not all of the useable magic from the world above. The small amounts that made its way safely to the surface were what he had been using in the few successes he had experienced.

"Were I able to free you, I assume you would be grateful and not try to eat me?" Alex asked with a tinge of sarcasm himself.

With so much magic to draw from, he felt himself more than able to protect himself, but had other motives in asking such a question.

"I am not so easily fooled Wizard; your white radiance is plain to me. What do you ask in exchange for my freedom?"

"Well, a couple of things. First, the world is a far different place than what you remember, perhaps you might consider a realm more familiar to the one you recall from the days before your imprisonment?"

"Perhaps."

Alex had a vision of this monster dragon appearing in the heart of London and couldn't see a happy outcome for anyone. Besides, he also needed a favor and this supported it.

"Second, my friends and I need transport to one such place. A realm where magic and dragons are still remembered and honored."

"It will be good to stretch my wings once more, agreed."

"Finally, while I do not ask you to pledge yourself to me, I do not wish to introduce a new enemy into the realms."

The dragon scoffed at the request before responding.

"Amateur. You reveal your true desires before attempting to place restraints. Your desire to return home far outweighs any concerns you have on my behaviors afterward. Do not fear, once free of my confines, the last thing on my mind is to entangle myself in the affairs of others."

It was at this point that Alex paused to consider his actions. Once the dragon was freed, he would honor their agreement, Alex was sure. It was the changes he was about to unleash on his old home that gave him pause. In a world that hadn't known real magic in a thousand years, he was about to reset that clock.

"Are you questioning your next actions?" Alex heard the dragon ask.

"No, just considering the ramifications," Alex replied honestly.

"You bear no responsibility for what happens afterward, that responsibility lies with the elves who chose to try and manipulate this realm for their own purposes."

"So how does this work?" Alex asked, committing himself to the action.

"First, you must remove the collar about my neck. Once free of its influence, I will show you how to deflect the magic of the spring just long enough for me to escape this chamber."

"And afterward?" Alex asked, referring to his promise to take the four home.

"Just summon me when you are ready and I will come. I warn you to dress warmly as the trip between realms can be cold and wet," the dragon advised.

"Let's get started then," Alex announced as he circled the magic well spring and approached the dragon.

The dragon did not move, but Alex could see the eye following him as he approached. This close to the creature he could really appreciate its massive size. He suspected he could be swallowed whole and never know it until he hit the stomach.

Examining the massive collar, he noted the similarities to the manacles he had slipped out of in the elven library. There was no way Alex was going to be able to move this thing on his own, but he could affect it. Placing both hands on the huge metal circlet, he slowly added energy until he could feel it growing just as the manacles had for his escape.

"Do not fear burning me, you can't create that much heat," the dragon said with a chuckle.

Alex could feel the ring growing even more as he turned up the heat, until it started to slide forward and away from him. Stepping back quickly, he watched as the dragon made a shrugging motion with its shoulders and the ring slipped over its head, crashing loudly in front of its nose.

"Wow, that feels wonderful," the dragon said as it shook like a dog shedding water from its coat.

The action had Alex back peddling as rock and dirt flew in all directions.

"What next," Alex asked, his impatience in returning to Cassie getting the better of him.

"You need to create a magical shield, to deflect the magic away from me. Do not try to absorb it, there is far too much for you to even try. Just let the energy flow around the edges, creating a barrier between me and the spring."

"How can you get out of here?" Alex asked, very sure the dragon was far too large to leave the way he came in.

"Once free of the spring's influence, I have abilities," the dragon replied confidently.

"How do I summon you when we are ready to leave this realm?' Alex asked as he started to form the shield to deflect the magic of the spring.

"Cast your thoughts to the wind, calling my name and I will come. Be ready to leave at once."

"I don't know your name; how can I call you?" Alex suddenly acknowledged.

"The reason we guard them so jealously," the dragon chuckled once more.

"I am named for the mountain of my birth, Vesuvius."

That was the last words Alex heard from the creature as his shield had done the trick and it disappeared from the chamber, leaving the collar and chain as a reminder of its absence.

----*----

An excited Alex returned through the portal, anxious to tell his companions they were going home. What he found as he passed back through the portal and into the library damped his excitement.

"Been making a bit of a nuisance of yourself, haven't you?" the elf asked without humor as he pointed to the men holding guns on his companions.

"Just in case you feel the impulse to use magic," he added.

"They appeared just after you left," Cassie explained.

"And surprised we were to find you all free of your bonds," the elf added.

"It's over. The dragon's free and so is the magic," Alex replied, attempting to influence the captors.

"It's never over, my friend, you are either winning or losing," the elf offered.

"By that measure, we are winning," Abrianna countered, then glanced at the gun pointed at her ribs.

"For the moment to be sure. OK, time for a change in venue," the elf announced while pointing back to the portal.

"On a positive note, your interference in events here will allow us to use the portal to a greater extent and save us a bit of walking."

Waving everyone toward the portal with his gun toting henchmen corralling everyone together, Alex caught Leander's eye. He passed a subtle nod indicating they should not make any attempts just yet.

"I concur, let's not try anything stupid. No point in risking wife and child needlessly," the elf affirmed.

Alex noted that the elf must have caught the exchange, but agreed now was not the time to try and escape. With that, everyone passed into the portal, leaving the library vacant once more. A moment later the candles went dark.

----*----

Ben's frustration was evident to everyone as he attempted once more to call the Red Dragon to his encampment. He was sure he was doing the spell correctly and had more than enough magical strength to reach the Dragon's Teeth across the

Western Sea. The problem was, the dragon had to come of its own free will and he had no influence over the beast beyond his relationship with Alex.

"No luck?" Amelia asked as she had been standing quietly by his side.

"Naga has no obligation to me, for her to honor the call. I have tried my best to impart feelings of good will but it appears she isn't buying it," Ben explained with a sigh.

Chapter 26

Emma had opened the shop early as the coven had called an emergency meeting late last night. Several of the members had experienced a change in the level of magical energy around them. Spells that had been impossible to perform were now responding with relative ease. They were all to gather first thing in the morning to evaluate the situation.

Sitting on a stool at the front counter, she was sipping coffee and nibbling on a bagel acquired on her trip in to work. A sudden bump on her leg reminded her that Kinsey was waiting patiently for her last bit of bagel. The little black dog had been a joy to doggie sit and was a bit of a chow hound as she begged to share whatever Emma was eating.

"Here you go," she said with a smile as she tossed the last bite for Kinsey to snatch out of the air.

The little dog had been a great house guest, but Emma could tell she missed Alex. Any time someone entered the shop or knocked on her door at home, she would rush to greet them only to show her disappointment.

That thought was interrupted as a familiar but unwelcome face appeared in the shop. Kinsey let out a low growl as she rounded the counter to face the visitor.

"What are you doing here?" Emma demanded of the blond shape shifter, the same she had befriended as a dog.

"I am here to help," She replied with a smile.

"Why would you want to help us?' Emma asked cautiously.

"I sense a change is coming and I want to be with the nicer side."

"It's gong to take more than a smile and a promise to make us believe you," Emma responded firmly.

"Give me a chance and I'll convince you I am telling the truth. There is nothing in it for me to keep working for the elves beyond being taken for granted," the little blonde explained.

"Besides, you have food at your meetings," she replied with a shrug and a smile.

----*----

"I am beginning to think I have been played," Avenstore announced to the four sitting nearby as he entered the room.

To Alex's untrained eye, their current prison appeared to be a typical English Manor sitting room. Wood paneled walls enclosed hardwood floors and area rugs that screamed old and expensive. On one wall, a broad fireplace with an exquisitely detailed mantle held a crackling fire. The adjacent wall held a rather large picture window framing views of a beautiful garden, bordered with tall hedges. The ceiling was a maze of beams and recessed panels that added to the ambiance.

Everyone held a beverage of some kind, Cassie with a hot chocolate, Leander and Abrianna sipping hot tea, while Alex had been offered coffee. A tray nearby once held finger sandwiches; the remnants still visible as crumbs. It was the first food any of them had eaten since entering the tunnels. While not filling, they dulled the edge he was sure Cassie was feeling by now. He and Leander had chosen to partake very little to insure plenty for the ladies.

"How so?" Alex asked in return as he watched the Dark Elf King cross the room and take a seat in an overstuffed chair by the fire.

None had offered to rise in the presence, an expected response to acknowledging his position. If Avenstore even noticed the slight, he gave no indication.

"I am want to believe that my demands to Elion that you be banished from A'nland played no part in this charade," the king said while staring into the flames.

"Charade?" Abrianna asked, curiosity in her tone.

"Am I to expect that your freeing of the dragon was not part of a greater plan? One intended to tip the balance once more here in this realm," Avenstore replied, finally turning to face the four captives.

"We needed the dragon to return home, nothing more," Cassie explained.

"Something Elion counted on I am sure."

"Vesuvius is the only remaining dragon here?" Alex asked in surprise.

"Don't be so shocked, dragons feed on magic and as it dried up, they went to greener pastures," Avenstore explained.

"So, you are admitting this is all your fault then?" Cassie asked Avenstore.

"I beg your pardon?" Avenstore replied, taken aback by the boldness of her statement.

"What my cousin means is that you placed us in a position where our only solution was to unravel all your plans for us to succeed."

"You were never supposed to be here at all, only him," Avenstore said curtly while pointing to Alex.

"You really haven't been paying attention, then, have you?" Leander offered up in a fashion that took all of his companions by surprise.

"Where have I been remiss?"

"You actually expected the honorable Alex Rogers of earth to abandon his duty to King Ben of Great Vale and the unquestionable love of his life to accept exile in a place he no longer calls home? Had he come alone or with a legion of followers, he would never have remained here a second longer than to took to discover a path to his new home and love."

"In a way, sending all of you was the only way he might consider staying," Avenstore said absently.

"A huge gamble at best, as I am sure Ben is doing everything in his power to get his daughter back," Alex observed.

"That notable is otherwise occupied at the moment," Avenstore responded firmly.

The comment caught all four by surprise and produced a deep frown on Abrianna's face.

"It was the baby, wasn't it?" Avenstore asked out of the blue.

"I'm sorry?' Cassie asked in return.

"Your desire to return home was driven by your coming child," he said more than asked.

"I would have no child here, willingly," she responded firmly.

"I did not see that Elion held all the cards in this hand," Avenstore said with a nod.

"What now?" Alex asked as he prepared himself for a fight, one he didn't think he could win.

He could feel the uncorrupted free magic flowing now as it had in A'nland.

"You are free to go, my man will see you delivered to the flat you rented in London," Avenstore replied as he rose from his seat.

"You're letting us go?" Cassie blurted out in surprise.

"Of course, I am. You think me heartless and bloodthirsty?" he replied with a laugh.

"A mother with child, newlyweds and a betrothal, far too much bright future to snuff out needlessly," Avenstore explained as he pointed to each of the four before him.

He turned to leave and then stopped once more. Spinning in place he faced the four before he spoke.

"You think me evil and Elion goodness? He and I are just two sides of the same coin, each intent on bringing our vision of the future to life. You, Alex, are better suited than the others to understand how replacing magic with technology brought your world out of the darkness and into the age of enlightenment. By retaining the old ways, Elion limits the ability of humanity to grow, where technology adapts to ever changing needs."

Avenstore paused as he waited for his words to sink in.

"A world with magic, expects magic to solve all your problems. Technology makes you think for yourself," he finished before turning once more and leaving the four in stunned silence.

----*----

Avenstore had been true to his word and all four were loaded into a vehicle and escorted back to London. Alex had cautioned them all to keep silent until they were safely back in the small apartment and off the busy street below. He wasn't sure how far the Dark Elf King had gone to ensure his people were no longer a threat.

"What do we do now?" Leander asked as the noise from the kitchen indicated their need to eat.

"We go home, pack out things, and then call Vesuvius," Alex replied.

"Why not just call him now and get home quickly," Abrianna asked as she looked up to see what meal Alex and Cassie were preparing.

"We need to get Kinsey and I don't think Vesuvius is going to like the thought of side trips. He warned me that when I called for him, we needed to be ready to be gone from here," Alex explained.

"Do you believe what Avenstore said, about him and Elion being the same?" Cassie asked as she assisted her husband, taking bites in between of whatever was at hand.

"I think he believes it. Remember what Naga said, the Elves are not my friend. She didn't qualify that," Alex added, inferring dark or woodland not specified.

"What about my father?" Abrianna asked as she held up a piece for Leander to taste, standing nearby.

"Yeah, I am worried about that too. As soon as we are done eating, I will call and get us the first flight home. I am afraid he might be in some kind of trouble back home."

"We need to get home as quickly as possible," she emphasized.

"I'll call the airlines, you all get us packed after eating," Alex instructed as he headed to the phone.

----*----

The latest reports Elion received from his people were worth celebrating over. It appeared he had achieved everything he hoped to accomplish without loss of life on either side of the conflict. He had long suspected it would take a wizard of exceptional strength and ability to overcome the magical wards protecting the master portal chamber in the labyrinth under London.

The chamber had been constructed long ago to protect the source of magic. Placed there eons ago by the elves, it was a way station of point to point portals, protected in its subterranean location. One had to first reach the chamber before passing into the library and finally on to the cavern containing the spring. Only the portal in the library was aligned to the one in the cavern.

Long known to the magical creatures of that realm, the spring's location had been a well-guarded secret. At first both the Dark and Woodland Elves had shared the task of diverting any considered a threat, human, animal or magical. Little by little that responsibility had dwindled as conflicts arose in other realms, until the cavern was left unguarded or so Elion had thought.

The humans had never understood their attraction to the location, their sense of magic unrefined as it was. It was the Romans that first started building structures there, the location drawing more to the site, until the stonework they constructed under the city reached close to the room of portals. That's when the age of magic was dying out.

Placing the dragon so close to the spring had its desired effect, but the nullification had been so very slow at first. By the time the Woodland elves had discovered the trick, it was too late and the prophecy was born. Dark Elves ran the show and the Woodland Elves had left the realm.

Only a magical human could free the dragon and restore magic to the realm.

----*----

The trip home was uneventful as Alex did his best expedite things. Before calling the travel agent, he had suggested they could go back to the room of portals and try to return home that way. The lack of enthusiasm all around convinced him that they would rather endure the time on the plane than try to find that place again.

He was able to book a flight for that evening and didn't quibble at the price the agent quoted him. The return flight back to Seattle was costly, but he could more than afford the upcharge for a last-minute reservation for 4 people.

A quick trip back to the bookstore had Alex updating Christina on all that had transpired. The delight on her face over the anticipated return of magic was only matched with the possibility that she might soon see a dragon in the skies over London. He did his best to downplay that prospect, as he still cringed at the chaos he envisioned, should that come to be.

A smooth flight and what little sleep they could manage provided a brief respite, the anticipation of returning home hanging over their heads. After a quick shuffle through US customs, he herded his charges through the parking structure and loaded the Jeep up with their meager luggage.

Everyone silently took their seats with Leander and Abrianna in the back and Cassie riding shotgun. One look at their faces told Alex that they were all as ragged as he, the jet lag mixed with the excitement of returning home soon weighing on them.

The red eye flight from London to Seattle had delivered the four travelers to SeaTac airport just before noon, thankfully avoiding peak commute time. Alex had them out of the parking structure quickly, and out onto the freeway, headed east. Traffic was reasonable and the short trip from the airport to the exit off the 405 for Renton came quickly.

Making a snap decision, Alex took a slight detour and hit one of the many coffee shacks for a badly needed pick me up, the one he had visited before.

"Hey, glad to see you're back! What can I get for you," the same young woman from his last visit asked enthusiastically.

"I could really use a Grande White Mocha, maybe a double shot?" Alex replied.

Before turning to his companions, a quick survey confirmed she was no more covered than she was on his last visit, however the shock of that had worn off long ago.

"Can I have one of those hot chocolates?" Alex heard Cassie ask at his shoulder.

"Whipped cream?"

"Oh, yes, please," Cassie answered, a flush of embarrassment on her cheeks.

During their travels, she had taken to the sweet hot drink over the tea she normally sipped. Having leaned back so Cassie could order, he noted the slight look of surprise as she scanned both the occupants of the small structure. The glance she passed to Alex was one mixed with curiosity and a tinge of disapproval. It was clear from the greeting that he had been here before.

"Tea for us, please," Abrianna slipped in from behind the pair.

"Right away," the barista said in a perky tone as she jumped to the task.

There was an awkward silence as the four watched the woman work, her practiced banter floating out the service window as she chatted with her co-worker.

"Sugar with the tea?" she asked as she paused in her work, popping up in the service window once more.

"Ah, no thanks," Alex replied after catching the nods in the rear-view mirror.

A loud squeal from inside the coffee hut drew everyone's attention, as they all caught the last of a soda shower from a newly opened seltzer bottle. Both young women were drenched from the spray, as the holder attempted to cap the fountain.

Giggles and false protests followed as the pair attempted to shake off the water rolling off their bare skin.

"Ah, Alex, do you see that?" Cassie asked in a hushed tone.

"I do," came Abrianna's response from the back seat.

"Hey, it's happening again," one of the girls said as she pointed to her workmate.

Alex nodded at Cassie's question, acknowledging the glow emanating from both the newly drenched baristas. It was the same light aqua that Cassie had, although definitely not as strong.

"Nymphs!" Cassie declared.

Chapter 27

Ailmer's arrival was filled with pomp and circumstance as his honor guard consisted of more than three times the number of troops as what Ben had on hand. Not one to underestimate a foe, Ben had secreted King Teivel's men into the surrounding woods. It took the better part of the afternoon before the Vassal King had settled into his camp and was prepared to parley.

"Ailmer, what's all this business then?" Ben asked his counterpart as they stood a few yards apart in the open expanse between camps.

"A good day to you, King Ben," Ailmer replied, ignoring the familiarity.

Each party had a small gathering of supporters at hand as they stood out away from the camps bristling with armed troops. Ben was unconcerned by the inequity of numbers as he feared little for poorly led men. His main focus was to find a way to nullify the battle by champions Ailmer was hoping to invoke.

All their research pointed to needing a dragon to overcome the Paladin and he was fresh out.

"I claim the right of Challenge by Champion," Ailmer shouted for all to hear.

"By what insult do you invoke the Challenge?" Ben asked in return, noting he was not going to distract the Vassal King from his course.

It had been a long-standing tradition that if two parties of noble blood fell into dispute, each could choose a champion to defend their honor. It was thought to level the playing field for old against young or weak against strong. Even bullies need fear the charisma of one wronged, able to attract a champion willing to fight in their stead.

For lesser offenses, they fought to first blood or until one yielded, and then the other was declared winner. Upon resolution, a penance would be paid, normally in a form of monetary restitution or public humiliation. In severe cases, one might lose title or holdings rather than their life. Ben was sure Ailmer had the latter on his mind but didn't have the slightest idea on what grounds he could proclaim such a prize against him.

"The Lord Protector of Windfall is sworn to you is he not?" Ailmer asked, once again in a tone that insured all could hear.

"He is, he is my representative in Windfall as I cannot be in both places at once."

"Yet he is absent, gone from these lands?" Ailmer asked, the question a leading one.

"Yes, a dastardly deed has seen him and others transported beyond my reach," Ben answered stone faced.

"Then, as his liege, you are to atone for his transgressions in his absence. I proclaim that said vassal to King Ben of Great Vale did attack my person, my family and my home in Gundor Stronghold. Guests under my protection were assaulted, and many a good soldier's blood was spilt."

Ailmer paused for effect and then took up once more before anyone else could speak.

"Lesser insults have led to war between kingdoms; however, I will not have more innocent blood spilled over the tyrannical actions of one. It is under these accusations I invoke the Challenge of Champions. Loser to forfeit crown and kingdom."

----*----

"Those women had nymph blood," Abrianna acknowledged as the four sat in Alex's living room, planning their next steps.

It had been decided that they needed to stop, take a break and think before they just jumped on the first dragon home. With that, each had grabbed something to drink and Leander one of Alex's Conan books.

"I would guess so, yes," Alex replied as he worried over a small list he had created.

"Now that magic is free here, things like that should happen more often. Is that going to be a problem?" Cassie stated in the form of a question to both Alex and Abrianna.

"Yes, people here are not used to seeing glowing Baristas," Alex provided in the way of an explanation.

"They had better start getting used to it, I saw a lot of those little buildings on our way here," Leander commented with a smirk, looking up from the book in his hand.

"When are we leaving?" Cassie asked the group, but looked to her husband.

"We need to collect Kinsey and then wait until dark. I don't want to summon Vesuvius in broad daylight for all to see. Also, it might be best if we did it some place with a little more room. He might wreck the neighborhood."

"What are you doing there?" Cassie asked as she pointed to the paper in his hand.

"Well, I am not sure if this will work, but I was going to try and take a few things back with us," he said with a grin.

"What kind of things?" Cassie asked suspiciously.

"Well, for starters your new sleepwear," he said leeringly.

"Do you think books might make the trip unscathed?" Leander asked while waving the volume in his hand as an example.

"Possibly," Abrianna replied for him.

"What else?" Cassie asked, waving off Alex's first reply.

"Our rings," Alex added while holding up his hand for inspection.

"Do you think they might not pass?" Cassie asked, her free hand clutching the ring bearing finger possessively.

"I don't know," interjected Abrianna as she considered her own ring.

"Well, it's pointless to take any technology with us," Alex said while pointing to one of the unused laptops nearby.

"But I have a number of books on engineering and marine science that just might be transferable to A'nland. Structures and ship building can't be all that different."

"It's a shame about technology, I was growing quite fond of this watch," Abrianna said sadly as she held her wrist up for inspection.

"They make a mechanical version, but I doubt it works properly back home. I never bothered to find out how time was measured there," Alex replied thoughtfully as he had a small revelation.

"Alright, I am going to go fetch Kinsey from Emma. Why don't you three get together, anything you want to bring along. Be mindful Vesuvius cautioned me that the trip between realms was cold and wet."

----*----

"Ben, this is absurd," Amelia whispered as the pair stood facing Ailmer and his entourage.

"Win a kingdom without a war, it's actually quite brilliant. That's why I know it's not Ailmer's idea," Ben replied in a soft voice.

"I demand satisfaction in this matter!" the Vassal King ended, apparently winding down from his tirade.

"I acknowledge your complaint Ailmer, however per the rules of Challenge of Champions both parties must sit down and try to resolve their differences before the Challenge is valid. We have not spoken on this issue, so I must insist we parley before such a challenge can be issued."

"You are stalling," Ailmer snapped back.

"Possibly, however it is still required, none the less," Ben said casually.

"Very well, we shall meet here in one hour to begin discussions. The challenge can commence afterward."

"No, by the rules, we must parlay until sunset, only the following morning may the Challenge of Champions commence," Ben explained.

"So be it!"

----*----

Alex pulled the Jeep up in front of the Tribal Elf, the afternoon traffic lighter than he expected. He questioned, with the return of magic, if he had any influence on the ease of which he had traversed the distance between his home and the shop, but had no evidence that he had. The internal dread he had of having to fight his way here was offset with the excitement of reclaiming Kinsey.

Stepping from the Jeep, he rounded the nose just in time to receive a verbal blast from the shadows near the building.

"What have you done?" he heard as the source of the question stepped into the light.

"Why Joey, you are the last person I expected to see today, or should I say the last Succubus," Alex said with a smile.

"Not funny Wizard, see I know things about you too. Now tell me what have you done to the magic of this realm? I was rebuffed by one of my regulars last night, how is that possible?" the woman asked, amazement written all over her face.

"You mean one of your regular meal tickets?' Alex rephrased the question.

"OK, yes. He was one of the humans I feed on in my regular rotation. I'm cautious and don't ever drain too much from anyone so no one dies and I get what I need," she explained.

"Well, did he perhaps suspect that was what you were doing?" Alex asked in return.

"Is everything alright Mr. Rogers?" Alex heard from behind as one of the Wiccan's approached the pair.

The concern on her face indicated to Alex that she recognized the succubus as a threat.

"Just fine, we were catching up," he said casually.

"Oh, and can you let Emma know I'm here for Kinsey please?"

"Um, I sure will," the young woman replied before backing away from the pair and quickly entering the shop.

Turning back to Joey, Alex could see she was still waiting for an explanation.

"So, when you say rebuffed?"

"We had sex, as usual, but I was left unsatisfied like I got nothing out of it from him. And then he had the nerve to ask me to leave, so he could get some sleep!"

"A man you were using for sex, left you unfulfilled and then told you to leave? Unbelievable!" Alex replied sarcastically.

"Wizard, he should not have been able to resist my charms, let alone ask me to go!"

"Was he wearing anything that might have been a Talisman? You know around his neck or maybe a bracelet?"

"Those things don't work in this realm!" Joey scoffed.

"You mean, didn't used to," Alex replied cryptically.

"You didn't?" she responded after a moment.

"Let's just say that Disney isn't the only Magic Kingdom here anymore," he replied with a smile.

"Be safe," he added with a wave as he turned and headed for the Tribal Elf.

He had no sooner entered the shop when he heard a yelp and a black flash darted across the shop to hit him below the knees.

"Kinsey!"

All Alex could do was wait as his little black dog did an excited dance around his legs, never stopping long enough for him to pet her.

"Someone is sure happy to see you!" Emma said with a smile as she emerged from the back room.

"It's mutual," he said as he knelt to give her better access.

After several minutes of doggie excitement, Alex looked up to a surprise.

"Why is she here?" he asked of the blonde shifter standing beside Emma.

"A funny question coming from you. With the changes about to rock this realm, I decided to play nice," she said casually.

"She in on probation until we are sure she is on the up and up," Emma explained.

"Well, you may find a succubus on your doorstep very soon as well," he added with a laugh.

"Not that nice," the blonde replied, before turning in place and disappearing into the back room once more.

"Kinsey was a good girl?" Alex asked of Emma while stroking the excited dogs back.

"Best houseguest ever!"

Standing, he followed Emma into the back room where he found several members of the coven all busy in various activities. Emma stopped in front of a workspace where he could see she had been working on her art. Specifically, she was doing a color rendering of a dragon.

"I have those drawings you asked for before you left, I hope you like them."

Emma then opened a folder and passed two colored drawings to him, both on heavy bond paper. Alex studied both carefully, looking for the details he had requested and was very satisfied with the results.

"Do you like them?" Emma asked hesitantly.

"They are perfect!"

"And these?" Alex asked about the other work spread about as she placed them safely back into the folder.

"We sell this out front, dragons are quite popular right now," she said as she pointed to several sketches she had in progress.

"How would you like to see a live model?"

----*----

By the time Alex and Kinsey returned home, he found the three still sitting in the living room. Now, however, each had changed into travel clothes and had a bulging pillowcase nearby. Setting a small package on the table, he looked to Cassie as she spoke.

"I found these cloth sacks in the closet and thought they made the best choice for our trip," Cassie explained.

Leander offered his for inspection. Inside the pillowcase was a plastic trash bag liner. In addition, Alex found what he suspected were all the Conan books he owned plus a few other similar titles mixed in.

"I hope you don't mind," he said with a sheepish grin.

Looking inside Cassie's sack, he found it had also been lined with a plastic trash bag for waterproofing. Inside her bag he found day and night wear, the latter containing all of his favorites. There were several bags of hot chocolate mix and a few other food items she had taken a liking to, all sweets. He was surprised to find her watch in the mix.

"You know this won't work back home?" he asked as he held it up for inspection.

"We know, but all agreed it was a nice memento of our trip to your home realm," Abrianna explained.

"Well, you might add this to your stash then," Alex said with a smile as he pulled the pocket watch he found in the Tribal Elf from his package.

Handing it to Abrianna, he explained.

"It's a mechanical watch, so I expect it will continue to operate back home. I make no promises to its relevance, however."

"These are for you two," he added as he pulled the folder from the bag.

He first handed Cassie hers and then Leander the other.

"It's beautiful!" Cassie exclaimed as she stared at the drawing of herself, a nymph in a white gauze dress emerging from an aqua pool. He had remembered her protests for the Franzetta Art book and had insisted on an appropriate dress. Truth be told, it looked suspiciously like her Victoria Secret nightgown, but provided appropriate coverage none the less.

"Leander?" Alex asked of his friend as he passed the artwork to him.

Alex had asked that his be in the Conan the Barbarian style, the long sword and shield in hand and helmeted head with Leander's face. It was a leaner Conan rather than the over muscled stereotype, and it suited him well.

"I am speechless, thank you my friend," Leander offered as he stood to embrace Alex.

"It's up to you to tell the story of that image," Alex pointed out.

"Oh my," Abrianna said as she reached for the drawing.

In typical fashion, Emma had drawn the warrior on a mound, his dead enemies all around and a very naked woman wrapped around one leg. The woman's face was Abrianna's.

"Sorry, that was the artist's idea, not mine," Alex added with a blush.

"Perhaps we can keep this one private?" Abrianna replied softly as she passed the image back to Leander.

----*----

Emma dropped the four off at Cedar Park, a community park that sat just below Alex's house in the Highlands. At 1am, the traffic was nonexistent and the park lighting had been conveniently shut down by a thought from Alex.

"It's a shame I couldn't' do this when I lived here," he smiled to himself, imagining all the trouble he would have caused in his youth had he been able to work magic like this.

Before leaving, he had parked the Jeep in his garage, assuming the elves would deal with everything else as they had before. It went against his grain to leave the house in disarray, so he had taken a moment to clean up as well.

All five people, including Emma, left the parked car and walked to the edge of the parking lot, with Kinsey running off in advance of the group to inspect the grassy field. In the distance, Alex could make out the structures that consisted of a water park and a baseball field.

"What now?" Emma asked excitedly as Alex had offered to let her stay and meet Vesuvius in exchange for the ride.

"Give me a sec," Alex replied as he closed his eyes and began to concentrate.

"Vesuvius, we are ready to go," he thought to himself as he tried to project his thoughts to the wind.

"No need to shout, I'll be right there," he got in immediate reply.

"Did you hear that?" Abrianna asked in surprise as she heard the dragon as well.

Before anyone could respond, there was a flutter of wings, very large wings, and Vesuvius lightly set down in the field, causing Kinsey to retreat back to the others. That was not to say he left no mark in the grass, however, as Alex noted beep rifts wherever the Dragon placed a foot, claws digging deep into the turf. Someone was going to have a hell of a time explaining that to the groundskeepers in the morning.

This was Alex's first real opportunity to see the entire dragon he had released onto the world from the cavern below London. He had tried to imagine the size of the creature based on what little he saw. His imagination was woefully lacking!

Like Naga, he was a true four-footed dragon, his wings separate appendages. Vesuvius was substantially larger in every way, two to three times larger. His body scales were bigger that the car they arrived in. He watched as the dragon settled onto its belly to make it lower to the ground, and then dipped one wing to act as a ramp.

"All aboard," Alex and Abrianna heard, passing along the instructions to the others.

With Leander leading the way, Alex took Emma off to one side.

"Emma, this is Vesuvius," Alex said as he led the young woman to the front of the beast.

"A snack?" Vesuvius asked optimistically.

"No, a friend. Smile nicely and she will immortalize you in ink and paint," Alex projected in thought.

"It's a pleasure to meet you Vesuvius, you are truly amazing," Emma said excitedly, unaware of the exchange.

Alex noted that the dragon dipped its head in acknowledgment of her complement. The gesture seemed to have the desired effect, as the young woman seemed to vibrate with excitement.

"OK, get your picture, and then we need to get out of here," Alex instructed, as the young woman began to backpedal.

Moving backwards, she began pulling out her camera while he climbed aboard the dragon.

Shifting to the center of the dragon's back, he found Kinsey was sitting between Cassie and Abrianna while Leander was behind the three. All had their pillowcase packages tightly in hand with Leander holding the one Alex had packed for himself before they left. A camera flash in the distance was the queue for Vesuvius to take flight.

"Hold on everyone," Alex shouted to his companions as the dragon took no more than three steps before launching himself into the sky.

As Alex looks back to see the receding lights of his old home town, he wondered if he would ever see it again.

Chapter 28

As Vesuvius banked, Alex could see the gathered masses in a field below. The early morning sun was just beginning to illuminate the clearing as he watched two individuals approach one another from opposite sides of the clearing. One he immediately identified as King Ben, his mentor and Uncle-in-law. The other was a large armor-clad behemoth.

Half again as tall as Ben, it carried a double bitted ax in one hand and a very large sword in the other. Ben stood before the aggressor, empty handed and apparently unarmed, but Alex knew better.

"Clear the way!" Alex shouted as Vesuvius made a low pass, scattering the onlookers and causing Ben and his opponent to retreat in opposite directions.

With all eyes upon them, the dragon circled once more before landing lightly in the center of the field. No sooner had they stopped than Kinsey leapt from the dragon, landing halfway between Ben and the dragon. She had returned to her wolf form and was apparently quite pleased with the change.

"Father!" Abrianna shouted, as she was the next to slide off the dragon's back, landing softly in the grass.

Leander was right behind his intended, leaving Alex to assist his wife until all four had dismounted. Rather than taking flight once more, Vesuvius simply folded his wings, sliding to one side, with his keen eyes scanning the area as if evaluating the situation.

"Abrianna, you are safe," Ben declared as he embraced his daughter while reaching for Leander's hand in acknowledgement.

Releasing Leander, Ben then waved Cassie to his side, wrapping a free arm about her as he continued to hold his daughter tightly. Alex swore he saw the hint of a tear in Ben's cheek as he rubbed his face in her hair. By the time he looked up, the evidence was gone and Ben was in control once more.

"About time you got here boy, I've been stalling as long as I can!" Ben shouted to Alex as he released both women and whispered to them both while pointing to his camp.

"Take the wolf," Ben added as he motioned for Cassie to take charge.

Ben moved up to meet Alex and shouted to those gathered on the far side of the clearing as he did so.

"Ailmer, as you can see the Lord Protector has returned. I suggest you reconsider your challenge before it is too late."

Ailmer appeared flustered as he realized Alex had in fact returned, and it was clear that this had never been part of the plan. There was a flurry of whispering between the Vassal King and his advisors before anyone spoke.

"This changes nothing, King of Great Vale, the Challenge remains, as does the penalty," Ailmer shouted from across the field.

"Ben what the hell is going on?" Alex asked in return.

"Ailmer is claiming the right of challenge after your rescue of Amelia. He says you dishonored him by a sneak attack and needlessly killed his men. Also, you attacked a guest under his protection," Ben provided.

"So, who cares? His guest was a kidnaper and a villain!" Alex snapped.

"In affairs such as this, that matters little. One can make a challenge for just about anything, most don't because the consequences can be most severe," Ben explained.

"In this case?" Alex asked suspiciously.

"Winner gets the crown and the kingdom of the loser."

"So that was Avenstore's plan," Alex responded.

"You saw Avenstore?" Ben asked.

"Yes. They sent me home, to our old home."

"That I know, Elion did his best to reassure me. He said you needed everyone with you to get back here again," he replied.

"Truer words were never spoken," Alex acknowledged with a nod and a smile.

"No more delays! Let the Challenge continue," Ailmer shouted, interrupting their conversation.

"Alex has returned. Your claim is against him, so he must be permitted to prepare," Ben replied.

"You can explain as you fight. I care not if he, you, or you both confront the Paladin. It will make no difference in the outcome," Ailmer boasted.

Shrugging off the coat he had worn for the trip home, Alex and Ben stepped out into the center of the clearing to face the approaching Paladin. Weaponless, Alex presumed his magical abilities were required for this and not steel. Standing there in his jeans and shirt he looked very out of place.

"What is that thing," Alex asked as it came close enough for a detailed inspection.

"Avenstore's gift to the Vassal King. We think its vulnerable to dragon's but haven't been able to confirm just how," Ben explained as he and Alex stopped midway.

Ben and Alex separated slightly, as they watched the creature cautiously close the distance until they were all within fighting range. It turned in place until Alex stood before the Paladin, squared off in a confrontation. The thing appearing to appraise him as he raised his shields up in defense. He sensed his opponent probing him for weakness, the unseen attack a form of mental pressure rather than magical force.

Alex deflected the images and rage the being attempted to force into his mind, the effort intended to strike fear into its opponent. The visual array did provide him with insight into how the creature viewed combat and victory. He caught fleeting visions of its victims sucked dry of their essence while the creature drained the life from them. In return, Alex sent images of puppies and bunnies, mocking the creature's fierceness as they chased him from the field of battle.

The armored knight appeared to glare at him in rage as it was denied the easy kill it expected from the unarmed prey. With a double bitted axe and sword still in hand, the challenger swung both with ease as he circled his prey. Alex had to weave and dodge as the knight worked to get its sense of distance from its opponent.

Ben had been working to keep the armored hulk between the two of them, positioning himself opposite Alex to better observe and contribute. Out of the corner of his eye, Alex could see the hulking dragon resting comfortably on its haunches as it watched the action before him. Alex recalled Ben's suspicions around the Paladin and dragon weakness.

"Vesuvius a little help please," Alex shouted as the dragon simply sat to one side, watching the engagement with amusement.

"I made no commitments to aid you in your fight once you returned home?" Vesuvius replied with a chuckle.

"True, but this creature was sent here by the very elves that enslaved you," Alex replied quickly as the Paladin took a swing at him with its axe.

"So you say, Wizard, but I have no proof of that," the dragon replied lightly.

Rolling away to avoid absorbing the impact on his shields, he returned with a blast of concentrated energy that staggered his opponent, taking him off his feet and squarely onto his back.

"Well done," Ben commented with admiration.

"Your dragon friend appears to be of no use in this fight, let me try my own dragon fire, then," Ben added as he blasted the Paladin with his best imitation Dragon Fire while it was down.

The flames wrapped themselves around the armored figure, causing it to begin to glow red. As everyone watched, the creature pushed itself up from the ground and faced its opponents once more, the glow still present in the daylight.

"Apparently there is no substitute for the real thing," Vesuvius said smugly from the sideline.

Still in his clothes from the trip, his sneakers were slick on the damp grass, making his footing less that stable. A growl from behind reminded him that Cassie was holding Kinsey by her side, now returned to her wolf form and anxious herself to fight. The Paladin was not something she could confront, though, and he knew Ben had asked Cassie to keep her safe.

The dragon's comment triggered a thought in Alex's mind.

"You are right, why not use the real thing."

Alex closed his eyes for only a second, seeming to concentrate on something before opening them once more.

"Ben, stand back, I got this," he said in a firm voice.

----*----

It had been a long time since Ben received instructions from others in that way, but there was something in Alex's tone that told him he should comply with his demand unquestioned. Those like Ben with magical ability, could see Alex was drawing in massive amounts of free energy as he stood in place. His white radiance was almost painful to the eyes.

Suddenly he sprang forward, shimmering blades of magical energy extending from both hands. The Paladin swung first, his sword meeting Alex's only to find itself half its original length, the free end falling to the ground.

"Alex watch out." Cassie screamed as the axe in the other hand had found its target in Alex's midsection.

The blow sent the young Wizard flying across the field, landing on his back a good ten feet from the Paladin. Alex had no more than hit the ground, when Ben saw him spring to his feet, anxious to meet his approaching opponent once more.

"You are going to need more than that big boy," Alex taunted as he swung another invisible sword at the Paladin.

The impact didn't sever the arm it contacted, but the ring of magic on metal caused Ben to flinch in pain. The Paladin stepped back with the impact, clearly not expecting the force of the blow, though there appeared to be little damage.

"Yield and live!" Ailmer shouted from his sideline, his bravado somewhat diminished.

"I'm just getting started," Alex replied as he rushed his opponent, battering it with blow after blow, forcing it to retreat.

"I have a lot of rage to work out!' He shouted over the hammering he was delivering to the Paladin.

Ben was at a loss to Alex's plan. While the young man was pummeling his opponent, in the end there wasn't any visible damage inflicted. He agreed Alex was getting quite a workout, but all it was doing was prolonging the inevitable. Sliding over to one side, Ben approached Vesuvius in hopes of shifting the battle in their favor.

"Is there nothing that will convince you to intercede?" he asked the dragon telepathically, as they both watched Alex go flying once more from the Paladin's blow.

Even wrapped in his shields, Ben knew Alex had to be taking a beating every time the Paladin scored a hit like that. The evidence of such was his slow recovery with the last blow.

"Why would I? Choosing sides has never worked out well for my kind. Besides, I haven't had this much fun in a thousand years!"

"You feel no debt to him for freeing you?" Ben asked, indicating Alex as he charged his opponent once more, the telltale ringing of his armor validating the repeated blows.

"That has been paid in full."

"What can I give you to change your mind?" Ben asked, hoping to buy the dragon's help.

"You have nothing I desire."

----*----

Alex knew he couldn't keep this up much longer. He had built himself up a magical armor that would take the best the Paladin had to offer, but in the end, his inability to even scratch his opponent was problematic. While not the death blows he was wishing for, he had hoped to be able to pummel him into some form of submission.

Selecting another tactic, Alex took a few steps back to gather himself. The Paladin seemed to grant him his pause, likely unsure of the ruse being planned. Once again, Alex drew in all the free energy about him, in such abundance in comparison to what he had been accustomed to back home.

In his mind, he imagined the energy in the form of a dragon, one he gained favor by returning with its treasured eggs.

"Abrianna look," Leander said in wonder as the ghostly shape of a dragon appeared, even to those not inclined to see magical constructs.

"Form of a dragon," Alex recited aloud as the phantom image took substance.

Channeling more and more of the energy about him, through his body and into his construct, the dragon took on color and substance.

"It's Naga, Cassie said aloud, giving a name to the shape.

"No, it's Alex's conjuring to look like a dragon," Abrianna explained.

As she spoke, the phantom dragon snapped its jaws at the Dark Paladin, causing the creature to dodge, and then leaps to one side. The false Naga took chase, swiping at the armored knight and tossing it to one side like a discarded toy.

Feeding the dragon the energy required to fight, challenged Alex in a way unfamiliar to him. Unlike in the past where he acted as a conduit, only redirecting the force, the dragon was actually an extension of himself. The phantom Naga only repeated the actions Alex performed. He swung his arm and it swiped a clawed talon. He gave a heaving exhale and it spits fire at his foe.

While it kept him at an arm's length, the Paladin unable to damage the construct, it still lacked the lethality required to end the conflict. The phantom Naga snapped and clawed at the Paladin, chasing it around the clearing, but the knight continued to come, seemly impervious to the continued battering it received. With a heavy sigh, he allowed the dragon to dissipate, absorbing the released magical charge to reinforce his own protection.

Closing in once more on his opponent, he began battering away once more. As he did, so he could feel his own hits getting less and less powerful. He continued to draw on the abundant magical energy around him, but it was only as good as his own health. It was then the Paladin managed a blow up side his head that sent him staggering, followed by a vice like grip around his throat.

"No, Alex," Screamed Cassie as she started to dart for the open field.

"Stay Back," He replied in a strangled voice.

Grasping the Paladin's arm with both his hands, he felt his feet, leaving the ground, as it raised him high. Focusing his energy on the shields at his neck, he once again closed his eyes, concentrating on one thing. As he did, he could feel the creature trying to draw his life force from his body.

In the corner of his eye, he could see Ailmer's delighted face as it appeared, he had won. It was then that something touched his mind.

"Shields up!" he heard shouting in his head.

Doing as he was told; he was instantly awash in flame as he felt the Paladin release its hold on him. Hitting the ground, he unceremoniously scrambled away as the Paladin was engulfed in flame once more. Sitting on the grass, he focused his shields to wrap the back side of his opponent, blocking escape.

"Another magical dragon?" Leander asked in confusion.

"The real Naga!" he heard Cassie proclaim as the Red Dragon landed next to Alex while flaming the Paladin for a third time.

With each blast, Alex would deflect the flame, directing what he could toward his adversary, while the knight could do not but absorb that flame directed at its core. Ah the heat increased, Alex backtracked to a safer distance without gaining his feet, but continued to concentrate the dragon fire around his foe.

With each blast from Naga, the Paladin seems to melt a little more, its armor liquifies in place as Alex circled the fire back onto the villain. Finally springing to his feet, Alex approached Naga as she finished off the Challenge once and for all. There in the center of the field was a glowing pile of red metal, no hint of the creature inside remaining. Both Alex and Naga stood side by side inspecting the smoldering metal, looking for any sign of life.

"You Cheat! Your win is invalid!" Ailmer screamed from his side of the field.

"No, the rules state each champion may use whatever weapons are available to them. Alex chose to use a dragon," Ben said in a clear calm voice.

"I will not yield!" Ailmer shouted in defiance as panic set in.

"Then I expect you and your men are prepared to face said dragon," Ben responded while motioning to the dragon still beside Alex on the field.

At that, both Alex and Naga looked up to face the crowd standing behind the Vassal King. As if on cue, King Teivel and his dwarves emerged from the surrounding woods, weapons at the ready and looking none too pleased with Ailmer and his men. Before either group could take a step forward, first one by one, and then entire groups behind Ailmer took a knee and bowed before the two.

"I expect you to be out of Gundor Stronghold before the next full moon," Ben said before dismissing Ailmer, who was now standing alone, with a wave.

----*----

"You were just delaying?" Cassie asked, standing by her husband, both her arms wrapped around one of his.

"Well, I was telling the truth; I had a lot of rage to work out after the last few weeks."

"How did you know she was coming?" Ben asked as he made his way over to the gathering crowd.

"I called to her just before I attacked the Paladin. That's why I needed you to stay back. If she came in hot and you were not prepared to deflect the blast, it might have been problematic," he said with a grin.

"Speaking of Naga," Alex said as he turned to look for his dragon rescuer.

On the far side of the field he could see the two dragons staring at one another. While others might assume it was in silence, Alex could hear the conversation passing between the two as they caught up with one another. Alex wandered over to the pair, Cassie still attached to his arm and giving no indications that the dragons would change her mind.

"Naga, I want to thank you for coming to my aid," Alex stated aloud so Cassie could hear.

"Wizard, you should have disclosed that it was Naga you freed, I would have been happy to avenge her," Vesuvius said before she could reply.

Alex paused for a moment; positive he had disclosed that fact to the dragon in the cavern before releasing him. With the statement, he watched as Naga rubbed her head on the larger male's neck in what Alex assumed was a sign of affection.

"Yeah, sorry I forgot to mention that. Perhaps I can call on you for help then some other time," Alex stammered in reply while indicating he would gladly cover for the implied omission, quid pro quo.

"Perhaps," Vesuvius replied with a nod of understanding.

So apparently it wasn't just human males that stretched the truth to impress a female.

"I was happy to disrupt the Dark Elf Avenstore's plans!" Naga added.

"What about them, need some assistance now?" Vesuvius asked, suddenly interested in Ailmer and his troops.

"No, I think they will be no more trouble. Feel free to use the caves under Gundor Stronghold as home if you like, I have a feeling they will be little used in the near future."

"No thank you, Naga was just telling me about her home in the Dragon's Teeth. I think I should like to see them for myself."

Chapter 29

"Alex, it feels so good to be home," Cassie said lazily from the hot bath in their chambers in Windfall Castle.

With Alex behind her, his arms wrapped about her as the two soaked in the steaming waters, she lay back against his chest. Kinsey, happy in her wolf form, had found a spot in the corner and curled up where she could both keep an eye on her charges and stay well clear of the water.

"You said it, no more elves, dragons, succubus or shifters!" he said softly in her ear.

Both his arms were resting on what was beginning to be what Alex called the baby bump. She could feel him lovingly rubbing the area, as if he were soothing the growing child within. Cassie could not remember a time where she had been so happy as now.

She held his left hand in her right, her fingers idly playing with the wedding band he had purchased himself when he bought hers. With that thought, she raised her own left hand, placing it on top of his. Her jewel encrusted band still sparkled brightly as she laced her fingers in his. Of all the things they had hoped to bring across the boundary of realms, these were the most important to her.

"Honey," she heard him say.

"Yes?"

"Um, you are really glowing. I mean way more than usual," he said, concern in his tone.

"That's because I am so happy."

She could feel Alex draw her in tighter as they two of them sat enjoying the moment.

"Cassie?" she heard her husband ask once more.

"What, my love."

"In the library, what was it that Abrianna wanted so badly that you objected to?" he asked, caution in his tone.

"She wanted my sex appeal. She worried that Leander would never desire her as much as you desire me," she said with a bit of a laugh.

"She truly doesn't understand love, does she?"

"Not even a little," Cassie replied, understanding Alex's meaning.

She knew Alex desired her because he loved her, not for her sex appeal.

"That poor woman has no idea what she she's in for, does she," Alex answered with a laugh.

"None at all."

----*----

The days following the return of the four saw a flurry of activity in Windfall as everyone tried to get back to normal. Ben had rushed Abrianna and Leander back to Great Vale, concerned that the absence of the princess had unduly upset the kingdom. He felt a celebration around their return would go far in restoring calm. To that end Amelia went with them, leaving the twins behind to help Alex and Cassie.

Alex had his own suspicions for their hasty departure. The growing familiarity between Leander and Abrianna had not gone unnoticed by Ben, and Alex wondered if the added sex appeal Abrianna had traded with Cassie had the two headed to an accelerated wedding schedule. As it was, Alex had a pile of work waiting for him, left undone by the mermaid twins as they focused on their pet projects.

"Kelby, Leena, look, I do appreciate the work you did while I was away. The help with the pirates was pure genius. That however doesn't mean you can forget to do all the other stuff that needs to be taken care of."

"Mom said it would be better if we stuck to things we understood," Kelby explained as she dropped the pile of papers on Alex's desk.

"This stuff we don't get," Leena added as she dropped an identical pile next to Kelby's.

"Can we go now, Cassie promised to tell us all about your adventure," Kelby asked with excitement.

"Perhaps it's better if you do," Alex replied as he started sorting through the papers, not liking what he was seeing.

It was several hours later that a knock on the door interrupted what Alex could only describe as a trip into bureaucratic hell. At this point any interruption had to be an improvement.

"Sire, Captain Regas is here to see you. He says he has urgent news," the guard outside his study informed him.

"Send him in," Alex instructed as he continued to sort through the stacks of paper piled high on his desk.

"Sire," Regas said, removing his hat as he entered.

"Please sit," Alex replied as he waved the man into a chair.

"Anything to drink?" he asked as he waved to the steward standing at the door into the room.

"Please," Regas replied, as the two watched the steward pour whatever was in the pitcher.

"I am told you have urgent news?' Alex asked after the man had taken his first sip.

"Nyland, Sire. There are reports of lawlessness since the exodus of the deposed King," Regas explained.

"Lawlessness, by whom?" Alex asked, the concern in his voice evident.

"Mostly former soldiers, demobbed by the King before his departure."

"There should have been no such action. Once King Ben assumes control there, they were to be put to good use," Alex snapped.

"I thought as much, but they were turned out nonetheless, and without pay I am told."

"Is he still around?" Alex asked, unsure of when Ailmer and his wife were to have vacated Gundor Stronghold.

"No, Sire. He and his entourage set sail for the west just days after your victory. I am told he took the royal treasury with him as well as many valuables from the castle," Regas added with disdain.

"Expected, I suppose," Alex commented as he gave the situation some thought.

Moving over to the window, Alex snatched up a small parchment and scribbled out a quick note to Ben explaining the situation in the North. Taking an acorn from a small bowl nearby, he performed the ritual and soon set the small bird free.

"Have you eaten?" Alex asked.

"Not since last night," Regas answered honestly.

With that, Alex ordered food for the two and they sat in conversation, waiting for Ben's reply. The books Alex had brought back had survived the trip and had been put to good use in the shipyard. There Captain Regas was looking forward to the first in a line of ships intended for coastal defense and policing of the waterways between Windfall and Nyland.

It was after the two had finished eating that a small black bird appeared at the window. Holding out his hand, Alex watched the bird alight on his outstretched hand before disappearing in a puff of smoke. Taking the rolled parchment, he opened it and did a double take before scoffing at its contents.

"What is it Sire?" Regas asked cautiously.

Without a word Alex handed the Captain the parchment. On it were the words.

"Your Kingdom, your problems"

Made in the USA
Middletown, DE
20 January 2024